M000288448

Fatal Risk

Jane Blythe

Copyright © 2023 Jane Blythe

All rights reserved.

No part of this publication may be reproduced, transmitted, downloaded, distributed, reverse engineered or stored in or introduced into any information storage and retrieval system, in any form or by any means, including photocopying and recording, whether electronic or mechanical, now known or hereinafter invented without permission in writing from the publisher.

All characters and events in this publication, other than those clearly in the public domain, are fictitious and any resemblance to real persons, living or dead, is purely coincidental.

Bear Spots Publications
Melbourne Australia

Paperback
ISBN-13: 978-0-6456432-3-7

Cover designed by RBA Designs

Also by Jane Blythe

Detective Parker Bell Series

A SECRET TO THE GRAVE
WINTER WONDERLAND
DEAD OR ALIVE
LITTLE GIRL LOST
FORGOTTEN

Count to Ten Series

ONE
TWO
THREE
FOUR
FIVE
SIX
BURNING SECRETS
SEVEN
EIGHT
NINE
TEN

Broken Gems Series

CRACKED SAPPHIRE
CRUSHED RUBY
FRACTURED DIAMOND
SHATTERED AMETHYST
SPLINTERED EMERALD
SALVAGING MARIGOLD

River's End Rescues Series

COCKY SAVIOR
SOME REGRETS ARE FOREVER
PROTECT
SOME LIES WILL HAUNT YOU

SOME QUESTIONS HAVE NO ANSWERS
SOME TRUTH CAN BE DISTORTED
SOME TRUST CAN BE REBUILT
SOME MISTAKES ARE UNFORGIVABLE

Candella Sisters' Heroes Series

LITTLE DOLLS
LITTLE HEARTS
LITTLE BALLERINA

Storybook Murders Series

NURSERY RHYME KILLER
FAIRYTALE KILLER
FABLE KILLER

Saving SEALs Series

SAVING RYDER
SAVING ERIC
SAVING OWEN
SAVING LOGAN
SAVING GRAYSON
SAVING CHARLIE

Prey Security Series

PROTECTING EAGLE
PROTECTING RAVEN
PROTECTING FALCON
PROTECTING SPARROW
PROTECTING HAWK
PROTECTING DOVE

Prey Security: Alpha Team Series

DEADLY RISK
LETHAL RISK

EXTREME RISK
FATAL RISK

Christmas Romantic Suspense Series

I'd like to thank everyone who played a part in bringing this story to life. Particularly my mom who is always there to share her thoughts and opinions with me. My awesome cover designer, Amy, who whips up covers for me so quickly and who patiently makes every change I ask for, and there are usually lots of them! And my lovely editor Lisa Edwards, for all their encouragement and for all the hard work they put into polishing my work.

CHAPTER ONE

October 2nd
6:19 P.M.

"We've got eyes on us."

Great.

Just great.

Damn, he hated this place.

Not the market specifically but the country they were in.

Every time they came here something went wrong.

Dominick "Domino" Tanner would be perfectly happy never to set foot in Somalia again. Not even four months ago, he and his team had been captured, held for two weeks, and tortured before finally being rescued. Then only weeks after that, they'd been back in this hellhole rescuing a teammate's woman who had been abducted and tortured.

In his mind, death and pain ruled this country, and he couldn't wait to get out of it.

"Domino, on your five o'clock," Luca "Bear" Jackson—Prey Security's Alpha Team leader—added.

This wasn't his first rodeo. At thirty-four, he'd spent most of his life serving in the military and then working hard to become a member of the elite Delta Force before moving to the private sector and joining Prey. The military had been the only way out of the life his family had planned for him, and he took his job seriously.

Many would say too seriously.

He might keep people at a distance, but there was one thing everyone knew about him; he was fiercely loyal and protective of

1

those he considered his.

The weapons trafficking ring operating out of Somalia had been responsible for almost killing his team and almost killing Prey's psychiatrist and was linked to a plot to overthrow the American government. That plot had almost gotten Bear's wife killed, and Asher "Mouse" Whitman's wife and daughter abducted.

There was nothing that would stop him from destroying anyone and everyone involved in this entire mess. If whoever was watching his team was one of them, Domino would gladly make sure they suffered, but not before he got every ounce of intel out of them that they could.

By whatever means necessary.

He was completely done with this. Every time they thought they had the pieces of the puzzle clicked into place, they found a whole other box they hadn't known about full of pieces that needed to be figured out.

Domino would love a chance to expel some of the anger that raged inside him. That fear that he would turn out like his family had been festering ever since the head injuries he'd sustained when he and his team had been held captive here in Somalia. Fear that he was one moment of lost self-control away from being everything he had spent so long fighting to get away from.

Maybe it was time to just embrace his genetics and stop fighting against them.

Starting with whoever was following his team.

Bring it on.

"Description?" he asked into his comms. If he turned to scope out whoever was watching them, he'd tip the person off to the fact that they were on to him. For now, he wanted the guy to think he had the upper hand.

"Hard to tell, they're in a vehicle," Antonio "Arrow" Eden replied, his voice tight with barely controlled anger. Antonio's girlfriend was Piper Hamilton, Prey's psychiatrist who had been abducted by a former Prey operative turned weapons dealer and brought to Somalia where she was tortured and almost killed before they could get to her.

Piper was the sweetest woman, brave and strong. She'd fought through so much and reminded him of someone he used to know. Another sweet woman who had fought through a lot of horrible things, only to wind up gone far too soon.

This was the first time Arrow had been away from Piper since they'd rescued her almost eight weeks ago, and it had been hard for both of them. If someone was tailing them, ready to cause more trouble for the couple, they had to be stopped.

"Vehicle description?" he asked.

"Black SUV," Arrow replied.

"Been on our tail since we hit the market," Christian "Surf" Bailey added.

"What's the plan?" Caleb "Brick" Quinn asked.

They were here following up on a lead on a couple of the men who had escaped the compound when Prey raided it to rescue Piper. Thanks to an undercover Prey operative who had access to the weapons traffickers, they had made it through the explosives and guards lining the perimeter without losing a single man. The traffickers hadn't been as lucky.

Nathan Miller had been working undercover, building his rep as a source of weapons for almost two years, yet when he'd recognized Piper, he had risked everything to help get her out. He had paid for that choice with his life.

No one else was dying.

"One of us circles around and moves in from behind. The rest of us keep doing what we're doing," Bear said.

"I'll move in," Domino said without hesitation. They'd been here for three days already, and so far, there had been no sign of the men from the trafficking ring who had supposedly been spotted here in the market.

Three days of waiting, watching, and he was about ready to

lose his mind. He needed to be doing something. Needed to try to work out the anger that was always simmering just beneath the surface before he lost control of it, and it bubbled over.

"We want him alive," Bear said, and it ate at Domino that his team no longer seemed to trust him the way they used to.

His fault.

Right now, his anger *wasn't* under control.

"Understood," he muttered, frustrated with himself for being annoyed at Bear all but calling him on the anger his entire team knew he was battling with.

Moving casually wasn't an easy task for a man like him. Not just because of his size, but because he was an intense guy, overly focused, it was hard for him to relax and let go. Scratch that, it was all but impossible.

Purchasing whatever it was he had in his hand, his attention was already so focused on the mission he couldn't even remember which stall he was at, Domino slipped it into his pocket and strolled forward. The market was made up of dozens of stalls and hundreds of people, men, women, and children all buzzed about. It should be easy enough to fade into the landscape, especially since he knew his team would make sure they drew the tango's attention.

Since he had to move cautiously and look like he was just another man with nowhere he had to be, it took much longer than he would have liked to circle through the market and around to the other side of the road.

As soon as he turned the corner, he saw the black SUV. It was parked toward the end of the market, but there were enough people around that there was no way he could grab the person and disappear.

"Going to get in the backseat, get them to drive out of here," he said into the comms.

"Abandoned apartment building about three klicks away, it's remote," Mouse said.

Strolling down the street, Domino slipped into the backseat of the vehicle like he belonged there at the same time that he covered his face and palmed his weapon.

Before the driver could even process what was happening, he had his weapon pressed to the back of their head.

"Drive," he growled.

A very feminine gasp caught him by surprise.

Not what he'd been expecting at all.

Not that women couldn't be every bit as evil as men, but there had been no indications there were any females involved in this particular weapons trafficking ring.

"Drive," he repeated when she didn't move.

Carefully, the woman turned the engine on and placed her hands on the steering wheel. As she took off down the street, a pair of the greenest eyes he had ever seen flickered to the rearview mirror.

Even though he knew she couldn't see his eyes through his sunglasses and the hat he'd pulled low down to cover most of his face, it felt like she saw right down inside his soul, reading every secret about his past and his family that he had worked hard to hide.

What the hell was with that?

Those eyes of hers were something else. Their shade was almost unnatural, accentuated by her creamy white skin and long dark lashes. The long, soft red waves tumbling around her shoulders caught the sunlight and shimmered like fire.

Bewitching.

It was the only word Domino could think of to describe her.

Bewitching but dangerous.

She'd been watching them, and he didn't believe in coincidences. This woman was somehow involved in the trafficking ring which meant she was also involved in the plot to overthrow the government. While she might look sweet as sugar, that didn't mean her soul wasn't black as coal.

"Eyes on the road, red," he ordered, somewhat impressed she'd navigated the street without hitting anyone while staring at him. "You try anything stupid, and I would love a reason to put a bullet in you."

Instead of showing fear, the woman rolled her eyes, making Domino grind his teeth in irritation.

The last thing he needed right now when his temper was on a hair trigger was a beautiful woman with plans to destroy the world.

* * * * *

October 2nd
6:52 P.M.

Don't let them see you sweat.

A mantra Julia Garamond had repeated to herself several times over the years.

Only this time, it felt a whole lot harder than it had in the past.

The man in the back seat of her rental was huge. He had to be well over six feet tall if the way his head brushed the ceiling in the car was any indication. His muscles strained against his shirt, and the hand that rested on the back of her seat had to be twice the size of hers.

Big and deadly.

It wasn't just his size that made him scary. Anger rolled off him in waves that seemed to wash through the vehicle. Julia wasn't sure how she could feel it or how she knew, she just ... did.

He was composed, still, his voice had been cold and hard, but despite the comment about loving a reason to put a bullet in her, his tone had been even and smooth. Like he was used to jumping into the backseats of cars and ordering strangers to drive while he pointed a gun at their heads.

Unfortunately, this wasn't her first time being kidnapped. Actually, it was her fourth, but trying to keep her eyes on the road, her fear under control, and her gaze from wandering to the man in the backseat made it hard to concentrate.

Wasn't like she hadn't known this wasn't going to be dangerous.

Of course she had, she was in Somalia for goodness sake.

Still, she hadn't expected the men she was following to catch on to her. Or at least not this soon, before she was ready.

She had no idea who they were, only that their plane had been in and out of a small private airfield three times in the last four months. The airfield was close to a compound owned by a weapons trafficker. That same trafficking ring was linked to a number of explosions that had been set off across America, she was sure of it.

Only no one else believed her.

So, she was here to find proof.

Perhaps not the smartest thing she had ever done, although no one could ever accuse her of being too cautious. Julia lived by her emotions and her gut. When a story called to her, she answered, making her a good investigative journalist. Add in the fact that she was more than happy to wander right into danger without blinking, and she was someone who could get a story no one else dared to touch.

Which often led to her finding herself in trouble.

Like right now.

"Pull in over there," the man in her car ordered, gesturing with his free hand at what looked like an abandoned building on their right.

As his hand moved, his knuckles brushed across her shoulder, and she felt a little flutter low in her belly.

Really, Julia?

You're going to be attracted to the man who wants an excuse to shoot you?

Because it was so utterly ridiculous, she rolled her eyes. Of course, the man noticed.

"You always roll your eyes when you got a gun pointed at your head, red?" the man asked, this time anger seeped into his every word.

Julia bit on her tongue to stop a sassy comeback from slipping out. Best not to antagonize the man holding a weapon on her.

She wanted to look at him, study him because even though she believed he would kill her without a second thought, she also felt kind of safe with him. Her gut told her this man wasn't who she'd thought he was.

It made no sense, but then again, emotions and feelings often didn't make sense, and she had long ago learned not to fight against them. Life was all about love. Loving the people who shared the journey with you, loving what you did, loving even when it meant taking the pain of loss along with it.

As she pulled the car over where he indicated, she saw five men approach with their faces covered and their weapons aimed at the car.

Six men, this *had* to be the men she'd been following, the ones connected to the trafficking ring. So why was her fear receding instead of increasing?

And why was it because of the man in the backseat?

"Stop there," he ordered.

For now, she had to obey their commands, they were still armed, and she wasn't, and they obviously knew she'd been following them, so they were a threat to her. It was stupid to want to believe they were good men. If they were involved in trafficking weapons and blowing people up then they weren't, simple as that.

Yet still, she hoped.

Once the car stopped moving, her door was yanked open, and she was dragged roughly out. Her hands were yanked behind her back and secured with plastic zip ties, and they threw a bag over her head.

The restraints didn't bother her as much as the bag.

It seemed to cut off her air supply although logically she knew it did no such thing. It was just that it brought back memories of being trapped in the rubble of a restaurant, the smoke and dust choking the oxygen out of the air.

Fifteen hours.

That was how long she'd spent trapped alone, injured, bleeding, and terrified.

The men dragged her inside the building where she was shoved onto the floor, the zip ties cut and replaced with a metal cuff around her right wrist securing it to what felt like a pipe. The ground was cold despite the warmth of the day, or maybe it was her body chilling as fear built inside her.

No one spoke, but she could feel them standing close by.

Watching her.

Trying to intimidate her.

This was by far her first rodeo. She'd been captured in Cambodia by a drug smuggler and almost killed. She'd gotten too close to a human trafficker in Mexico once and almost found herself sold. And just last year when she'd been investigating a survivalist who planned to destroy the government and build his own utopia, she had been abducted by a weapons dealer.

That time someone had helped her escape. The same someone who might very well be dead now because he was a good man who couldn't stand seeing someone suffer unjustly.

This was personal for her, and if these men were involved, she would do whatever she could to take them down even if the one from the car did make her feel weird things.

"Why were you following us?" one demanded. Not the one from her car.

"Because I know who you are," Julia replied honestly. Well, kind of honestly, she knew they were involved she just had no idea how.

"Then you have the advantage," another voice said.

She huffed a chuckle. "Yeah? Because six on one, me unarmed and restrained, certainly doesn't seem like I have any advantages."

"You know who we are, and we have no idea who you are. I think that's a pretty big advantage," another man spoke like they thought it would confuse her if they all took part in her interrogation, which she was pleased so far hadn't involved torture.

Yet anyway.

It could definitely be coming.

"Not one that will help me though," Julia said. "Let's cut to the chase. You're involved with the traffickers who are setting explosions across my country. Your country, too, by the sounds of your accents. I was caught up in one of those explosions. That makes this a personal mission for me as much as a work one. Even if you kill me, what I know so far will be sent to my lawyer who will pass it along to my publisher. I might not have enough to take you and your friends down, but I have enough to get the public talking."

For a long moment there was silence.

Guess they hadn't expected her to be so forthright, but Julia saw no benefit from beating around the bush.

The bag was removed from her head, and Julia blinked to clear her vision before looking around at the six large men.

Huh.

Turned out she knew them after all.

"Oops." She shook her head, realizing she had made a big mistake. "I didn't realize I was following Prey guys. Which team are you? I recognize you, but I don't know your names." Everyone had heard of Prey Security, the world-renowned security firm. They worked hostage rescue, some bodyguard work, and black ops missions for the government. That was likely why she had pinged their plane as suspicious. They were probably working to do the same thing she was. Bring down the trafficking ring.

Instead of answering, the blond one asked, "And you are?"

"Oh, I'm Julia. Julia Garamond. I'm an investigative journalist. Were you involved in rescuing the woman? The one who was being held captive at the compound?" She'd wanted to reach out to Prey to ask about her, but she hadn't been sure if it was appropriate or if they would give her an answer.

"How did you know about that?" the large, gruff, growly one asked.

"Because I'm the one Nathan reached out to," she replied. Nathan had saved her life last year, almost breaking his cover in the process. Julia was not at all surprised he'd risked it again to try to save this woman. "Is he …?"

"Are you a relative of Nathan's? A friend?" the growly one demanded.

"No, but I owe him my life. When he reached out to me and asked me to pass on intel to Prey, I didn't hesitate. I'm only alive right now because he saved me." While she had no regrets, it was possible that if Nathan's cover had been broken and someone knew he'd reached out to her, it could have put her on these men's radar. But life came with risk, and she always did the right thing no matter the potential consequences.

"He didn't make it, I'm sorry, but we did rescue the woman," a man with blue eyes told her. The tone of his voice told her the woman meant something to him.

"Then he would have been happy," she said softly. It was true, Nathan would have considered that a good trade. "Sorry for following you around. Like I said earlier, this is personal to me, and when I saw your plane had been here three times in four months, I had to look into it. Didn't know it was a Prey plane. Eagle should have his logo printed on the side," she joked.

The guys chuckled, and she felt the lingering tension ease away. Almost.

When one of them stepped toward her, another of the guys

stopped him. "You going to cut her loose?" he demanded. Ah, seemed the guy from the car wasn't willing to trust her yet.

"Think we're on the same side here, Domino," the blond one said.

"Domino? What an adorable nickname," Julia said. "When I was a kid, I always wanted a dog, a Dalmatian. I would have called it Domino."

Again, the guys laughed, more heartily this time. And Julia beamed. Already she liked them, they had reacted to a threat, she couldn't fault them there, but once they learned she was no bad guy, they were quick to change their minds accordingly.

All except for Domino.

"We should check out her story first." Domino huffed.

"Don't believe me, tough guy?" she asked, amused. It looked like whatever weird spark had lit between them in the car wasn't one-sided. He'd felt it too. And he didn't like it.

Domino glared at her, heavy shutters on his dark eyes. Still, she felt his suspicion and anger come shining through.

"It's okay," she told the others. "Let's put tough guy's mind at ease. Call Eagle, tell him you found Julia Garamond in Somalia, see if he's the least bit surprised to learn I'm here."

With amused smiles, the other five men headed out of the room, leaving her alone with Domino.

He looked none too pleased about that.

"You suspicious of everyone, tough guy?" she asked, wondering if she could tease him into cracking a smile. His face was handsome but so hard and controlled it looked like it had been cut from stone. "Or just pretty redheads with amazing green eyes?"

His glower darkened. "I see you're modest."

Julia threw back her head and laughed. "You think I don't see the spark of attraction in a guy every time he looks at my eyes? They may as well be possessed, drawing in men against their will. Am I having an off day or am I right when I see that same attraction in your eyes?"

"You should have an off switch," he muttered.

She laughed again. "Not the first time I've been told I talk too much. Not the millionth either. Why do I get the feeling *you* don't have that problem?" There was something about this man that intrigued her. She loved a challenge and suspected that cracking Domino's tough shell would be one of the hardest she'd ever faced.

When he didn't respond except to scowl at her, she opened her mouth to try again to tease a smile out of him when the world around them suddenly exploded.

As debris rained down around her, Julia found herself trapped in a horrible déjà vu.

CHAPTER TWO

October 2nd
7:24 P.M.

His head hurt.

Again.

Domino was getting sick of head injuries.

Slowly, he blinked open heavy eyes, taking in the dark and debris littered about him. Dust and smoke were heavy in the air, clogging his lungs and making it difficult to breathe.

It took a moment for his memories to return.

He and Alpha team were in Somalia tracking a sighting of two men who had escaped the raid at the weapons trafficking compound.

Instead of getting any leads on the men, they'd found someone following them.

A woman.

A firecracker of a woman with red hair and green eyes. A woman who turned out not to be an enemy. A woman who seemed to possess armor-piercing capabilities because she was somehow managing to break through the shields he'd built around himself with each smile, each laugh, each word she chattered.

That woman had been chained to a pipe in the wall just half a dozen feet away from him.

Planting his hands beneath him, Domino pushed up. The world spun, the dizziness making him instantly nauseous and he battled not to throw up. Last thing he needed was to add that stench to the mix.

It took him a moment to get to his feet.

A long moment.

Not a good sign.

Although when he gave his body a mental onceover, no significant pain emanated from any one location. He was achy, and his head throbbed, but otherwise, he felt okay.

Except for the rock sitting in his gut.

The rock was fear, but not for himself.

Not for his team either.

His fear was for Julia.

The spunky little woman who had chattered away at him and his team like he hadn't just carjacked her at gunpoint. Like she hadn't been cuffed to a wall, like she wasn't surrounded by a team of special forces operators who could kill her in a hundred different ways, many of them long, slow, and painful.

None of that had seemed to faze her as she openly told them who she was, who she thought they were, and why she was here.

She'd laughed and teased, had been completely unconcerned by his anger and hostility, and in those impossibly green eyes, he'd seen determination. Focused on him.

He didn't like that, and yet …

No.

No and yet.

Turning in a slow circle, he found he was in a small pocket of space. A metal beam had fallen, landing at an angle that had protected him from the worst of the explosion and subsequent collapse of the building. There was just enough height for him to stand, but barely two or three feet on either side of him.

If the beam hadn't landed the way it had, he would have been crushed.

Domino looked over to where Julia would be if he could see her through the pile of bricks and concrete piled like an impenetrable wall between them.

Had she fared as well?

He'd been lucky. There was no other way to describe why he was alive right now and virtually uninjured.

There were no guarantees Julia had been lucky too.

At least his team had been outside when the explosion hit. He prayed they were all okay. They would do whatever they had to to get to him, but he was worried about Julia.

Worried.

Him.

About a woman a mere half an hour ago he had fantasized about torturing for information. Now knowing he'd held a gun to her head made his stomach revolt, and he ruthlessly shoved it down.

Emotion of any kind hadn't been allowed in the home he'd grown up in.

Tears got you beaten as did taking joy in anything.

Anything his father had perceived as a positive in Domino's young life had been ruthlessly snatched away. Toys, broken. His car, sold. The dog he'd loved, killed.

Domino had been groomed to follow in his father's footsteps only he had rebelled. Formed a life as far away from his family as he could get. Yet those lessons, learned in the formative years when his brain was developing had stuck.

So why did he now feel fear for a woman he didn't even know?

"Julia?" he called out as he carefully tested the debris walled up between them. He couldn't just go knocking it down because he had no idea what things were like on her side. The last thing he wanted to do was cause her further injuries.

There was no answer.

"Julia," he yelled again, louder this time. "It's Domino. Can you hear me?"

Nothing.

His gut tightened.

Was she dead or merely unconscious?

For some reason, the idea of her being dead didn't sit well with him. Of course, he took no pleasure in the death of the innocent, but it was more than that.

Her death felt like a loss.

Only it wasn't one.

He didn't know her; she meant nothing to him. Absolutely nothing.

Love hadn't been a part of his childhood, at least not from his family. The only person to ever love him had been brutally ripped out of his life.

Domino had vowed to never let anyone else get that close. The last thing he needed was more pain.

Women were there when you had an itch you could no longer ignore. There was no need for emotions to be involved. Sex could absolutely be a purely physical activity, mutually beneficial, there was no need to be catching feelings.

"Julia, answer me," he barked. Fear made his voice come out harsher than he intended.

Damn fear.

He didn't like this.

Not one little bit.

"D-Domino?" a weak voice filtered through the rubble. The sound of it literally knocked him to his knees.

She was alive.

"Julia, are you injured?" Heaving himself back to his feet, he began to feel around the debris separating them, he needed to get to her.

"I ... ah ... no ... not really."

"Is that a yes or a no?" he snapped. Now was not the time for her to play games or downplay how seriously she was hurt. It was not time to be a martyr.

"It's a not really," she replied, and he found he was almost smiling at the sass in her tone. He'd take that as an any injuries she had were not life-threatening.

"Not really sounds like you are," he said because he felt this need for reassurance. Reassurance he could only get by hearing her voice.

"Bumps and bruises. Are you okay?"

"Fine."

"I can't tell by your voice if fine means actually fine or you know your arm is half hanging off, but tough guys like you don't complain no matter what."

Her voice was growing stronger—as was his smile—and reassured he started working with more fervor, some sort of primal urge driving him forward. "What do things look like on your side. Do you have any space in there? If I work on getting through to you, am I going to send debris falling down on you?"

"I guess I can assume both your arms are properly attached."

"Julia," he warned. As much as her bantering reassured him, he also needed to get to her and get them both out of there. Since he was stuck in there, he had no intel on what had caused the explosion or if tangos were descending on the building.

"Okay, okay. I have a little pocket of space around me, not a lot, maybe three by three. I can't move to check the wall though because the pipe I'm cuffed to won't budge."

"I'm going to work at getting through to you. I need you to watch the wall. If it looks too unstable on your side, you let me know. Immediately," he added.

"Yes, sir." Her tone was teasingly mocking, and he could almost imagine her doing a two-finger salute.

For several minutes he worked in silence, making slow but steady progress. Thankfully, the building was old, already dilapidated before the explosion. A lot of the bricks and pieces of concrete had been close to breaking anyway and were crumbling with more ease than if the building was newer and in better condition.

"Domino?"

He froze.

There was a tremor in her voice on that one word.

"Yeah?"

"I'm … scared," she admitted, and he remembered that she'd told them she had been in an explosion recently. This was likely giving her major traumatic flashbacks.

"I'm working as fast as I can," he promised because that was really all he could give her. If Julia was expecting comfort and reassurance, she had the wrong guy. He couldn't give her any of those things. Didn't know how to give her any of those things.

"Domino?" she asked again after a few more moments of silence.

"What?"

"Do you think you could maybe talk to me? About anything. I just … it's being alone. Last time, I was trapped for fifteen hours by myself while rescue workers dug through the rubble to get to me. I … I need to know I'm not alone this time."

Julia's openness, her honesty, how freely she admitted her fears without shame, got to him in a big way. That was the complete opposite of everything he had always known.

"Please," she whispered when he didn't say anything.

That one little word, said in a trembling tear-filled voice, was all it took.

Domino started talking.

* * * * *

October 2nd
8:43 P.M.

The walls were closing in on her.
Silence.
Dark.
Panic.
"Julia?"
The voice was like a life ring being thrown out to her when she

19

was trapped in a relentless ocean with nothing to help keep her head above the water.

"I'm okay," she assured him. They both knew that she wasn't, but they accepted the lie because it was easier. If she allowed herself to think too much about the fact that she was once again trapped beneath the rubble of a building, Julia knew she would fall apart.

Falling apart wasn't conducive to their current situation which meant it wasn't an option.

"Julia."

"Said I was okay," she reminded him, smiling despite the terror she felt trapped like this. She hadn't been entirely honest with him. While it was true that she wasn't suffering any sort of life-threatening injuries, with her wrist locked to the pipe her body was twisted at an awkward angle that had her shoulder cramping. One of her legs was pinned beneath a pile of debris, not enough that it was crushing it, but enough that it hurt.

If Domino knew she was in pain, she worried he would work faster to get to her, and while she wanted out of there ASAP, she didn't want him hurt in the process. The building had collapsed, a beam had protected them from being crushed to death, but that didn't mean they weren't in danger.

One wrong move and Domino could send brick and concrete raining down upon himself.

Don't ask her why, but she kind of liked the guy beyond just being attracted to him. Definitely wasn't because of his charming personality, maybe it was because behind the blankness in his eyes that carefully covered his emotions, she sensed pain and loneliness.

Julia was no stranger to either. She'd had her fair share of loss, had definitely been in her fair share of dangerous situations, and found herself wanting to soothe his hurts.

"You *said* you were okay," Domino agreed.

"Saying I'm lying to you, Dom?"

"Yes. And it's Domino. Not Dom."

He was so darn serious it was adorable. Julia had never been a particularly serious person, odd given her line of work and the things she investigated, but she looked for joy in the world. However dark things got there was always a spark of light somewhere, sometimes you just had to search to find it.

Could she help Domino learn to find the specks of light that existed in the world?

"You going to tell me where the nickname Domino came from?" Julia asked.

He grunted. "Dominick Domino."

"Your name is Dominick?" Why did it sound like a lie when he told her his nickname came because it was close to his given name? Reading people was an important part of her job, reading between the lines was too, and Domino had a whole mess of stuff he was doing his best to hide. Did he ever let anyone in?

"Yes."

"Do you ever say more than necessary?"

"Never saw the point."

That was kind of sad. Hadn't he ever had anyone in his life who he could just talk to for hours?

As an only child sent to live with an aunt and uncle after her parents' deaths, the thing she'd missed the most was the long talks she and her mom used to have at night, sitting outside under the stars. Her childhood had been unconventional and being sent to live with elderly relatives and to a normal school at fourteen had been a huge adjustment. She hadn't yet found someone she could talk to like she had her mom, but she hadn't given up.

From the closed-off way Domino seemed to approach the world, she suspected there had never been someone he trusted to share his deepest secrets with.

Her heart hurt thinking about it.

"Julia."

"Don't worry, tough guy, I'm not going to go and die on you.

I'm not that easy to get rid of."

"Worst luck," he muttered under his breath, making her laugh.

"Tired of my winning personality already?" she teased. "Give me a chance, and you might find the best friend in the world."

"Yeah, sure." While she couldn't see his face, she could hear the eye roll in his tone. Domino didn't seem to believe in people, which while she understood made sense in a way because working at Prey meant he saw the worst of humanity, he also had a team he had to trust to always have his back.

She'd met that team, had no doubt they worked together like a well-oiled machine, he did trust them, but did he have anyone who was just his? Julia suspected he didn't, and she didn't like the idea and wanted to change it, but reality was as soon as they got out of there, he and his team would go off about their mission, and she would go back to looking for links to the trafficking ring.

Her gaze scanned the tight space. Memories of four months ago filtered through her mind, and each one seemed to suck a little more of the oxygen out of the space.

Tight spaces never used to bother her.

After all, she had grown up living in camper vans and tents.

But no matter how small their home had been, she and her parents had spent most of their time outside in the fresh air.

That was the problem.

There was no fresh air in here.

Hardly any air at all.

Her chest felt like it was tightening, and Julia pressed her free hand to it, holding it above her heart, willing it to keep beating. Now was not the time to fall apart.

"Deep breaths, you got this," she coached herself. Later. She could fall apart later when she was safe in her hotel room.

"Did you say something?"

Of course, the tough guy heard her whispered words. However, she had no intention of telling him how precariously she was balanced on the ledge of hysteria. Not only would it endanger him if he stopped working his way through to her carefully, but she doubted dealing with a hysterical woman was something a guy like Domino would appreciate.

"Julia."

A weary smile touched her lips as she rested her head back as best as she could at this weird angle against a piece of the wall still standing behind her. "You keep saying my name, and I might start to think you like me."

"Never said I didn't."

"Well, not in so many words, although telling your team not to trust me kind of made the point anyway."

Domino was silent for a moment, and then a puff of powder filled the space as he shoved aside a small pile of bricks and looked through at her.

A rush of relief left her feeling drained. She wasn't alone anymore. It was one thing to know Domino was just on the other side of the wall of rubble, but it was another to be able to see his face, even if it was shadowy and hard to see in the dark.

Because the guy didn't seem to possess an ounce of softness in his perfectly sculpted body, he immediately frowned at her. "Your leg is trapped."

Although his words came out accusingly, Julia smiled. "But not crushed."

"You should have told me."

"Didn't think it was useful information."

"I decide what's useful information."

"It's my leg," she reminded him. Why she was arguing with him she didn't know, maybe it was because the pain was beginning to become unbearable. Julia knew her ankle wasn't broken, but the pressure of the rubble weighing down on it was starting to get to her.

"Hold on, I'm coming," Domino said in that arrogant tone that said once he was there everything would be okay.

Strange thing was, she believed him.

Now that he was mostly through to her, it didn't take him long to make a hole big enough that he could squeeze through it.

Next thing she knew, he was crouching at her side. When his large hand curled under her chin so his fingers could press to her neck and check her pulse his touch was so gentle it brought tears to her eyes.

"Let's get this unlocked." His fingers circled her wrist, warm and strong, the pads rough telling the story of the battles he had fought, and he unlocked the handcuff. With more care than she would have expected he would take, he moved her arm around in front of her. While one of his hands rubbed the bruises on her wrist, the other massaged her shoulder. His touch was tender, gentle, and sweeter than she had realized he was capable of being.

Being here, trapped inside another exploded building so soon after the last time had her feeling vulnerable, tender gestures like that were enough to push her into meltdown mode.

"Careful, tough guy, you keep being sweet like that and you may have a crying woman on your hands."

There.

Was that a smile?

"Can't win with you, huh, red? Either I'm a jerk who doesn't like you or a nice guy who makes you cry."

Julia huffed a small chuckle even as a couple of tears tumbled free.

"Do you think your leg is broken?" he asked as he set her hand in her lap and started removing the debris pinning her leg in place.

"Just bruised."

"You sure?"

"Positive."

A moment later, she sighed in relief as the pressure on her leg disappeared as he freed it. While her leg might no longer be trapped, it wasn't like she could just get up and walk out of there.

They were still stuck.

"You crying, red?"

"Sorry," she said with a shrug.

Domino hesitated for a moment then brushed the pad of his thumb across her cheek, catching her tears. "My team will come for us."

"You're not going to leave me alone in here, are you?" Tough guys like Domino didn't like sitting still and letting someone else do the work, and she wouldn't be surprised if he left her here to go and try to find his way through to his team.

"Love my company that much?"

She playfully punched him in the arm. "As if. I just don't want to be alone. Memories, you know?"

Slowly he edged her sideways so he could sit beside her in the small space. "Wouldn't do that to you, red."

Why did those words hit her straight in the heart?

He didn't mean he wasn't ever going to leave her, he just meant he wouldn't leave her alone trapped in here, yet her heart took it way out of context.

Snuggling into Domino's side, Julia decided she didn't care how he meant it, for now he was here, and he was hers, and she liked it.

CHAPTER THREE

October 3rd
12:02 A.M.

He shouldn't be enjoying this.

They were trapped in a building, he had no idea who had set the explosion or why or if they were still a threat, the woman beside him had been following him and his team and there was every chance that in doing so she had painted a target on her back by catching the wrong person's attention.

And Domino did like this.

Julia was warm and soft against his side. She was small, dainty, and fragile, and yet at the same time, she was larger than life and strong enough to own her emotions and fears without trying to hide from them.

He admired that a hell of a lot.

"Domino?" Julia's voice was soft, and it washed over him like a stream of warm water, heating a place inside of him he'd had no choice but to allow to grow into a barren, ice-covered wilderness.

His survival as a child had depended on his ability not to feel.

A lot of his adult life had as well.

You weren't a very good soldier if you were constantly bogged down by your emotions. To function, deal with victims, and deal with evil, you had to have yourself together and locked down tight.

So that was what he did.

What he had always done.

It wasn't a pleasant feeling to know that the woman at his side very well might be in possession of a key that could unlock the vault his emotions were locked in and send them spewing out.

"Yeah?"

"You don't think your team was hurt or killed, do you?" she asked somewhat tentatively.

As if that thought hadn't already entered his mind a time or twenty.

Since he had no intel on who or what had caused the explosion, there was no way he could know the impact on his team.

Best case scenario, they hadn't been near the building when it went down and hadn't been injured. They had called in assistance or were working on their own to get him and Julia out.

Worst case scenario, they had either been injured or killed in the explosion, or whoever had blown the building up had come in to make sure that they—Alpha team or Julia, whoever the target was—was dead and his team had been slaughtered.

Neither of those two options was good for him and Julia.

While there was a chance he could find a way out for both of them, it would involve leaving Julia behind, and he wasn't sure she could handle that.

Or that he could.

"They're not dead?" she asked it like she needed to hear him say it in order to even allow herself the possibility of believing it.

What was worse was he wanted to offer her that reassurance.

Her emotions weren't his responsibility.

Hell, *she* wasn't his responsibility.

Still, his mouth opened, and reassurance tumbled out. "No, they're not dead."

"You're sure?"

"Yes."

"Positive?" The woman sure had a need to talk things out, and while Domino couldn't say he was used to the constant chatter, he'd spent enough time around his teammates' women to at least tolerate it. Especially when it was this woman chattering.

"Yes."

"Okay then." Julia rested her head on his shoulder, her face pressed against his chest.

Maybe sitting down beside her hadn't been the smartest idea. There wasn't a lot of room in here, so it wasn't like he had a lot of options, but he could have sat across from her. Or stood. Standing over her would have been a lot more comfortable.

Well, it wouldn't have been, he was bruised and achy and sitting conserved strength, but he hadn't anticipated that Julia would take it as an invitation to use him as her personal pillow.

Or anticipated that he would actually like it.

Potential terrorist or not, this woman practically had dangerous tattooed on her forehead.

"Did you hear that?" Julia shot upright. "I thought I heard something."

He had too.

Carefully, he eased himself upright and moved to the partially demolished wall that had separated them when they first regained consciousness.

Someone was coming.

"Stay here," he ordered as he slithered back through the hole he'd created and into the space where he'd been trapped.

There was every probability that it was his team searching for him and Julia. They knew where they'd been in the building so they would have worked at getting to them the quickest way possible. It had been going on five hours since the explosion. If his team hadn't been injured and had started the search right away there was a chance that they could be closing in on his position.

Palming his weapon, he whistled.

"Domino?" Julia asked, obviously wondering why he was whistling.

"Don't you ever stay silent?" he muttered, making her laugh. She seemed to find his somewhat surly attitude amusing, which was both grating and somewhat comforting. Usually, he did his best to put off anyone who might even think about trying to get close to him. He liked the Oswald family who owned and ran Prey Security, and he liked his teammates and their women. In particular, Arrow's girlfriend, Piper, felt like a little sister, but what he felt for Julia definitely couldn't fit into the sister category.

Another whistle echoed through the dark, and he relaxed.

Help was on the way.

The quicker he got out of here and they sent Julia Garamond back Stateside, the better.

He whistled back, and a moment later, he heard Bear call his name.

"We're here," he called back.

"Julia with you?" Arrow asked.

"Yeah, she's here too."

"Injuries?" the medic asked.

"Relatively minor." While Julia claimed her leg wasn't broken, she also hadn't informed him that it had been pinned in place by bricks and concrete so he wasn't sure he could believe her.

"Won't take us much longer to get to you," Bear said.

Locating which direction they were coming from, he headed for it. "I'll work on things from this side."

"Are they coming?" Julia asked from behind him.

"Didn't I tell you to stay there?"

"Yep, you did," she agreed cheerfully. "Oof."

Her oof had him spinning around, and he found her trying to clamber her way through the hole he'd created.

"What are you doing?" he demanded, hurrying to assist her.

"Coming to help."

"Don't you ever do as you're told?"

"Nope." She was grinning at him, and he felt his own lips wanting to echo that smile.

To curb the impulse he scowled, then reached out and very gently lifted her, easing her through the hole and setting her down on her backside on a relatively clear bit of floor. "Stay there."

"I'm not a dog, Dom," she said, sounding highly amused.

Domino merely grunted and went to work. It probably took them another thirty minutes of hard work, but finally they had a hole in another section of wall, and there was his team.

"Hey, man," Arrow said, first to climb through the hole.

"She hurt her leg," he said, directing the medic's attention to Julia first.

"She's fine," Julia said, limping toward them.

"Let's take a look and confirm that," Arrow said smoothly, taking Julia's elbow and easing her back down to the ground.

Domino was completely unprepared for the rush of jealousy he felt at seeing another man's hands on Julia. Didn't matter that Arrow was madly in love with another woman, a woman he planned to marry and have babies with. Didn't matter that he never got close enough to anyone to be jealous over them.

"Easy, man, he's just checking her out," Mouse soothed from behind him, causing Domino's temper to spike.

"I know that," he ground out.

"Then stop acting like he's stealing your favorite toy," Surf said.

"She's not my anything," he growled. Just as he was turning his back on the pair, he saw Julia get to her feet. No way. "She can't walk out of here, she's in pain."

"I'm not a baby, Dom," Julia said patiently. "I can handle a little pain if it means getting out of here."

Maybe she could handle the pain, but for some reason he found he couldn't.

"We'll carry you out," he said in a tone that allowed for zero argument. His father had used the same tone when dealing with his underlings. "Then you're getting straight on a plane and going home."

"You are crazy if you think I'm leaving before I get what I came to Somalia for."

"You aren't cut out to be in a country like this?"

"No?" Her voice had taken on a mocking tone. "So, I guess I didn't get caught by a drug smuggler in Cambodia and almost got my head blown off. Would have if a rival hadn't shown up and a shoot-out gave me a chance to slip away. Or got too close to a human trafficking ring in Mexico, who kidnapped me and would have sold me if his house hadn't been raided by the cops. Or been captured by the very same people linked to the explosions back home, and probably this one tonight, and was only saved because Nathan risked everything to get me out. Trust me, Dom, I can handle anything life throws at me."

It felt like his blood was slowly oozing out of some unknown injury.

Julia might believe she could handle anything, but he wasn't sure he could stomach the idea of her in danger.

"You're not helping your case with those stories, red."

"Wasn't aware I had to build a case. I'm a big girl, and I make my own decisions."

"We'll talk about it later," he muttered as he stalked over to her and snatched her up, cradling her against his chest.

"Okay, but it's going to be a pretty short talk," Julia said. She didn't sound angry with him for attempting to make decisions for her, nor did she sound like she was going to be backing down any time soon.

Domino had no idea how to convince her that going home was her best bet at being safe. His father had issued orders, he didn't discuss things, same thing in the military and at Prey, you followed orders and did as you were told.

So how was he going to figure out a way to talk the firecracker in his arms into going home when he had zero of the skills required to do that?

* * * * *

October 3rd

2:43 A.M.

Julia let out a breath as they emerged from the rubble of the building.

Free.

As relieved as she was to be out, at least this time around she hadn't been trapped alone. Domino had been with her, and it had helped a whole lot more than she would have thought it would. The man was angry and closed off, usually downright hostile pretty much every time he talked to her or about her.

Until he touched her.

Then he was almost impossibly gentle.

The dichotomy didn't just intrigue her, it made her want to do something about it.

But how could you soothe someone's anger when that person didn't want to be anywhere near you? Maybe didn't even want to let go of their anger.

"So, am I going to have an argument on my hands if I drive back to my apartment?" Julia asked only half-jokingly as Domino set her on her feet. Just because the other guys on Alpha team believed she was who she said she was—and she had been vouched for by Eagle Oswald—Domino seemed determined to be a holdout.

She had no idea why he was so adamant about not trusting her. Like she got that he had to be careful, trusting the wrong person in his line of work meant the death of himself, his team, and innocent people, but she was a well-known and respected investigative journalist, and she'd helped Prey just two months ago. It was pretty obvious she was no bad guy, so why was he so determined to paint her as one?

"You think you're going back to your apartment?" Domino snapped. His face was dirty, streaked with dust and smudges of blood, with a bruise developing on his temple, but you wouldn't know he'd just been blown up from the strength and confidence

32

emanating from him.

"Umm ... yeah," she said like it was obvious.

"Someone tried to blow you up."

"Well, we don't know they were after me, do we now? I mean no offense, but you guys were here too, maybe they were trying to blow you up." The guys had told her and Domino that the explosion had been set on the opposite side of the building from where they were. Likely the reason they weren't dead. They'd heard cars leaving right after but had stayed to dig her and Domino out.

"Right, we don't know," Domino said like she was reiterating his point. "So, for now, you're coming with us."

"Oh, I am, am I?" she asked, amused more than angry by his demands. If someone was after her, she didn't really mind sticking with Alpha team. She could shoot and hit what she aimed at and had done a lot of self-defense training, but her skills were nothing compared to these warriors.

Domino took a step closer. "You are."

"And if I say no?" She took her own step closer until they were eye to eye. Her leg hurt but Domino carrying her out meant it wasn't as bad as it could have been.

"Then I cuff you and take you with us anyway."

Julia threw back her head and laughed. "Dom, you are too cute. I'm just messing with you. I'm actually grateful for the offer to hang with you guys, but I'm not going back home when there is more information here that I need. We need," she added.

When Dom huffed in irritation she laughed again. The man needed to learn to do that. No one had to be in control of themselves that rigidly all the time. She bet if he learned to let go, laugh, and have fun, he'd find that anger he seemed to cling to might just fade away.

"Thanks so much for coming for us," she said, turning to face the rest of Alpha team. Her smile faded and emotion clogged her throat. They didn't realize how much she would forever be grateful to them for getting her out. Being buried alive had never really been anything she thought about, but after being trapped in that last explosion on her own for so many hours it had become a huge phobia.

One by one she approached the men—whose names Domino had told her while they were trapped in the apartment building—and kissed each of their cheeks.

"Why are you growling?" she asked Domino, looking over her shoulder to see him glowering at her.

"Think he doesn't like you kissing other guys, darlin'," Surf said, clearly highly amused.

"Ah, I see." Closing the distance between her and a growly Domino, she stood before him. "You don't want me to thank your friends for saving our lives?"

If looks could kill, he would have just slaughtered her.

"You should know I'm an affectionate person," she warned. If there was going to be anything at all—even friendship—between them then he had to know the score up front. While she didn't cheat and she didn't share, she would continue to be the person her parents raised her to be, and that was someone who embraced her emotions and showed the people in her life that she cared.

"Don't care."

"I might believe that if you didn't look like you were about to beat up your team." When she nodded at his fists, he uncurled them slowly. With a grin, she placed her hands on his shoulders, used them to help her balance, and stood on her tiptoes so she could reach up and kiss his cheek. "Thank you for being there, I'm glad I wasn't alone. I'm glad *you* were there," she added. Then very softly feathered her lips across his.

If she hadn't been watching so closely, Julia would have thought he had been unaffected by her kiss, but she saw the flare of life in those dead eyes of his.

The real Domino was hidden somewhere in there, and she hoped she could help him break out.

"You should get off your leg," Domino said briskly.

"See, guys, he does care," she said with a laugh as she allowed Domino to take her elbow and help her to one of the vehicles.

Once they were settled inside, Julia immediately opened her window, allowing the fresh air to roll over her, reminding her that she wasn't trapped any longer. Domino sat in the back beside her, and although Surf and Arrow were talking neither she nor Dom participated.

Even though he said nothing, she could feel his attention on her. It sounded strange, but it was like she could feel it warming her like a soft caress.

It felt good to sit on the comfortable leather and relax. Her muscles were tight, she was achy all over, her leg throbbed from the small amount of time she'd spent standing, and when Arrow passed her a bottle of water she sipped at it, then tilted her face toward the window and closed her eyes.

Maybe if she worked with Prey they could actually find these guys and stop them before they killed anyone else.

When the car slowed, she opened her eyes, then did a double take when she saw where they were.

Betrayal burned hot inside her.

"An airport? I said I wasn't going home."

"And I said we'd talk about it," Dom said so calmly she wanted to hit him.

"So, you're going to tie me up and put me on a plane against my will? Don't you think if you try, I'm just going to get right back on a plane and fly back here?" She thought they understood that it wasn't up for discussion.

Guess they wouldn't be working together after all.

Which didn't matter, she was used to working on her own anyway. It was how she did her best work.

"Let me out," she ordered, grabbing at the doorhandle the second the car stopped moving.

"So, you can lose your temper after all," Domino said,

sounding amused for the first time since they'd met.

There was no point in answering. If he thought she would just go quietly and allow anyone to manhandle her and make her do something she didn't want to, he was crazy. Her parents had raised her to be independent, tackle problems, work to find a solution, and that was what she would do now.

This was the same airfield she'd tracked the plane entering the country, she knew where it was and could find her way back to her rental.

"Hey." Domino snapped an arm around her waist before she'd taken more than two steps and yanked her up against his chest. "You need to get off your leg."

"Let me go." Julia struggled against him even knowing it was pointless.

"Calm down."

"You tricked me into coming here. I thought you guys were going to help me find these people and stop them." Domino and Alpha team's betrayal shouldn't hurt, but for some reason it did. They hadn't outright said they'd work together she had just assumed. Her mistake, but it still sucked.

"I didn't say we were putting you on a plane."

"But ... you brought me to an airport."

Setting her down, Dom kept his hands on her shoulders and turned her to face him. "You shouldn't make assumptions, red. This is where my team and I have been staying."

"Oops," she said sheepishly. "Guess I shouldn't have jumped to conclusions. I'm sorry. Forgive me?"

His brows furrowed and his expression told her he thought she was some sort of alien species he had no idea what to make of. "Sure. I guess. Yeah. The guys are waiting. You want to come and tell us what you know?"

"Do I? Is that a rhetorical question? Yeah, I want to come and share what I know." Excitement replaced the betrayal that just a moment before had been burning a pit in her stomach. "Come on, hurry up, slowpoke."

"I don't get you," Domino said as he caught up to her.

"I know, I hear that a lot."

"You come to dangerous places, you've faced death more times than you should have, and here you are so excited about working to bring down men more dangerous than you realize. You don't make sense."

Julia laughed. "Life doesn't have to make sense, it's fun and awful and confusing all at the same time. But it's also short. *Too* short. You have to make the most of it while you can, otherwise you're missing out. You're missing the point."

She could feel his eyes on her as they entered a hangar and walked through it to a large room with a small kitchen, a table and chairs, and a couple of couches. The rest of Alpha team was waiting for them.

"You two kids get everything sorted out?" Mouse asked.

"Sure did," she said, joining them at the table. "And Dom said you want me to share my intel with you. That means you're sharing with me too, right?"

"We'll share what we can," Bear said.

"Good enough." There was likely classified intel Prey couldn't share, but she was sure together they could do this. Bring down a terrorist ring before they could destroy the country and steal innocent lives. "The first thing you should know is that this weapons trafficking ring based here in Somalia, I'm pretty sure it's connected to the Russian Mafia."

Everyone was looking at her so no one else likely saw the flash of horror on Domino's face.

Horror that said he had some sort of personal connection to the Bratva.

CHAPTER FOUR

October 3rd

3:58 A.M.

The Russian mafia.

Bratva.

Domino felt like the world had opened up beneath him.

Was it possible?

Could they have sent Julia after him?

It had been a long time since he'd walked away from that life.

Leaving had cost him everything he had loved, the only good thing he had, and in a horrific twist of fate, the only thing that had allowed him to remain free for almost a decade and a half.

If Julia was involved, nothing would stop him from making an example of her. If she was involved willingly at least. If she had been dragged in against her will, he would leave it to Prey to help her get out.

But if she had come here to play games with him, do his family's dirty work for them, then she would pay a hefty price.

Everything that had been done to his dear, sweet, innocent Rosie he would do to Julia then leave her body on their doorstep. Same thing they'd done to him. They'd viciously tortured the woman he loved, then had her body delivered right to the door of his apartment.

Sixteen years later and the images hadn't faded.

Every detail from the stark contrast of the bright red blood on her too-pale skin, to the pain in her eyes, locked open in death, to the fearful o her lips had formed.

Rosie's death was supposed to be a message. It was supposed

to remind him that he could never leave, instead, it had given him the leverage he needed to blackmail his family into backing off. Her death had bought his freedom, and he had used that freedom to help make the world a better place and end suffering like the kind his own family inflicted.

Like she didn't have a care in the world, Julia shot him a funny look, then began to ramble excitedly. "Follow the money. You *always* follow the money. It always leads you to the truth."

"And it led you to the Bratva?" Surf asked, sounding intrigued.

"Not at first. At first, all I had was a bunch of pieces, and I couldn't figure out how to put them all together," Julia replied. "It started when I decided to look into Storm Gallagher last year after he went on the run. I told you that I ended up getting too close. I thought I'd look into the weapons and where he got them. I did some investigating and found some links about the trafficking ring here in Somalia. I obviously got too close because I was grabbed one night. I heard things while I was there. Russian. I wish I spoke it, but I remembered a few words, and after Nathan got me out, I found out what language it was."

"So, you thought the Russian mafia could be involved," Arrow said, sounding like it was quite a leap.

Julia shrugged. "It sounded logical."

"Let me guess, you then did some more digging?" Mouse asked with a grin.

"You guess right." Julia grinned back.

"I like this girl, she goes after what she wants with a tenacity that would put most people to shame," Surf said. Surf's gaze moved to him, but Domino ignored it. It was taking all he had to keep his feet rooted to the spot so he didn't go and do something stupid.

Like grab Julia, drag her out of her chair, slam her up against a wall, and demand she tell him if his family had sent her here to mess with him.

"Tenacity is the only way to get the story," Julia agreed. "And this one is personal for me. For all of us, I guess. These people are dangerous. I suspect you know more than I do, but I know they're going to hit more targets back home. That means more innocent people will lose their lives. I won't stand by and let that happen. No way. We have to stop them."

Fire shot from Julia's green eyes, determination that said there was no way anyone was going to make her back down.

She looked so sincere.

Sounded sincere too.

But how could he know it wasn't an act?

Even if she had been forced into this against her will, she could still be a threat to him, his team, his teammates' partners, and children.

Unable to stand here a second longer, Domino spun and stormed out of the hangar, not caring what his friends would think of his behavior.

Bursting out into the muggy early morning he sucked in a long, slow breath, then held it for a moment before expelling it equally as slowly.

Ever since he'd been in Somalia four months ago, held captive and tortured, receiving head injuries he still had lingering issues from, his family had been at the forefront of his mind. After years of banishing them from his thoughts and his life, these last few months they seemed to be shoving their way back in.

It was the last thing he wanted.

If it was possible to scrub their DNA right out of his body that was what he would do.

"Dom?" A gentle hand touched his bicep and he jerked away.

The movement wasn't voluntary, he was just balancing on a knife's edge right now, and the last thing he wanted to do was take out his anger on Julia.

Of course, she wasn't some spy sent in by his family. If his family wanted to mess with him, they wouldn't play games they'd just kill him. Or if they wanted to teach him a lesson or make an example out of him, they'd abduct him and torture him first.

Julia's hand hovered in the air for a moment and hurt flashed on her face, but she didn't yell at him, lose her temper, or tell him off for being rude. Again.

"Are you okay? You stormed out and I was worried about you," she said softly.

There was no way she could know how deeply those words struck.

Growing up, nobody had worried about him. He was a tool to be groomed and used, nothing more. An irritation because he hadn't cowered and done as he was ordered.

But Julia wasn't lying when she said she cared.

He could see it in her eyes.

Why, he had no idea. Wasn't like he had been anything even remotely close to friendly, he'd barely even been civil.

Do something.

Despite his internal urging, he didn't know what to do. Had no idea what he should say to her. Thank her for caring? That was appropriate, right?

Problem was, Domino had shut down emotion in order to survive.

Sure, he'd bonded with his Delta team and trusted them with his life. Same when he came to Prey, the men on Alpha team were family to him. He loved them and their families as though they were his own, but he rarely interacted in any meaningful way with anyone who wasn't part of Prey.

Julia made him feel like he was spinning out of control. He didn't like that she sparked feelings in him, and while he resented it, he also … kind of liked it. In a way it felt freeing. Julia didn't shy away from anything she was feeling, she embraced it, processed it, and moved forward. What would it be like to live like that?

"Do you want to talk?" Julia offered. He still hadn't said anything, he was just standing there staring at her, yet she hadn't backed away. There was no pity in her eyes, but there was empathy and understanding. He actually believed that she wanted to help him, and he never believed in people who hadn't rigorously proved they were trustworthy.

"I don't talk." Domino hated that his words came out harsh, that wasn't what he wanted, but he was floundering well out of his comfort zone here.

Apparently unoffended, Julia just smiled. "That's okay, we could just walk around, or we could just sit here and look at the stars. Well, it's cloudy and it feels like it's going to rain, so we could wait for the rain. Maybe we could even dance in the rain, I've never done that before, but I'll admit it does hold a kind of weird but fun appeal."

Domino could picture Julia in the rain. Arms held out wide, welcoming the onslaught from nature, head tilted back, taking the full force of the downpour. Soaked clothes would mold to her slender form, highlighting her soft curves. Raindrops would slide down her face, trailing along her lips.

Lips he found himself wondering about. Were they as soft as they looked? What did they taste like? Would she be a tentative kisser? No, there was nothing tentative about Julia, her kisses would be infused with the same energy that she lived the rest of her life with.

"If I can't convince you to dance with me then we could always—"

Whatever Julia had been about to suggest was lost when a loud crack split through the night.

A gunshot.

Launching himself at Julia, he tackled her, taking her to the ground and covering her body with his own, praying that she hadn't been hit.

* * * * *

October 3rd
4:31 A.M.

Bullets whizzed by them.

Slamming into the concrete and sending sharp shards flying into her and Domino.

Since Dom had covered her body with his own, pressing her down into the concrete so hard it hurt her already bruised body, Julia knew he was taking the brunt of the punishment from the concrete shards as well as putting his life on the line for her.

Was whoever was shooting at them aiming for him or her?

Both?

Random?

Domino shifted slightly, and then more gunshots splintered through the night. The sound was loud since he was firing from just above her, and with the way she was pinned down, she couldn't even lift her hands to cover her ears.

Whatever else Dom was, however, he felt about her—and she actually had no idea whether he hated her, was attracted to her, or completely indifferent—he was a protector at heart, and he hadn't hesitated to put himself between her and danger.

Footsteps indicated that the rest of Alpha team had heard the shots and come to help. Julia didn't have any doubts that whoever was shooting at them was no match for the elite men who worked for Prey.

"We have to move, there's no cover out here," Dom told her, his lips right against her ear and she shivered. Not in a scared way, but his warm breath on her skin did things to her. Tingly things to her lady parts.

Great timing, Julia.

The rebuke did little to quell the attraction humming through her body. Maybe she'd been doing this too long if she could be in the middle of a firefight and still be able to lust over her sexy savior.

"When I tell you, I want you to run back into the hangar," Domino said.

"What about you?" Of course, she didn't want to get shot, but she didn't want Domino to get shot either. Especially not because he was more worried about her than he was about himself.

"Don't worry about me. Don't look back, don't stop no matter what."

His orders were given briskly and without concern like he had done this a million times before and was completely confident in his abilities.

That cool confidence bled into her as well, and she found she wasn't afraid. Well, she was a little, but she trusted Domino and his team.

When Domino slowly levered his body off hers enough that she could wiggle out from underneath him, she didn't stop to think about why it seemed important, she just placed her hands on his cheeks and pressed her lips to his in a quick and fiery kiss.

Sliding out from under the protection of Dom's large, muscled body, Julia did exactly as she'd been ordered to.

She turned and ran.

Her bruised leg protested violently, but she clamped her teeth together and ignored the pain. They hadn't wandered far from the hangar so it didn't take her long to close the distance.

Bullets continued to fly from all directions, and she felt absolutely trapped in the middle.

Good guys and bad guys were all shooting in her direction, although only the bad guys were aiming at her. The good guys were laying down cover fire so she could get to safety, but it didn't ease her fears for Domino.

He was still out there.

Risking himself for her.

Julia wanted to believe it was because he cared, but she suspected it was simply because he saw it as his duty. She was a mission, a task to be completed, a problem to be solved, something to take care of so you could move on, only for some reason she didn't want him to move on.

Crazy, but she liked the guy.

As she approached the hangar a pair of hands grabbed her, snatched her up and pulled her back behind cover.

"You hurt?" Arrow asked, setting her on her feet and running his hands over her body in search of injuries.

"I'm okay," she assured him. "But what about Domino?"

Finishing his examination of her, Arrow straightened. "Don't worry about Domino, he'll be fine."

She hoped that was true, but there was no guarantee. "Where are they going?" she asked as the others moved out of the safety of the hangar.

"To find the men shooting at you."

"At us," she corrected.

"They were shooting at you, Julia," Arrow said gently. "When you got up, they shifted their aim from where Domino had you pinned down. Whoever it is followed you here, you're the one they want, not us."

It had to be the trafficking ring, they knew she was still looking into them. If they knew she was in Somalia, they must have followed her, which also meant the explosion was likely a way to eliminate her. Domino could have been killed twice now because of her.

Was still in danger because of her.

"We're moving out as soon as the guys take out the shooters," Arrow told her, ushering her toward the plane.

"No. Wait." Julia tried to push back against him, but he was so much bigger and stronger than her that he easily maneuvered her forward. "I can't leave now."

"You really want to give these guys another chance at you?"

"Well, no, of course not. But …"

"No buts, Jules. Get yourself in the plane and stay down low. I have to grab our stuff then as soon as the guys get back, we're out of here."

Nobody could say that Julia didn't put herself in dangerous situations, often without blinking or giving it a second thought, but she also wasn't stupid. If she stayed, Alpha team would stay, and she had already put them in danger twice. They could go back home and figure everything out, then Prey could get the bad guys, and she'd get her story, and no one else would get hurt. Simple.

"Go." Arrow nudged her toward the plane, then when she started climbing the steps he disappeared inside.

Her leg ached, her entire body was covered in bruises that throbbed, adrenalin was draining from her system leaving her lightheaded and shaky, and exhaustion was settling in.

It had been a long few months tracking down every lead she could find to try to identify the men involved in the plot to blow up targets in the country she called home. Obsessive enough at the best of times, this story being personal to her meant she wouldn't give up. No matter what. Threats and intimidation wouldn't work, but that didn't mean she was unaffected by everything that had happened the last twenty-four hours.

And it was all starting to hit her at once.

"Sit down," Arrow said softly as he took her elbow and guided her into a chair.

"Are the others okay? Are they back?"

"They can take care of themselves, let's just take a moment to check you out." Arrow took her wrist, checking her pulse, then shined a light in her eyes before turning his attention to her leg. As he eased her sneaker off and rolled up her pants, she saw the bottom half of her left leg was almost entirely black and blue. No wonder it hurt so badly.

The smart thing to do would have been to keep off it, but then Domino had gone storming off and had looked so angry and alone. There had been no choice but to go after him and do what she could to soothe him. For some reason, his pain really bothered her.

While Arrow wrapped an ace bandage around her leg she stared at the door, willing Domino to return.

How would she feel if he was killed because of her?

What would have happened if she hadn't stumbled upon Alpha team?

Likely these men would have caught up with her, kidnapped or killed her, and this time there might not have been a rival gang, a police raid, or an undercover operative to get her out alive.

Sooner or later, her time would be up. There were only so many times you could tempt fate before it finally caught up with you. Before it had never bothered her, she'd always lived knowing that it was important to enjoy every day because in a second it could be over. But now the thought of dying before getting a chance to be with Domino made her feel like she would be missing out on something amazing.

Arrow moved in front of her a split second before she saw Bear enter the plane. Mouse was behind him, then Surf and Brick.

Julia's heart tightened in her chest when Domino finally emerged.

His dark hair was mussed, tired lines bracketed his mouth, and exhaustion was etched into every pore. Immediately his gaze roamed the plane, settling on her.

Their eyes met, and she didn't think.

Flying across the plane, Julia threw herself into his arms. They closed around her, and even though she had no idea where they stood or if they were even on the same page, she felt him relax.

This man had her all twisted into knots, confused, and even a little uncertain, not something she was entirely accustomed to.

But as he held her, she got a sense of home that had been missing since her parents' deaths.

CHAPTER FIVE

October 4th
2:12 A.M.

He couldn't tear his eyes away from her.

Domino wasn't even trying to hide it.

Julia was stunning. She laughed and talked with his team like she had been a part of them since the beginning. The guys all teased her affectionately like she was a little sister, and she gave as good as she got.

She should be resting.

They were going on thirty-six hours since he'd slipped into the back of her car and held a gun to her head. All of that appeared to be forgotten. Julia had slipped seamlessly into Alpha team, and no one but him seemed to have any doubts about her.

All right, so he didn't really have doubts.

He just had to cling to the notion that she might not be who she said she was because if he didn't, she would blast through all of his defenses without breaking a sweat.

Despite her sparkling eyes and bright smile, he could see the toll the last day and a half had taken on her. He didn't know how. Other than cuts and bruises there was no outward evidence that she was about to hit a brick wall built of exhaustion and trauma.

No one could go through what she had in such a short amount of time and not be shaken up. She'd had a weapon pointed at her, been in an explosion, and been shot at. One, two, three and he knew she was about ready to be down for the count. Add in the fact that being buried alive was her worst nightmare given that she had been in another explosion, trapped alone for hours just months ago.

How he knew she was struggling he didn't understand.

Emotions—his or other people's—often eluded him. Groomed from childhood not to have any, it was no wonder he didn't know how to process them, it was easier to just shut them out. Didn't mean he didn't get angry at the atrocities he saw perpetrated in his work at Prey, or that he didn't care when the people in his life were hurting, it was just that he always felt removed.

Until now.

Now Julia's emotions were coming screaming through at full volume.

Her gaze roamed the plane until it settled on him. It hovered there for a moment before returning to Surf, who was trying to teach her to play poker, only Julia couldn't seem to catch on. Her face was too expressive, the woman couldn't bluff if her life depended on it.

He noticed she did that a lot. Searched him out. Domino got the feeling that he was somehow keeping her anchored.

A shocking feeling.

A *terrifying* feeling.

How could he be her anchor when he was adrift himself?

"Brick, can I come help land the plane?" Julia called out, ruffling Surf's blond locks on her way toward the cockpit.

Apparently, Julia had wanted to learn to fly, and the second they were in the air she started bugging Brick to teach her. Shockingly the man who was even more closed off than Domino himself had agreed.

Julia had been thrilled to pieces, her excitement contagious, and everyone had watched her childlike glee as Brick gave her a lesson in some basics. He was pretty sure that one of the first things she would do after she got her answers was hit Brick up for more lessons. It was clear she was the kind of person who craved new experiences, and once she set her mind on something wasn't going to change it.

Which meant there was no chance she was walking away before she found the people responsible for setting those explosions.

That meant there were only three options as far as he could see.

One, they could walk away and forget they ever met her, leaving her to her fate.

Two, they could forcibly lock her away somewhere she would be safe while they found every person involved in the plot to overthrow the government and ensure Julia's safety.

Or three, they could work with her.

Domino already knew which option Prey would choose.

Standing, he followed Julia toward the cockpit, propped himself up against the wall, and watched her.

There was something special about the way she lit up a room. He had never seen anything like it. The way she just embraced emotion, wore her feelings so freely, it baffled him, but he also found it appealing.

Probably more appealing than he should, given there would never be anything between them except perhaps one hot night of sex.

Could women like Julia who were all about emotion do meaningless one-night stands?

Should he care?

As they started to descend, Domino took the seat closest to the cockpit where he could watch Julia help Brick land the plane. The way her brow furrowed into cute little lines as she concentrated intrigued him, and he found he couldn't tear his gaze away from her.

"Wow, that was *so* cool," Julia exclaimed the second they were on the ground and the plane had stopped moving. As soon as she bounced out of her seat, she threw her arms around Brick and kissed his cheek. "Thank you so much. That was the best thing ever. You'll teach me to fly, right?"

Brick shot her a bemused smile. "Sure thing. But perhaps hold off on the hugs, yeah?"

"Hold off on the hugs?" When she followed Brick's gaze and saw him glaring at her, she tossed back her head and laughed.

Next thing he knew she was in his arms. "Did you see how I helped Brick land the plane? That was so amazing. I've wanted to learn to fly for so long, but you know how it is. Not enough hours in the day. I'm super excited for Brick to give me some lessons."

"I know how to fly, I can teach you." The words were out of his mouth before he could stop them. Forget the possessiveness of his tone, the ugly jealousy that reared its head at the sight of her touching Brick and thinking about the two of them alone together on a plane. The real problem was the fact that he had just invited himself into her life when the best thing for both of them was to spend as little time together as possible.

The smile she shot him was brighter than the sun. "I would *love* for you to teach me how to fly. Thank you, I accept." She touched a quick kiss to his cheek, and he found himself wishing she'd kissed him properly.

Like she had back in Somalia when they'd been shot at.

The timing couldn't have been worse, yet instead of focusing on eliminating the threat, he'd been replaying that kiss.

It was nothing more than a brief touch, and yet he felt consumed by it.

"You need rest," he said briskly. Dealing with Julia's constantly bubbling over emotions was more than he could cope with, so instead of telling her what he was feeling—something he couldn't even articulate—he fell back on issuing orders.

That was so much easier.

Julia yawned, and he saw a tiny crack in her armor. She wasn't as unaffected by everything that had happened as she wanted everyone to believe. Knowing that brought out an odd protectiveness he hadn't experienced before.

Of course, with his job he wanted to protect the innocent, but it was always emotionally distant. Even with Piper, Arrow's girlfriend, who was like a little sister to him, he hadn't felt like this.

This was overwhelming.

Her emotions, his emotions, it was all too much.

He needed to escape.

Standing and setting Julia away from him, he turned to head out of the plane, needing distance, space. He had to figure out what was going on with him.

Instead of getting his need for space, Julia pressed up against his side, resting against him. "I feel like I could sleep for a day straight."

"Maybe you should have napped on the plane instead of trying to learn to play poker."

"I asked you to play," she reminded him, obviously picking up on the fact that he hadn't liked her hanging with his team.

Well, that wasn't quite true. Problem was he liked it *too* much.

She fit in too well, and this was all happening too quickly.

Domino tried to shake her off, but she didn't budge so he had no choice but to walk beside her as they disembarked.

"Surf said I just need a few more lessons and then I'll be a great poker player," Julia added.

"If you want to learn so bad, *I'll* teach you," he muttered, not liking the idea of Julia and Surf alone together. Ever since they'd been held captive and tortured in Somalia four months ago, Surf had been on a mission to sleep through the female population of Manhattan.

Not that he thought Surf would sleep with Julia. All the guys had made it clear with each little grin they'd shot his way that they knew he was enamored with her.

Even if the two wanted to have sex it was hardly any of his business.

Still, Julia didn't even glance Surf's way as they stepped out into the chilly early morning. It was his side that she stayed by, snuggled closely against him.

While the touch was simple, certainly nothing extraordinary, the feel of her against him stirred something deep inside. Awakening a part of himself he thought was long since dead and buried.

Like a horribly repeating nightmare, the crack of a gunshot once again sliced through the air.

Different country, same situation.

Wrapping an arm around Julia's waist, he tackled her to the ground.

* * * * *

October 4th
2:59 A.M.

Someone was shooting at them.

Again.

How?

Why?

Who?

Julia would love an answer to even one of those questions.

This shouldn't even be possible.

Okay, she could see how someone might have followed her—or Alpha team—from the market to the building where Domino and his friends had been going to interrogate her. And she could see how they then might have followed her to the airport where Alpha team was staying.

But they weren't in Somalia anymore.

They were back Stateside having just landed a plane in a small private airfield close to New York City.

There should be no way anyone knew she or Alpha team were even here.

Yet they had.

Which could only mean that whoever was after her or Alpha team had men here in the States, and men who had enough intel to know she was with Prey and to expect her to turn up at their private airfield.

Whoever was after them obviously wasn't going to just give up.

The control she'd been clinging to began to slip.

She was shaken by the explosion and being shot at, but she was surrounded by big, tough men who gobbled up danger for breakfast. If she wanted them to take her seriously and work with her, she had to show she was every bit as big and tough as they were.

Even if it wasn't true.

Now fine tremors were wracking through her body, which felt achy and drained. All she wanted was a hot shower, some painkillers, and a comfortable bed. Hell, she'd settle for just a couch and some sleep if she had to.

But no more bullets.

"I'm going to provide cover fire. I want you to get back on the plane," Domino told her. His voice had lost the sweetly confused tone he'd been using with her the couple of times he'd spoken to her on the plane. Now it was all cold and hard again, his operator mode. She knew it, knew it was needed, still she liked it better when he dropped his guard and allowed her glimpses at the man underneath the former special forces operator.

Panic hit harder than she was anticipating.

Her running for cover meant Domino was in danger.

She didn't want that.

She just wanted him to stay here where he was. His large body covering hers, warm and strong, it made her feel safe.

Knowing he would so easily put his own life on the line for her made her feel safe in a different way, but right now, scared was edging out any warm and fuzzies.

"No!" she said a little shrilly, aware she was being ridiculous, putting them all in more danger, but she was feeling a little hysterical. Seemed like her body had done all it could to hold in her emotions and was now doing a dump.

"What do you mean, no?"

"I'm not leaving you."

Domino's head lifted just enough that she could see his face. For once he didn't have that impenetrable mask in place. His dark eyes softened. "It's going to be okay, Julia."

When he said it, she almost believed it.

Because there was nothing else to do but pull herself together, Julia nodded.

"Going to have to let go of me," Dom said, sounding almost amused as he nodded at her hands clenched into fists tangled in his shirt.

Slowly, she forced each finger to uncurl. She didn't want to, but right now it didn't matter what she wanted. It only mattered that they all made it out of there alive.

"Straight to the plane," Domino reminded her.

Julia gave a shaky nod, willing herself to hold it together just a little longer. Later she could fall apart. In her hot shower or once she was tucked beneath the covers of a big, cozy bed.

"Go."

On Domino's command, Julia rolled to her feet and ran back the way they'd come just a few minutes before.

Had it really been just a few minutes since she'd actually felt like she was making progress with Domino? He hadn't liked the idea of Brick teaching her to fly or Surf teaching her to play poker, and on the flight back here she'd felt his gaze on her almost the entire time. He was possessive of her even if he didn't realize it. While she'd never allow a man to own her, she knew that wasn't the way Domino meant it. He liked her, he was just confused by it.

His gut was guiding him, telling him not to run from her but toward her. Who knows, maybe they could both find something pretty amazing. Or not. However things worked out, Julia just knew this was a chance she wanted to take, no matter whether there would wind up being anything between her and Dom or not.

Just as she reached the steps leading up to the plane, her bruised leg gave out on her.

She cried out as she went down on her knees.

Why did it have to choose right now to give out?

"Julia?" Domino sounded borderline panicked as he called her name.

"I'm fine," she hurried to assure him. The last thing she wanted was for him to get hurt because he was worried about her. It was bad enough knowing that he and the rest of his team were in danger very likely because of her. While they didn't know for sure she was the target, there was every chance she was since they knew the trafficking ring had known about her, already abducted her, and tried to kill her once already.

Grabbing the metal railing of the steps, she started to drag herself up. There was no point in trying to stand again, she barely had enough energy to move. It seemed her body had hit a brick wall and decided that from here on out it was doing absolutely nothing.

All of a sudden, she was swept up into a pair of strong arms.

Domino leaped up the few steps and got them both inside the cover of the plane. Gunshots continued to fire outside, but once again she had confidence in Alpha team, she just hoped this time they were able to get one of the men alive so they could get some answers.

"Were you hit?" Domino demanded as he set her on her feet.

When she swayed, he quickly maneuvered her into a seat. A good thing since she knew if she didn't get some sleep soon, she was going to crash. Not a good thing when there was someone who might be out to kill her.

"Do you …?" The question died on her lips when she got a

good look at Domino and saw the blood.

Blood.

On Domino.

Streaked down his left arm.

"Y-you w-were shot," she stammered, somehow finding the strength to get back on her feet. Julia began to frantically unbutton his shirt, desperate to see to his wound. How bad was it? Was he going to bleed out? If they didn't take out the men shooting at them, they couldn't get Domino to the hospital.

"It's fine, Julia. A scratch."

While she heard the words, they sounded distant and couldn't penetrate the haze of panic that swamped her.

Hands closed around her shoulders, and she was eased away.

"Stop! I need to see it," she shrieked.

Instead of letting her go, Domino sat her down again and crouched in front of her. Pinning her hands to his chest with one of his, with his other he palmed her cheek, his long fingers stroking gently but firmly across her forehead. "Listen to me, Julia, it is just a flesh wound. A scratch. Nothing more. Stop panicking and calm down."

"A s-scratch?" she asked, not quite ready to relax yet. What if he was lying to her?

Releasing her, he stood and unbuttoned his shirt, pulling it off and tossing it onto the floor. When he crouched before her again his biceps were at her eye level. "See?"

Carefully, she reached out and swept a finger across his skin, right above where the blood started. Not that she was by any means an expert in gunshot wounds, but he was right, it did look like it was just a scratch.

Relief hit her hard.

"You're not bleeding to death."

"Not today anyway," Domino said, sounding amused.

Amused.

While she was scared out of her mind, he thought this was

funny.

Unexpectedly, tears filled her eyes.

Too much had happened over the last day and a half, and she was exhausted and emotionally strung out.

Any amusement that had been in his expression faded and panic took its place. "Are you going to cry?"

Domino's absolute horror at the idea made her laugh, the need to cry fading away. "I think I need sleep."

His gaze softened, and there was something close to affection in it. "Here, lie down." He stood and reclined her seat for her.

"The shooting has stopped," she said, already feeling sleep pulsing at the corners of her mind.

"You stay here till the guys say it's safe." Domino used his no-arguments voice.

"Are you leaving me?" Even though Julia was more than used to being alone, even in the most terrifying of circumstances, for some reason today she couldn't handle the thought.

Somehow his face softened further. "No. I'm not leaving you. Now close your eyes and get some sleep. I won't let anyone hurt you, Julia."

"Not me I'm worried about," she mumbled sleepily as her eyes fluttered closed. "It's you."

CHAPTER SIX

October 4th
3:20 A.M.

"Tell me we got one alive," Domino growled as Bear entered the plane.

Julia had passed out into an exhaustion-fueled sleep, curled up in a seat in the plane. She'd folded her hands beneath her cheek, and despite the bruises and dark circles beneath her eyes, she looked peaceful in slumber.

He wanted to keep her that way.

She had been playing a good tough girl game, and he had zero doubts that she was every bit as tough as she looked, but underneath he sensed her vulnerability.

It called out to him like a whisper in the wind.

So faint he almost wasn't sure that it was there, but he had been taught to trust his gut. It was the only way you could survive in his world, and his gut said that as strong as she was, she needed someone there to stand at her side and help hold her up.

"One was dying when we got to him," Bear replied.

"And?"

"He was persuaded to talk."

Bear didn't have to elaborate to let him know just what that particular form of persuasion had been.

Domino wasn't squeamish. Never had been. Even if he had, his father would have beaten it out of him as a child. He was always prepared to do whatever was necessary for the safety of his team and his country, but he wasn't bloodthirsty. He took no pleasure in other people's pain.

At least he never had before.

Now he found himself wishing he had been the one to extract whatever intel they could out of the man shooting at Julia.

Someone had to pay for the fear in her eyes and the panic in her voice when she hadn't wanted to leave him to get to safety, and when she'd asked him not to leave her alone before falling asleep.

"What did he say?" Domino asked, his gaze still fixed firmly on the sleeping woman he was standing guard over.

"Not a lot. Confirmed he was one of Pete's men. Said they'd been told some reporter was sniffing around who knew too much and had to be eliminated. Updated intel said she was with Prey, so they staked out our airfield. Orders were to bring her in alive so she could be questioned if possible, but if it wasn't then she's to be killed."

Domino said nothing.

Couldn't for the life of him cut through the emotions clouding him to figure out an appropriate response.

Julia had been marked for death.

Wasn't like he hadn't suspected as much. In fact, he'd told her she was the likely target of both the explosion and them being shot at at the airfield in Somalia.

But hearing it confirmed …

"What's our next move?" he asked.

"You really have to ask?" Mouse demanded.

"If it wasn't for Nathan passing on intel to Julia about Piper then we would never have found her in time," Arrow added. "As far as I'm concerned, Julia is one of us, that means she's under our protection till we get the target off her back. I don't think any of the guys feel differently."

Domino turned slowly to find his entire team had entered the plane and were looking at him with dead serious expressions. It was beyond clear that Alpha team had well and truly adopted Julia into their little family.

"Thank you," he said softly. Domino wasn't quite sure what he was thanking them for since they were doing this for Julia, not for him, and she wasn't anything to him, yet still he needed to verbalize his gratefulness.

"I spoke to Eagle, he's sending in a cleanup team, and he's arranged a safehouse for Julia until we can get a better handle on her situation," Bear said.

"I'm staying with her." There had been no conscious thought behind the words, they'd just come out, but now that they were out Domino found he had no desire to drag them back in.

He wanted to stay with Julia.

Perhaps even needed to.

Whatever this weird thing he felt brewing like a storm between him and Julia was, he knew one thing for certain.

No one else was going to lay a hand on her.

No one.

Not on his watch.

"I suspected you would want to. I've cleared it with Eagle. Since whoever is after her is linked to the men who escaped Pete's compound, Alpha team is assigned to Julia until this is over. Maybe by working together we can finally bring these people down once and for all," Bear said fiercely.

There wasn't a man on Alpha team for whom this fight wasn't personal.

Some more than others, but they were a team, and when you messed with one of them you messed with all of them.

This mess had started with Storm Gallagher, a mentally disturbed man with plans to destroy the government and bring in a new age. The man had abducted Dove Oswald and her now husband Isaac but managed to escape. Kidnapping his sister Mackenzie, Storm had fled the country.

When Bear met Mackenzie, the man was smitten, and although he fought it at first, he'd ended up with the girl, and they'd managed to take down Storm, only to learn that he was merely a puppet.

Links to a family law firm as a potential financial backer had brought Mouse's now wife Phoebe into their lives. Her abusive ex had been up to his neck in the whole thing, and while Dexter Hunt had been eliminated by the men he'd been working with once he became a liability, they still hadn't found the man—or woman—in charge.

Former Prey operative Pete Petrowski had set his sights on Prey's on-staff psychiatrist Piper Hamilton because he blamed her for losing his job with Prey and being committed to a psychiatric institution. What none of them knew was that Pete had been building a weapons trafficking empire for years and had been supplying Storm Gallagher with the weapons he'd planned to use to take down the government.

Now once again they were chasing their tails, trying to work an op where they only had bits and pieces of the intel they needed, and once again his team was at the center of things.

Because of Bear and Mackenzie.

Because of Mouse and Phoebe.

Because of Arrow and Piper.

Because of him and Julia.

Kind of.

Sort of.

"We should go. She needs a bed and proper sleep," he said briskly, hoping the emotion he felt didn't seep into his tone.

As he gathered Julia into his arms, he shoved away thoughts of her in bed for an entirely different reason than sleep with a ruthlessness his father would be proud of.

Avoiding the looks he knew his team was giving him, he carried Julia out of the plane and into one of their vehicles. Arrow got into the driver's seat while Domino settled Julia in the back and buckled her in. No sooner had he sat beside her, and she was shifting to snuggle into his side.

While she looked all sweet and sleepy now, Julia was a

firecracker, and Domino knew she would fight them on the safehouse idea.

A fight she would lose.

When he'd allowed Rosie to grow close to him, fallen in love with her, he'd known that he was flirting with disaster, but he'd believed he'd found a way to circumvent his father's grip on his life. Rosie hadn't realized just how grave that danger was and since he hadn't wanted to stifle her beautiful bright shining light, he hadn't done what was necessary to keep her safe and alive.

That wasn't a mistake he would repeat.

Of course, he wasn't in love with Julia, but there was something there, something he wasn't interested in attaching a label to. But he did care about what happened to her, and he would do whatever it took to ensure she stayed safe and alive.

Julia might not like it, might even fight against him, but he was prepared to do whatever it took.

If that involved chaining her to a bed and locking her up then so be it.

She could hate him and never want to see him again, but at least she would be alive.

The alternative was to find her body, beaten and mutilated almost beyond recognition, and know that he had to live with the guilt of not having done enough to protect her.

That wasn't an acceptable outcome.

Domino had no idea if there was actually anything between him and the too-sexy-for-her-own-good reporter, nor was he sure that he wanted there to be. In his experience, love was a rare occurrence, and even if you managed to find this almost mythical being it could be snatched away far too easily.

Once upon a time he had given his heart away and had it returned in pieces. Were there even enough pieces left to offer Julia anything like she deserved?

The pain in his chest as he stared down at the woman snuggled at his side suggested that the answer to that question was a resounding no.

* * * * *

October 5th
9:16 A.M.

Julia blinked awake, feeling like she was finally back in the land of the living instead of the sleepy, hazy land of slumber she'd been stuck in for …

She glanced at the clock on the nightstand, saw it said it was nine in the morning, and realized she had been asleep for over twenty-four hours.

Wow.

Obviously, she'd been more wiped out than she had realized.

Still, she definitely felt better after all the sleep. The cobwebs in her head had been cleared away, her fear had receded to a much more manageable level, and she was ready to get back to tackling the problem and bringing these people down.

Shoving back the covers, it wasn't until she swung her legs over the edge of the bed and her bare feet touched perhaps the softest carpet in the world that she realized she wasn't at her apartment. From the looks of the expensive rustic furnishings in the room, she wasn't at a hotel either.

Her memories of the last twenty-four hours were hazy at best. All she really remembered was complete and utter exhaustion and a crushing need to sleep but interspersed with that were hints of memories.

Strong arms cradling her against a hard chest.

A hand palmed the back of her head, lifting it, and holding a glass of water to her lips.

A woman helping her change clothes.

A presence beside her as she stumbled toward a bathroom, desperate to pee.

Julia had no idea how those images fitted together, but there was only one way to find out.

Standing up, she found a robe lying over an armchair by the window. Not just *a* robe, but *her* robe. And she was wearing her favorite pair of fuzzy mermaid pajamas. Ever since she was a little girl, she'd had a fascination with the mythical creatures. There was something about the freedom of roaming the wild ocean that called to the wandering side of her.

The side that couldn't sit still, sought out dangerous stories to investigate and had to fill up the rest of her time with the highest adrenalin-pumping pursuits she could find.

As a child, her home hadn't been a place, it had been with her parents. Once they were gone, she'd been left with no place to call her own, and nothing to hold her in place.

Pulling on her robe, Julia headed out of the large bedroom and found herself in a long hall. There were three other closed doors, one across from her and two further down the corridor. Since a bathroom was attached to her bedroom, she assumed the other three doors led to more ensuite bedrooms.

There were stairs further down the hall, so she headed for them. "Wow," she breathed out as she took in the full magnificence of wherever it was they were.

The downstairs opened into a huge double-height living room below her with huge picture windows that showcased a stunning view of trees and mountains. As she descended the stairs, she saw a kitchen and large table beneath the second floor, along with two doors behind them.

"This place is amazing," she said as she headed to the table where Alpha team and a woman she hadn't met yet were all sitting. "Where are we exactly?"

When no one immediately answered she narrowed her eyes.

She knew what kind of men worked for Prey. They were protective to the extreme. There weren't a lot of lengths they wouldn't go to in order to make sure someone under their protection was safe.

Julia didn't even have to ask to know they had put her in the under their protection category.

"This is a safehouse," she said as she pulled out a chair and dropped into it.

"Told you she'd figure it out without you telling her," the lone woman said with a grin. The woman was gorgeous with big brown eyes and soft brown waves hanging past her shoulders, her features were delicate, and her smile was warm. Julia immediately decided she liked her.

"I'm Julia," she said, reaching across the table to hold out her hand.

Tears shimmered in the other woman's eyes as she took Julia's hand and squeezed it. "I know who you are."

It hit her who the woman was. "You're Piper, aren't you?"

Piper nodded. "Thank you for what you did."

"I didn't do anything, it was all Nathan. He is … was … a great guy."

"I feel so bad he died because of me."

"No," she said fiercely. "None of that."

"But …"

"No buts," she cut off the other woman. "That was who Nathan was. He would have sacrificed himself for an innocent every time. Trust me, he would be so happy that you're okay, free, safe, and able to live the rest of your life and be happy."

"You knew him well?"

"Not really, but he saved my life too."

"I'll forever be grateful that because of him I got my happy ever after." Piper looked to her left where Arrow was sitting, his arm around her shoulders. The smiles on their faces as they looked at one another reminded her of the way her parents used to look at one another. That was love. Real love. The kind of soul-deep connection that defied logic.

"I'm so glad." She meant it too. Whether she ever wound up

finding the kind of love Piper shared with Arrow or not, she always wanted people to be happy.

"And I'm thankful for you as well. If you hadn't passed along Nathan's intel, I'd be dead. So, thank you."

"It was nothing." Julia brushed off Piper's thanks, really she hadn't done anything, Nathan was the hero of that story. "So," she drew the word out as she fixed a glare on each one of the guys before settling it on Domino, whose dark eyes were watching her carefully. "Safehouse?"

The guys looked to Domino before answering.

Honestly looked to him for permission.

Like it was up to him to decide what information they doled out to her.

Uh-uh.

She wasn't having any of that.

"Don't look to Dom. Tell me. Now. Did you bring me to a safehouse?"

"They confirmed they were after you, Julia," Domino said unapologetically.

That took a little of the wind out of her sails. "They did?" Since she'd passed out in the plane, she hadn't heard that at least one of the men shooting at them must have survived.

"Yes. There's a hit out on you. Orders are to bring you in for interrogation if possible, but if not, then to ensure you're dead," Domino explained.

Well, she'd wanted information, and now she had it.

Too bad it wasn't anything good.

She wasn't sure how she felt knowing there was a hit on her. Obviously, it wasn't a good thing, and there was definite fear involved, but somehow, she felt perfectly safe here with Domino and Alpha team.

Along with the fear, there was also a sense of empowerment. She knew something that the people involved in this conspiracy were worried about. That meant she held the power to bring these people to their knees.

That was something to be pleased about.

"I need to go to my apartment," she announced, shoving away from the table.

Domino was there, standing beside her before she even got to her feet. "What part of there is a hit out on you and you need to stay here in the safehouse did you miss?"

"None of it." She threw in an eye roll for good measure. "But I obviously know something. I took all my electronic notes with me when I went to Somalia, but there are a few hard copies of things at my apartment that I'm going to need."

"Are you under the impression that you are working with us to find these guys?" he asked, his voice deadly quiet, anger infused into each word.

"Are you under the impression I'm not?" If that's what he was thinking, they were about to have their own little war on their hands.

"My job is to keep you alive."

"Right," she agreed. "And what exactly is the best way to do that?"

From the storm brewing in his dark eyes, she knew he knew the answer to that.

"It's to use me, right? Not keep me locked up. I can help. Whatever I already know is the key to this because otherwise, they wouldn't care about bringing me in to interrogate. They know I have them, they just need to try to stop me before I figure it out and tell someone. The only way I'll ever truly be safe is for these people to be caught and stopped. They have more targets, they're going to set more explosions, and you told me those explosions are supposed to be used to destabilize the government. This isn't just about me, Dom."

Something else flared in his eyes this time, but it was gone before she could figure out what it was.

Regardless, she thought she had made her point.

"I won't—I can't—just hide away while other people die, not if I can do something to stop it from happening, that wasn't the way I was raised. So, you have a choice. You can lock me up here like some helpless little prisoner. Or you can use me, work with me, and help me bring down a whole lot of bad guys."

CHAPTER SEVEN

October 5th
11:49 A.M.

Domino punched his pillow.

Like that was going to alleviate the ball of frustration sitting heavily in his gut.

Never before had he felt this conflicted.

On the one hand, he wanted to be anywhere but here, in one of Prey's safehouses, with a sexy reporter who made him question everything he had ever believed about himself. On the other, he couldn't imagine being anywhere else.

If Julia was here, he had to be here.

How absolutely ridiculous was that?

With a growl, he shoved back the covers with a lot more force than necessary and all but threw himself out of bed. Since he was stuck here at the cabin on babysitting duty it wasn't like he could go anywhere to blow off steam, but he couldn't lie in bed pretending he was going to eventually fall asleep for another second.

Snatching up his sweatpants from the floor where he'd dumped them when he'd gotten into bed a couple of hours ago, he shoved his legs into them. Usually, he slept naked, but since he was technically working, he could hardly wander around without any clothes on.

Not bothering to correct himself on his lie—him being on bodyguard duty had nothing to do with why he wasn't going to walk around naked. It had everything to do with the woman asleep down the hall—Domino headed downstairs.

There was nothing to do down here, the safehouse didn't have a gym, and he couldn't leave Julia alone to go for a run, maybe he'd ask the guys to pick some gear up from Prey and bring it by when they came over later.

Despite his desire to keep Julia away from anything to do with this case, she'd made valid points the rest of his team had agreed with. If there was a hit out on her then it was because these people believed she knew something that could identify them, it only made sense that she was a resource Prey had to utilize.

Didn't mean he liked it.

And he didn't.

At all.

But he'd been outvoted. Everyone else seemed fine with it, and as soon as one of the guys had gone to her place and got her notes she'd been animated as she'd gone through it all with them in great detail.

She was kind of cute when she talked shop. It was obvious that she adored her job, and from her detailed and organized notes, she was good as well. While she'd been sleeping the day before, he'd spent a little time looking her up and reading some of the pieces she'd written. Julia was good. Really good.

Reading had been his escape as a child. Usually, he read science fiction or the occasional fantasy, but he never bothered reading non-fiction. He'd always thought it was too dry, with no passion, no spark. But not Julia's work. In everything she'd written, she hit just the right amount of emotion and used enough imagery to bring her words to life. It was like she was painting a picture only she was using words to do it.

Perfect.

Just what he needed.

Another reason to like her.

The pro column was growing quickly while the con column had virtually nothing in it.

Stubborn and reckless.

Those were about the only negatives he'd been able to find, and even those were debatable. If she wasn't stubborn, she wouldn't have survived what she'd been through, and if she wasn't reckless and full of life and energy then she wouldn't be Julia.

Irritated with his train of thought, Domino stomped to the kitchen and began to make himself coffee. Not the best drink to have when he was already too wired for sleep, but besides water, it was basically the only thing he drank.

Movement on the stairs caught his attention, and he spun around to find a sleep-rumpled Julia dressed in the same mermaid pajamas Piper had packed in the bag of clothes from her house. Her hair hung down her back in a fiery mane, and her green eyes possessed their usual bright spark even if it was blurred a little by fatigue.

"Is there a reason you're banging around down here at," Julia made a huge show of looking at her watch, "almost midnight?"

"You're supposed to be keeping off your leg," he snapped, not in the mood to make small talk.

As always, she didn't appear to be offended by his rudeness and merely limped over to one of the stools at the breakfast bar and sat down. "You making coffee?"

Every time she ignored his attitude another piece of his protective walls crumbled.

Did she know she was doing that?

Was it her plan?

The smile she gave him was sweet and sincere, and he knew she wasn't manipulative, she was just a good person who cared, even about people who didn't deserve it and had done nothing to earn it.

He had to tone down the attitude. It wasn't fair to her, and it made him look like a jerk.

Domino didn't want to be that guy.

Standoffish was one thing, but outright rude was something

else. The idea of Julia thinking he was some cold, hard, uncaring, unfeeling man hurt somehow. It shouldn't. It was a pretty accurate depiction of the man he was, but still, he didn't like it.

Softening his tone, he even attempted a smile. "You want something to eat with your coffee?"

Julia's mouth dropped open and she stared at him.

"What?" he asked, suddenly self-conscious.

"Wow."

"Wow, what?"

"When you smile your entire face changes, you are breathtaking."

No one had ever called him breathtaking before. Was he used to women ogling him and flirting? Of course. Domino wasn't modest, he knew he was a good-looking guy, and his body—which he worked hard to maintain so he was at peak physical fitness for his job—was the kind that got women drooling. Usually, the dead look in his eyes was enough to send all but the bravest of them scampering away.

"You should totally smile more. In fact, I'm going to do my best to make you smile as often as I can while we're staying here together."

Something shifted inside him.

A weird sort of pain at the finality of the statement.

Julia might think he was breathtaking, but it was obvious she intended to never see him again as soon as this mess was cleared up.

"What just happened?" Julia's brow furrowed. "One second you're smiling and looking absolutely gorgeous, and the next you look like I kicked your puppy."

Shaking off the odd sense of loss at never seeing Julia again, Domino opened the fridge and pulled out the leftover cherry pie from earlier. It was better this way, better that he didn't allow Julia to mess with his head more than she already was.

Nothing was happening between them, and it would bode well

for both of them if he kept that at the forefront of his mind.

He was here to keep her alive not to have sex with her and certainly not to bond with her.

"We should make popcorn and watch a movie," Julia said enthusiastically as she bounded off her seat.

A movie night?

The two of them sitting side by side on the couch, sharing a bowl of popcorn, their fingers brushing as they reached into the bowl at the same time, nothing and no one here to stop him from doing something stupid?

Yeah, no.

"Actually, I think I'm going to head back to bed." Returning the pie to the fridge he was halfway to the stairs when Julia spoke.

"I didn't take you for a coward, Dom."

"It's midnight, going to bed doesn't make me a coward."

"Running from this thing between us does. I don't know what it is, and I've never felt anything like it before, but it feels like the universe is trying really hard to push us together and you're the one running away. I get it, it's clear you've been hurt before, maybe even really badly. But you know what? We all have pain in our past, it's what shapes us and makes us into the people we become."

Everyone had pain in their past, sure, but not everyone had a family like his.

"I see you, you know. The real you. The one you try so hard to hide from the rest of the world. You pretend like you don't care about anything, that you don't feel anything, but I know that's not true. You love your team and would do anything for them. You love their women, too, I saw how you were with Piper. You care about people you don't even know or you wouldn't have joined the military and then Prey."

He heard her behind him, moving closer until she was millimeters from his back.

Domino wanted so badly to turn around and take what she

was offering. Allow her warmth to thaw the ice inside him, but he couldn't.

What if he lost her the same way he lost Rosie?

"You care about me too," Julia said softly. "If you didn't you wouldn't have sat beside me when we were trapped in that building in Somalia. You wouldn't be so adamant about not wanting me to help Prey with this case. You wouldn't look at me like you're starving and I'm the only person in the world with food. I'm not a complicated person and I don't play games. What you see is what you get. If you want me, I'm right here, all you have to do is say so."

Careful not to touch him, she edged past him and headed up the stairs. With her bruised leg it took her a while to make it up, and he watched her take each step, knowing it would be so easy to scoop her up and carry her off to bed.

So easy, but he couldn't break free of the chokehold fear had on him.

Julia paused at the top of the stairs but didn't turn to look at him. "Just so you know, Dom, I'm not going anywhere. You're scared and need time, I can deal. But I don't run away from things, and I'm not going anywhere until I know what this thing between us is and if it can go anywhere."

With that, she disappeared leaving him standing staring open-mouthed after her.

* * * * *

October 6th
8:28 A.M.

"Thanks, Dom," Julia muttered to herself as she slipped into a pair of jeans.

Thanks to the too sexy and appealing for his own good Dominick Tanner, she hadn't gotten more than snatched pockets of sleep throughout the night. Mostly she had tossed and turned, uncomfortable and way too worked up for sleep.

There was sexual frustration there. Domino managed to turn her body on in a way no other man ever had. Julia had slept with a few men since she lost her virginity when she was sixteen. One or two had been average lovers, but a couple had given her amazing burn-up-the-sheets kind of sex. She knew her body, knew what she liked and how to satisfy herself if there wasn't anyone else around to do it.

None of that compared to how Dom could make her feel with a single look.

He wasn't even trying to turn her on and he managed to do it.

Along with the sexual frustration had been a heavy dose of heartache. Domino was hurting, and she didn't know how to help him.

How did you make someone feel worthy when they didn't believe it?

Right now, she was at a loss on how to get through to him. She understood pain and loss. She'd been only fourteen when both her parents had been killed in a freak parachuting accident. Not only had she lost them, but she had been there when they died.

Literally.

After going to live with her aunt and uncle and attending a normal school for the first time, she'd been mocked and bullied. It had gotten to the point where she refused to go back and had finished out high school online.

By college she was stronger and more confident in who she was. Her parents' lessons on how being yourself was important, and that you should never try to change who you were just to fit in with the crowd had finally sunk in. She had blossomed, made lifelong friends, and spread her wings to fly on her own path.

Now at thirty-two, she knew who she was and embraced it, quirks, weaknesses and all.

But to help Domino she had to understand where he was

coming from, what had shaped him, what his fears were, and why he felt like he was unworthy of love and pre-emptively shut everyone out.

While she couldn't force him to talk to her, she could prove to him she wasn't giving up.

Dressed and hair done, Julia added a touch of makeup, gave herself a scrutinizing once over in the mirror, and then headed downstairs.

Domino was in the kitchen, his back to her, standing at the stove cooking. His gray sweatpants hung low on his hips, and his black t-shirt molded to his chiseled torso. Who knew your back could look so muscled and sculpted. Chests, yes, she knew those could look like works of art, but she'd never even really thought about a guy's back. Domino's was everything, and she'd love nothing more than to walk right up to him and run her hands over every inch of that deliciousness.

Since she didn't want to scare him off, she sidled up to the breakfast bar instead. "Morning."

"Hope you're hungry," Domino said, looking over his shoulder and giving her a smile. It wasn't a full one like last night, but it still transformed his appearance from merely handsome to drop-dead gorgeous.

"I could eat," she agreed. Honestly, she wasn't all that hungry, there was too much going on, and she tended to lose her appetite when she got consumed by a story, but Dom had cooked for her, so she was going to eat every single bite. "What's all that?" Julia pointed over her shoulder to where weights and a punching bag had been set up in front of the large wall of glass.

"The guys dropped off some gear earlier this morning."

"Earlier? It's only eight-thirty."

Domino shrugged. "We're used to being up early. Since there's no gym, and I can't leave you alone, I wanted to keep up on my PT so I asked if they could drop off a few things."

"That's a great idea. It's been ages since I ran through any self-defense moves. Do you think we could go over a few things later?" Because of the kind of life they lived her parents had insisted that she learn how to protect herself from the time she was old enough to understand that safety wasn't guaranteed. She'd done some Taekwondo as a child, and when she was home, she went to her gym to work out and run self-defense drills once a week. But she'd been fixated on Storm Gallagher, the bombs, and Somalia for months now and everything else in her life had kind of been dropped.

Dishing them both up plates heaped with bacon, eggs, sausage, and hash browns Domino studied her for a long moment. While she would hardly describe his expression as open, it wasn't as shuttered as it had been even just a few hours ago when they'd talked at midnight.

Progress.

"Sure. I could run through a few drills with you," Domino said.

"Awesome, thanks. I've never done any boxing before, but I was thinking it could be good exercise and helpful for self-defense. Do you think you could teach me?" Spending time together was the only way to prove to Dom that she wasn't going to hurt him. He had to get to know her, and maybe if they kept busy, he would lower his guard down and let her in. All she needed was one little opening, and she was sure she could prove to him that she wasn't like whoever had hurt him so badly in his past.

Breakfast passed in companionable silence, and she didn't push him to talk even though a million different topics of conversation were ruminating in her mind. Once they were done, Domino offered to clean up, so she went upstairs to change into something more suitable for working out. It was so nice of Piper to pack her a bag of her own clothes, it made being stuck in the safehouse much more comfortable.

"Self-defense or boxing first?" Domino asked when he heard

her approaching.

"Boxing," she replied without hesitation.

"I assume you know how to throw a punch since you've done self-defense training?"

"I know how, although I'm not very good. I can never get much power behind it."

"Because you're such a tiny little thing." Domino beckoned her over to the mats, and although she wouldn't say he was being warm and friendly, he was in teacher mode and certainly looked attentive. "Are you a leftie or righty?"

"No way you don't already know that. I know what you special forces guys are like, you notice everything," she teased.

Domino gifted her with a small smile. "You're a leftie."

"Yep."

"So, you have that advantage right off the bat. Anyone you have to defend yourself against will automatically assume you're a righty because most people are. Show me your fist, thumb on the outside remember."

"I know," she said with a grin. "Trust me that is not something I'll forget. Ever. First self-defense class I ever went to I rammed my fist into the bag right off the bat with my thumb under my fingers. I dislocated it. Not fun. Nothing I want to go through again."

Dom winced in sympathy. "All right, fingers curled into your palm, thumb wrapped around the first knuckle of your ring finger. Good." He nodded approvingly at her fist. "All right, let's see your stance."

Facing Domino, Julia tried to remember everything she was supposed to do. Feet apart so she couldn't be thrown off-balance, but not too wide or she'd lose any power to her punch.

Immediately, Domino shook his head. "Nope, no wonder you don't have any power to your punch, your feet are way too wide. Like this." He moved behind her, his large hands resting on her hips, and used one of his legs to nudge her back leg closer to her front.

With his hands like that, curled so closely to the part of her that was literally throbbing for his touch, it was hard to concentrate, but Julia did her best. As nice as sex with Domino would be, she really did need to be on her game, there were people who wanted her dead after all.

"Better," Domino murmured. "Hips turned a little this way." His hands guided her so she faced slightly away from where her opponent would be. "If you have to move backward or forward slide don't step. Arms up, in front of your face to protect yourself. Elbows in. Abdominals tight." One of his hands moved to brush lightly across her stomach, and she could swear that her lady parts sighed in delight at his touch.

She was falling way too fast for the sexy special forces operator.

Her body of course disagreed, but it wasn't the one that would have to deal with the broken heart.

As though he were immune to the sexual tension humming between them, Domino continued with his lesson. "You need to punch through your hips. It's a whole-body thing, not just your hand. You punch from your arm or shoulder, and you won't get any power in it. Pivot your back foot, not exaggerated or you'll lose balance, but twist your hips and throw your punch. Most important thing to remember is to keep control of your body and yourself balanced. You ready to try one?"

When he moved from behind her, she almost cried out in disappointment. Instead, she nodded. "I'm ready."

Domino stood in front of her. "We'll tape you up later but let's try a few now. You're going to hit with your first two knuckles. Remember to try to keep all the bones in your forearm down to your knuckles aligned."

"I'm going to hit you?" she asked when he didn't move the bag closer.

"Since we're working this on a self-defense basis, yeah. You aren't going to be attacked by a punching bag, you're going to be attacked by a person. Better to practice on the real thing so if you have to defend yourself, you're ready."

That made sense.

Of course, she hoped it didn't come to that, but she knew there was a hit out on her, she had to be prepared to do whatever it took to stay alive. Relying only on Domino and Alpha team to protect her would put her at a disadvantage. There were any number of reasons why they might be unable to, and she had to be ready to defend herself if that happened.

Remembering everything she had learned, everything Domino had just said, she took a slow, deep breath, found her center, and focused on her body, using it as one tool instead of a number of independent ones.

Then she threw a punch and plowed her fist into Domino's abs, stunned and thrilled when he grunted and stumbled backward.

"Ha!" she squealed. "Look at that. You weren't expecting me to hit so hard."

"Well, you did tell me you lacked power in your punches."

"Guess my new teacher is pretty good," she teased.

"The best," he teased right back, shooting her one of those rare wide, genuine smiles that hit her right smack dab in the middle of her heart.

That kind of smile was going to be far too hard to walk away from when he eventually shattered her heart into a million tiny pieces.

CHAPTER EIGHT

October 6th
2:08 P.M.

"Ready to give up?" Domino asked.

"Nope," Julia grunted her response. Her breathing was ragged and given they had both been battered and bruised in an explosion not even four days ago this probably wasn't the smartest way to spend their day, but he was having fun.

Imagine that.

Domino couldn't remember the last time he'd actually had fun.

He loved his job, enjoyed every second of it, and couldn't imagine doing anything else with his life. He also enjoyed spending time with his friends and their families. But having fun … the very thought was so foreign to him it almost made him laugh to realize that hanging with Julia was in fact fun.

"Come on, no way you can beat me."

"I might," Julia panted as she did another sit-up.

"Yeah? You really think you stand a chance?"

"I like to be positive."

"Positive is one thing, I'd call you delusional," he teased. Shockingly enough not only was hanging out with Julia fun but so was teasing her. And it was surprisingly easy.

How could a man like him who had spent his entire life surrounded by darkness, death, pain, and destruction slip so easily into this persona? Julia had been in his life for only four days, and already it felt like he was losing the edge that had been his only way of surviving. There was a new Dominick waiting in the wings. A man he hadn't thought existed or ever would, yet every second in Julia's company that man was phasing out the old Dominick. The one born in the depths of human depravity.

"Delusional?" Julia echoed. On her next crunch, she reached over and smacked the top of his head.

Since he hadn't been expecting it and he was mid-sit-up, Domino toppled sideways.

Immediately, Julia cheered and jumped to her feet. "I won! Told you I could win, and I wasn't being delusional."

With a grin on his face that felt completely natural, he pushed to his feet. "Doesn't count, little flame. You cheated. You're not allowed to knock the other person over. We both know I would have wound up doing more crunches than you."

Planting her hands on her hips, Julia shot him the most adorable little pout. "I didn't cheat! You were insulting me, I can't help it if you fell over. And you really want me to believe a guy who falls over doing sit-ups could have beaten me. Ha! No way." The pout faded, transforming into the brightest smile the world had ever seen. "Little flame?"

The nickname had slipped out without him realizing it, and despite the fact he felt a need to backpedal, draw the words back in, and pretend he'd never said them, he didn't offer any excuses. Julia had told him she wasn't playing games and she wasn't going anywhere without figuring out this thing between them. It seemed like only a coward would turn away from a woman offering him everything.

"Thought it fit you," he said nonchalantly.

"Because of my hair?" She ran a hand over her fiery mane, which she had pulled back into a ponytail for their boxing lesson earlier.

There was a hint of self-consciousness in the move, and for a moment he fumbled. Julia always seemed so confident and in control, he hadn't even realized that she had any doubts at all about how beautiful she was, how amazing, how strong, and courageous.

Needing to soothe this fear he hadn't known she had, Domino reached up and gently circled her wrist with his fingers, tugging her hand away from her hair. "No, not because of your hair, stunning though it is. Because of your spirit, your heart, it burns so brightly I'm positive it can be seen from space. You're passionate and dedicated, you don't give up, you face your fears. I respect all of that."

Pleasure danced in her eyes, but she shot him a cheeky smile. "So, you gave me that amazing compliment hoping I'd miss the fact that you tacked on the word little. You saying I'm short, tough guy?"

"Are you even five feet tall, shorty?"

"Hey!" Julia swatted at him. "I'll have you know I am five feet one and a half."

"Gotta remember that half, huh?" he teased.

"I'm sure I don't have to remind you that any extra inches are always appreciated." Her eyebrows waggled, and heat flared in her bewitching green eyes.

The sexual tension that had been humming between them since he slid into the back of her car in Somalia and held a gun to her head turned up several degrees.

It would be so easy to haul her into his arms, push her up against the nearest wall, and take what he knew she would willingly offer him. They'd touch each other, have hot sex, and get each other off, but that would be all there was to it. If they had sex now there would be no emotional connection, and while they might continue to sleep together as long as they stayed in the safehouse, once the danger was gone so would whatever could have been between them.

That was what he would do with any other woman.

He wouldn't care in the least that sex was all that would be between them because that was all he wanted.

But not with Julia.

Julia deserved more. She wanted more, she'd already made that clear. If all she was after was sex they would have had it already, Domino was sure of that. But Julia wanted something deeper, and although it utterly terrified him, he found himself wanting the same.

"I'll bear that in mind, little flame." Brushing his thumb across the inside of her wrist, he slowly released her and took a step back.

There was a moment of surprise in Julia's eyes, but it was quickly replaced by respect, and if he wasn't mistaken a warmth that touched him deep in his soul.

"So, tough guy, what are we doing for our next challenge?"

"You really want to get beaten again?"

"I won the last one," she reminded him, all sass and fire.

"You cheated." Domino ruffled her hair, making her dodge out of the way. "And I beat you at push-ups, one armed push-ups, push-ups with claps, chin-ups, jumping jacks, planks, and burpees."

"Okay, so you're winning so far. Excuse me for not working out ten hours a day, but I'm still on the board, and I know one thing I can win at."

"Yeah?" He arched a brow, wondering what she thought she could possibly beat him at.

"Tree climbing."

That surprised a chuckle out of him. "Climbing trees?"

"I was like a little monkey when I was a kid. I bet I can climb higher and faster than you. You game?" Her expression was pure challenge, and he knew that when they did find themselves in bed together—which at this point was pretty much inevitable—she was going to be an absolute firecracker.

"All right then, little flame, let's see if you're also the little monkey you claim to be."

Clapping in delight, she went skipping off—yep, the firecracker was actually skipping, albeit lopsidedly with her bruised leg—to find her shoes.

Domino was laughing as he found his shoes and shoved his feet into them. He grabbed his coat since it was cold out today, and Julia's as well then waited for her. Her eyes were sparkling, and even though he'd beaten her at every single one of her challenges—and they both knew he would have beaten her at sit-ups, too—she hadn't been upset or frustrated. He got the feeling that even though these little games were her idea she actually wasn't very competitive and was rather just trying to break the ice between them and get him to relax.

And it was working.

After helping her into her jacket they headed outside. The cabin was a couple of hours away from Manhattan, in upstate New York, hidden deep in the woods. It was beautiful out here, peaceful. The only sounds were the rustle of leaves and the chirp of birds. In the distance, you could hear the trickle of water over rocks. Maybe later they'd go for a walk by the stream, that would be romantic.

Had he really become that guy?

The guy who thought only of a woman and wanted to make her smile, wanted to make her feel special.

"What about that tree?" Julia asked, pointing to a large one just off to the right of the cabin.

"You're the monkey, your choice."

"It's the biggest one around so definitely that one."

"Okay, little flame. On three."

"I like ten better."

Domino laughed. "Ten it is."

They counted in unison, and the second they hit ten she was off with more speed than he would have expected given that her leg was still bothering her.

By the time he'd swung himself up only a couple of branches, Julia was way ahead of him. He had no idea how she did it, she was a tiny little thing and still covered in bruises, but it was like she really was part monkey. She swung and climbed with such ease as though she was born to climb trees.

Giving up, this time she was honestly going to beat him, instead Domino just admired the view of her perky little backside as she shimmied from branch to branch. It wasn't until the branches started to thin out and she kept going that he started to worry.

"Okay, little flame, you win. You don't need to go any higher," he called out.

Julia paused for a second and looked down at him. "I stop when I get to the top."

Shaking his head, he watched as she continued on until she was right up in the very top branches. Only then did she stop, hanging off the tree like she wasn't twenty feet off the ground.

"I'm the queen of the world," she called out at the top of her lungs, and Domino felt his heart do a weird little flutter in his chest.

She might not be queen of the world, but she was quickly working her way up to queen of his world with as much ease as she'd just climbed this tree.

* * * * *

October 6th
5:44 P.M.

Julia hummed to herself as she chopped vegetables.

It had been a fun day. Not only did she feel like she'd worked on her self-defense skills and felt much more confident in defending herself if it came down to it, but she was also making progress in cracking through Domino's shields.

While she wasn't a particularly competitive person—she liked to do her best at everything she did, but that was a personal thing, she never cared what other people were doing—she knew alphas like Dom often were. Deliberately, she had chosen games where she knew he would almost definitely beat her. She worked out as often as she could and was in reasonable shape, but Domino looked like a model with perfectly sculpted muscles.

Each game he won he relaxed a little more. Julia knew it wasn't because he felt superior to her, but because he could see that she was trying to get him to have fun. And he had. She'd even got him to laugh.

A real, genuine laugh.

More than once.

Those laughs, the crinkles around his eyes, the rich sound, the way the shutters he kept up to hide what was going on inside his head finally lowered, it gave her this warm, cozy feeling. It was like when she was a girl, and she and her parents would be living in a tent or campervan in some remote location somewhere in the world. They would always sit around a campfire in the evenings, watching the stars, talking and laughing, and sipping coffee or hot cocoa. When they did, it always gave her a feeling of peace, happiness, and tranquility like everything in the world was perfect.

Contentment.

That's what it was.

Domino was the first person to give her that same feeling since her parents, and she knew he would be shocked to hear that.

"Need any help?"

Looking up, she smiled at Dom. He'd disappeared for a while into one of the upstairs bedrooms set up as an office. She hadn't asked what he was doing, and he hadn't offered, but she had decided to trust that he and Alpha team wouldn't cut her out of this case.

"Sure, you can help. I'm making vegetable fritters to go with our steaks. They need to sit in the freezer to harden before I crumb them and pop them into the frying pan. If you want to finish chopping, I can get started on the cinnamon rolls, they need to proof for a while."

"Cinnamon rolls? That's fancy."

"You don't like them?" She'd just assumed everyone liked cinnamon rolls, but if he didn't like them, she could whip up something else.

"I love them."

"Good. My opinion of you dipped for a moment there, tough guy," she teased. "Cinnamon rolls are my absolute favoritist favorite. When I was a little girl, I used to beg my mom to make them all the time. Luckily, they were her favorite too or I think she would have gotten annoyed with me."

Something flickered in his eyes, gone almost before it was there, but Julia had grown good at reading the brooding, emotionally shut-down man, so she noticed it. Had his home not been a happy one? Was that why pain and anger had flared when she mentioned her mom getting annoyed with her? Abuse— physical, emotional, verbal, or sexual—could definitely make someone shut down their emotions and lock them away.

Continuing on like she hadn't noticed anything, Julia laughed. "Actually, my mom never got annoyed with me about anything. She was the sweetest, happiest, most easy-going woman you would ever have met."

"Was?" Domino asked as he nudged her sideways with his hip and took the knife from her hand.

"Yeah, was. She and my dad died when I was fourteen."

"I'm sorry. That's a rough age to lose parents, just as you're moving from childhood to adulthood, stuck in that in-between stage."

"It was hard. Really hard. Not just because I lost them and was all alone. We lived a very unconventional life. We traveled the globe and lived mostly in tents or campervans. I did my schooling online and spent most of my time learning about the world and the places we stayed in. Nothing about how we lived was what anyone would consider normal."

"Why do I not doubt that, little flame?"

A rush of heat flushed through her, settling between her legs.

At first, she'd thought he was poking fun at her hair when he called her flame. Julia liked her red hair, but she could be a little sensitive about it if she thought someone was mocking her, it stirred up some memories best left buried.

"Hey, you saying I'm a weirdo?" she teased, swatting at his backside.

"I reserve the right not to incriminate myself."

Hearing him make jokes was everything. Julia knew she was getting in too deep, too fast; she could much too easily become addicted to this. Teasing, seeing Dom come out of his shell, cooking side by side in the kitchen. Neither of them was conventional, their jobs were unpredictable at best, but there could be happy moments between them just like this, a little bit of domestic bliss if only Domino would open up and let her in.

"You lost them both together?"

"Yeah." Julia swallowed the lump forming in her throat and began to gather ingredients for the cinnamon rolls from the well-stocked safehouse kitchen.

"It's okay if you don't want to talk about it."

"No, it's okay. It's been almost twenty years. I can talk about it, it's just getting through that first moment of grief whenever I think about them. They were into all kinds of crazy things, abseiling and cave diving, canyoning and paragliding. They also loved skydiving. Since I was a minor, I wasn't allowed to go on my own. Actually, I was too young to go at all, but we were in Peru, and I'd been whining about not wanting to be left out. I think they paid someone off but anyway I was with them."

Even though she knew her being there had nothing to do with what happened, Julia couldn't help a small twinge of guilt. Maybe if she hadn't been so insistent on wanting to go along, her parents would have canceled that day.

"We jumped. I was with my dad, there was this freak wind, and it damaged the parachutes. My mom crashed into the ground. My dad managed to aim us at a tree and angled his body so it took the brunt of the crash. They both died. I survived."

It didn't matter how many years passed, the pain of losing your parents, especially in such a traumatic way, never went away. Time had dulled her wounds, and she was able to think about her parents, the amazing life they'd given her, and the invaluable lessons they'd taught her without bursting into tears, but it still hurt.

Taking the bag of flour from her hands, Domino set it on the counter, then folded her into an embrace.

For a second Julia was so surprised by the gesture that she didn't react. Her arms hung limply by her sides and her body remained stiff, filled with grief and sorrow. Then his lips touched the top of her head and she melted. Lifting her arms, she curled them around Domino's waist, pressed her face against the hard planes of his chest, and sank into his hold.

"I'm sorry for your loss."

The simple words opened a floodgate, and before she knew what she was doing, Julia was sobbing into Dom's shirt.

She didn't try to hold back. Tears were a natural part of human emotion, everyone needed to cry sometimes. Holding back those feelings wasn't healthy, and even though it had been a long time since she'd wept over her loss, today she cried as though it had happened just days ago instead of years.

Instead of pulling away at her messy display of emotions like she thought he might have, Domino stood still, a tower of strength for her, holding her as she wept. He didn't murmur consolations in her ear or stroke her back. He didn't touch his lips to her head again, he just stood there and held her.

For a man like Domino to take her emotions so stoically made her fall even harder for him.

What was she doing here?

Other than a few heated gazes and the very slow lowering of his guard, Domino hadn't given her any indication that he was interested in anything with her.

Well, sex maybe.

Julia was pretty sure he wouldn't turn down sex if she offered it, and she'd come close a few times. But to sleep with a man she needed not just to feel a connection with him but to know that he felt one with her too.

The connection with Domino was there on her end, and she was pretty sure it was on his too, but was he going to acknowledge it?

She'd told him she wasn't walking away until she found out what this thing was between them and if it could go somewhere, but he hadn't said he felt the same way.

To him, this could just be passing away the time while they were stuck here together.

If that was the case, she was pretty sure her poor heart wouldn't survive.

CHAPTER NINE

October 7th
12:39 A.M.

He had no hope of falling asleep so long as he was hard as a rock.

He had no hope of not being hard as a rock so long as the gorgeous redhead was asleep down the hall.

Domino groaned and shifted, trying to find a comfortable position.

Only there was none.

Maybe if he thought the most unsexy thoughts he could muster it would help. That shouldn't be hard given the life he had led, but for some reason, at the moment, he couldn't seem to think of anything but Julia's bright smile, her plump lips, her soft skin, her toned limbs ... and now he was harder than he'd been before if that was even possible.

What was even worse ... or maybe better ... was that watching Julia break down and cry as she told him about her parents' deaths hadn't put a dampener on his feelings. Usually, seeing a woman cry like that would only irritate him and turn him off. He didn't like emotions, wasn't comfortable with his own or other people's, and being alone with a sobbing woman would have been his worst nightmare.

Somehow with Julia it hadn't been that way.

Instead, he'd found himself wanting to absorb her pain, take it from her and carry it so she didn't have to be weighed down by grief.

In typical Julia fashion, after weeping into his chest, she'd then shrugged off her sorrow, dried up her tears, and been laughing and teasing him minutes later as they worked side by side in the kitchen cooking dinner.

The woman amazed him.

Confused him too, but not in a bad way.

Since sleep was a lost cause again tonight, he found his sweatpants and pulled them on, trying to shift so there wasn't a huge tent in the middle of them. Heading downstairs, he thought he'd make some coffee, then he could work out for a while now that they had equipment.

Although of course working out would only remind him of his self-defense training session with Julia, and all the silly games she'd wanted to play afterward. That kind of defeated the purpose of trying to take his mind off her so his body could get over its obsession and he could get some sleep.

"So, sleeping with you around is going to be impossible, isn't it?"

Despite the fact he was highly trained, could usually feel the shift in the air that indicated another presence long before they were able to be seen or heard, and he was here on bodyguard duty so he should be extra cautious, he hadn't known Julia was there until she spoke.

"I hardly made any noise," he told her, glancing over his shoulder to throw her a casual smile.

Big mistake.

How did he think he could throw a quick glance her way and then turn his back on her?

How did he think he was ever going to be able to turn his back on her and walk away?

"Uh, Dom?"

"Yeah?"

"Do you really have that much milk in your coffee?"

Turning back to the counter, he realized he'd continued to pour milk into his mug while staring at Julia's scantily clad body.

A delicious treat covered only by a skimpy pair of pink short shorts and a white tank top that molded to her perfect set of breasts. One he could hardly wait to unwrap and devour.

Domino didn't even have to taste her to know she would be delicious.

"Uh, Dom?"

"What?"

"You do know you're still pouring, right?" Julia asked, trying to fight back a giggle.

Actually, he hadn't.

What was she doing to him?

Everything he thought he knew about himself, his life, and what he wanted for his future had been changed by the tiny flame of a woman standing a few yards away, amusement dancing in her bright green eyes.

Milk was now spilled all over the counter and dribbling down onto the wooden floorboards. Setting the carton down, he grabbed the dishtowel and quickly mopped up his mess.

Since he was awake, and Julia was awake, he thought it was all but inevitable where this was going to end. The two of them in bed. But he wanted to try to derail things before they got started. Neither of them was ready for the next step.

Strike that *he* wasn't ready.

From the look on Julia's pretty face, she would be more than happy if he shoved her up against a wall and ravished her, but he wasn't ready to accept the emotional ramifications that he knew were bound to come when he finally joined his body with hers.

Emotions he wasn't ready to deal with.

Might never be ready to deal with.

"Want some coffee?" he asked.

"Made by you?" Julia snorted another laugh.

Damn, she was adorable. There wasn't a single thing about her that he found unappealing. Even the things that in someone else would have driven him crazy, in Julia he barely even noticed or actually liked.

"I think I'll pass, tough guy. Coffee is obviously not your forte."

"And what is my forte?" he asked as he began to stalk toward her.

Heat flared in Julia's eyes, but she didn't back away. If anything, her body drifted forward as though drawn toward him by some invisible force.

Her tongue darted out to wet her bottom lip, and a growl rumbled through him. "You shouldn't do that if you don't want things to get messy between us, little flame," he warned.

"I like mess," she murmured breathily. "I like you."

"Why?" Although he made sure the question didn't come out with any emotion whatsoever, Domino found himself wanting to know the answer.

What was there about him to like?

He was cold, hard, uncaring, and unfeeling. He had nothing to offer her and wouldn't say or do the right things. He would spend more time away than he would at home, didn't want kids, and didn't see marriage in his future. Yeah, he could see just why Julia liked him. Not.

"Well," she said slowly as she took a step toward him, closing the last of the distance. Her hands lifted to rest against his pecs, her fingertips brushing softly across his bare skin, lulling him into a sort of trance. "I like that you don't pretend to be something you're not. I like that you don't pretend the world isn't full of darkness. I like that you're strong, not just physically but that you survived whatever it is that made you think you had to shut down your emotions. I like that even though it made you uncomfortable, you held me last night when I cried. I like that your body responds to my touch because all I have to do is see you and mine feels like I'm about to catch fire I'm so hot and bothered."

One of her hands left his chest to brush against his erection. It twitched at her touch desperate for more. And it took all his self-control not to lift her up, shove her against the wall, and plunge deep inside her hot, wet center.

Instead, he moved his hands, which had been fisted at his sides, and tangled them in her hair. "As soft as it looks," he whispered, making her smile.

That smile did weird things to his heart.

Warmed it.

Cracked the shell that protected it.

"These pecs are as hard as they look," she teased. Her eyes sparkled as her fingers on his chest stroked in time with the hand she still had on his length.

"Julia, we shouldn't."

"Why? I know you want to, and I want to. We're two grown adults, I think we can handle things if they don't work out between us."

Tenderly he massaged the back of her neck. "That's it though, things won't work out between us. They can't."

She didn't get angry, didn't try to convince him otherwise, or argue her case. Julia just framed his face with her hands and lightly brushed her lips against his. "I won't hurt you, Dom. I promise."

Maybe.

Maybe not.

There was no way to tell the future.

If there was, if he could know for sure that he wouldn't lose her and she wouldn't betray him, then perhaps he could take a chance.

Her eyes met his, holding his gaze as though in a spell, and he felt like she had thrown open the gates to her soul to allow him to see deep down inside her. See every part of her, she was holding nothing back, showing him that she had nothing to hide from him.

Now or never.

Let her in or let what could be his only chance at peace pass on by.

Was it even a choice?

Was there any way he could resist the woman standing before him offering him everything?

With a growl, Domino lifted her up, one hand kneading her bottom, the other tangled in her hair as he kissed her with a ferocity that felt very much like he was claiming Julia Garamond as his.

* * * * *

October 7th
1:01 A.M.

This kiss was everything.

Julia clutched his shoulders and tried to draw him closer.

She needed more, so very much more.

"More," she pleaded, the word falling from her lips without any conscious thought. She had moved to a different plane of existence where all that mattered was her and Domino and them doing a whole lot more than kissing.

Dom pulled back enough that she could see his face and he gave her this ridiculously sexy one-sided smile.

How did he manage to get the perfect balance of alpha and vulnerability that made him insanely irresistible?

She didn't even want to attempt to resist him.

Not even if it meant walking away from this with a broken heart.

In this moment, she would take her heart being shattered into a million pieces if it meant just one night of indescribable passion with Dominick Tanner.

"I'll give you more, little flame." His rock-hard length was pressed flat across her center. She could feel its heat through the thin material of her sleep shorts, and when he rolled his hips just enough to create some friction she moaned and pressed down, trying to absorb more of him.

Out of her mind with need, she reached out. She had to touch, it was a need that had to be satisfied. But just as she closed her hand around him, he reached for her wrist, tugging her away.

"No, not here. I'm not taking you up against a kitchen wall. We need a bed."

He looked so serious that she was filled with tender affection. Touching a light kiss to the tip of his nose, she said, "Up against a wall is fine. I'm not some delicate little flower, Dom."

"No, you're not," he agreed. There was something in his eyes she didn't get a chance to decipher because his lips were on hers again and he was carrying her up the stairs.

Domino carried her into the bedroom she had been staying in and set her on her feet. His eyes were like fire, scorching her with every touch. His gaze roamed her body, and while she knew she didn't have huge breasts or a nice round backside, she was a little scrawny and lacked the curves she'd always thought made women attractive, Julia had never felt more beautiful than in this moment.

When he reached for her, he stripped her out of her sleep shorts and tank top with a fervor that matched her own. Once he'd practically ripped them from her body, he picked her up and laid her out on the bed with a reverence that made her heart flutter. Despite his cold side, he could be warm and gentle when he wanted to be.

When he allowed himself to be.

There was no sweet talk, no dirty talk either. Domino just stretched his large body out above hers and took one of her breasts in his mouth. With his tongue lapping at her, suckling, the tip swirling against her hardening nipple, her hand automatically moved between them, searching out his length.

As soon as her fingers curled around him, he pulled back.

"I don't like to be an inactive participant," Julia warned him.

"Then I should have brought ropes to tie these dainty hands of yours to the bedpost," he said. Lifting her hand to his lips he took each one of her fingers into his mouth, one at a time, running his tongue along each one before swiping his tongue across the sensitive skin on the inside of her wrist.

"You're into bondage?" Julia had never been tied up for sex before, had never even thought about it because like she'd told Dom, she liked being an active participant, not just lying back and allowing a man to have his way with her. Although with Dom she admitted there was a certain level of appeal she hadn't been expecting. Maybe because she knew for certain he would never hurt her, just bring her more pleasure than she could imagine.

"I ... don't like people touching me," he admitted, giving her a rare glimpse of vulnerability.

"My touch won't hurt, not ever," she promised, once again reaching for his length.

With the kind of self-control she expected from a man like Domino, he held himself still and allowed her to explore. She stroked him, memorized every jerk his length made, the way her touch made his pupils dilate and his jaw tighten. The more she touched him the wetter she got, but when she lifted her hips and tried to guide him to her entrance, he pulled away again.

"Not yet, little flame," he told her as he shifted down her body until he was settled between her spread legs.

That first touch of his tongue against her most intimate areas made her gasp.

Then she no longer had the ability to think. All she could do was feel. He ate at her like he was starving, his tongue doing the most wonderful things, stroking deep inside her, and sucking on her needy little bundle of nerves. At some point, he added his fingers and sensations built until they were almost too much.

"Come for me, little flame, don't hold anything back," the murmured order was enough to send her spiraling into a pleasure-filled vortex.

But Domino didn't pull away.

He didn't stop.

He was relentless, licking and touching her until her lingering orgasm began to build all over again.

"No, too much," she begged, not sure her body could take another burst of sensation like that when she hadn't even recovered from the first.

"Come again, Julia," he ordered.

The use of her name this time made her feel like he was reaching inside her chest, curling into her heart, and taking residence inside. There was nothing she could do but give in to his command and come all over his face again.

Julia was still reeling, still locked into a pleasure-filled haze when he sheathed himself and entered her in one smooth thrust. There was one moment of stretching that almost hurt as her body accommodated his large size, but then once again there was nothing but pleasure.

This was Domino's show, and all she could do was hold on for the ride.

His lips found hers, and she clung to his shoulders as he set a fast pace, thrusting into her as his fingers found her overly sensitive little bud and somehow managed to get a third orgasm building inside her in just moments.

How was he doing this?

She'd never come three times in such close succession.

But somehow Dom managed it. She could tell he was holding back, waiting for her to come yet again before he would allow himself to find any release, and his thoughtfulness was the final push she needed before she fell through a myriad of shooting stars.

This man could crush her, and she didn't even think he realized it. Domino was more worried about protecting himself from pain that he couldn't see how deeply she was falling for him.

Hard and fast.

And she wasn't talking about the sex.

It could be a good thing or her downfall, that remained to be seen. It all depended on whether or not Dom decided to give her a chance. To do that, he would have to admit his fears to her, let her see his scars, and allow himself to be completely emotionally naked, and she wasn't sure that was something he was ever prepared to do.

"I'll be right back," he said as he slowly eased out of her.

Immediately she missed his warmth, but he leaned down to drop a kiss to her lips before disappearing into the bathroom.

It was only because she was watching him walk away that she saw it.

A tattoo.

One she had seen before when she was researching the Mikhailovs, the Russian mafia family involved in the bombings. The bombings that had almost killed her twice now.

The tattoo was of a lion with the devil's face and horns.

Every member of the Mikhailov Bratva had this same tattoo.

The placement depended on the person's position in the organization, different ones for different roles.

Domino's was on his bottom.

The right side.

It meant one day he would sit on the throne, and until then, he was to be his father's right-hand man.

The man she had just had sex with wasn't just working for the people involved in a plot to destroy the government, the people who had put out a hit on her, he *was* those people.

She had to get out of there.

This had to be a plot of some kind to get information out of her before they killed her. She had no idea if all of Alpha team was in on it or if Domino was a mole at Prey Security, there to gather intel for his family and further their interests.

Not that it mattered.

Whatever game he was playing, Julia knew she had only seconds to make her escape.

Flying from the bed, she fumbled to throw on clothes. Jeans, sweater, a jacket, comfortable shoes, she was going to have to trek through the woods to get somewhere safe.

Behind her in the bathroom she could hear the tap running; any second now he would come out. If he knew she was onto him, he wouldn't try to seduce information out of her, he'd resort to torture, and then he'd kill her.

The thought of being killed at the hands of the man she was falling in love with was too much.

Fighting back tears, she ran down the stairs and out into the night, ready to fight for her life however she had to. Even if that meant killing the man who had already crept into her heart.

CHAPTER TEN

October 7th
1:21 A.M.

She had ghosted him.

Domino stood in the bathroom doorway looking at the empty bed where just moments ago he had been buried deep inside Julia having the best sex of his life.

Now she was gone.

What the hell?

"Julia?" he called out, hoping she had just gone to use one of the other bathrooms or maybe downstairs for some water.

There was no answer.

Anger bubbled to life inside him.

The towel he'd wet with warm water to clean her before they both got some much-needed sleep dropped from his hand, hitting the floorboards with a thwop.

The same sound he imagined his heart was making at the very moment as it fell from his chest and landed alongside the towel.

Never before had he cleaned a woman after sex. Usually, he cut the bonds he'd used to tie them to the bed, got dressed, and walked out the door.

Damn.

He'd let Julia touch him.

Touch him.

She had no idea what a big step that was for him. Usually, a woman's touch made him ill. Forcing memories of Rosie and all the ways he'd failed her flooded into his mind in an uncontrollable stream.

But not with Julia.

With Julia he hadn't even thought of Rosie.

Was that why this hurt so badly?

A one-two punch. Realizing what they had just shared meant absolutely nothing to Julia, and then that he had forsaken the only woman he'd ever loved and allowed her to become a distant memory.

With a howl of pain, Domino slammed his fist into the door, pleased when the wood splintered.

This was why he didn't allow anyone to get close to him. The resulting pain was too much.

Stalking over to where he'd dropped his pants, he shoved his legs into them and then headed downstairs to find his phone. He needed to track where Julia was going. Once he had proof that she'd played a good hand and really was involved in the terrorist plot he would do whatever it took to make sure she was punished to the fullest extent of the law.

The woman would never see the outside of a prison cell again.

And for her involvement with his family, he would exact his own form of justice.

Once he'd located his phone he dropped down into a chair at the table and brought up the app that would monitor the tracking device he'd implanted in her on the car ride to the safehouse. She'd been exhausted and passed out sleeping. He'd had a feeling that things weren't going to end well, so he'd inserted a tiny tracking device near her elbow.

It was similar to the kind of microchip people put in their pets, only more advanced. It would allow him to track her anywhere in the world and she would be none the wiser that he was watching her every move.

A sense of satisfaction made him smile when the red dot appeared on his screen. She thought she had the upper hand, and it was going to be fun wiping that smirk off her beautiful face.

As he watched the dot, he typed out a 911 text to his team,

knowing they would drop everything to get here as quickly as they could.

The dot moved slowly. Obviously, Julia was on foot making her way through the woods. Did she even know she was going in the wrong direction if she wanted to get to a road in a timely manner?

He would have thought she'd have called her contact in the Mikhailov Bratva to come and pick her up, but obviously, he was wrong because she continued to move slowly across his screen.

A trickle of doubt edged through the anger.

Why was she alone out there?

Why was she going in the wrong direction?

If Julia had been sent by his father as he suspected she had been, why wasn't she reaching out to someone to come and get her?

Domino knew his father, and whatever game he was playing here, whatever he hoped to gain by sending Julia in to infiltrate his life and Prey, he'd want that information as soon as possible. Konstantin Mikhailov was not a patient man. He would want Julia's intel immediately and wouldn't be pleased if she kept him waiting to go traipsing through the woods.

Stupid woman was going to earn herself a punishment.

"What's wrong?" Bear demanded as Alpha team burst through the front door.

"Julia ran," Domino replied.

"Huh?" Mouse asked, switching on more of the lights. "What do you mean, she ran?"

"I mean, she's gone," he growled. What did Mouse think he meant? "She must be working with the Bratva. I told you that she was bad news, that she was involved in this terrorist plot somehow."

For a long moment, nobody said anything. Instead, they all just stared at him like he'd lost his mind.

"There is no proof she's involved in anything," Surf said

slowly.

"Then why else would she run?" he demanded. If someone else had a better theory, he would love to hear it. "She's a liar, a plant of some kind. I don't know what information she hoped to get from us, but she must have gotten it, and now she's gone. We should have taken her in to Prey, locked her up until we knew more about her and why she was really in Somalia."

"I don't think you're right about her, Domino," Arrow said after another long pause. "Piper really liked her, and she's pretty much a perfect judge of character."

"Then Piper can visit Julia in prison," he snapped. Why was his team ganging up on him? They were supposed to be his friends, not Julia's.

"What's she going to prison for?" Mouse asked. The fact that his friend actually sounded amused only served to add further fuel to the fire raging inside him.

"Whatever she's done wrong." As far as he was concerned, he'd have as many charges as he could thrown at her. If she was working with his family, she deserved to spend the rest of her life in prison for their sins. He might not be able to get his powerful father locked up, but he'd get his vengeance by proxy through Julia if he had to.

Someone had to pay for Rosie's death.

"And if she hasn't done anything wrong?" Surf asked gently.

Then the future he'd just started to imagine would be gone forever.

"Then I'll apologize," he growled.

Only they all knew an apology would never be enough. If he continued down this road, labeling Julia a member of the Bratva, and treating her as a threat to their country, he would lose her forever.

Both he and Julia would know that he was working a vendetta against her because when she'd run from their bed just after making love, she'd taken his heart along with her.

Hurt his feelings.

Hell, he sounded pathetic.

"Julia isn't a runner," Mouse said. "She stands and fights for what she believes in no matter how dangerous. For her to have left like she did means she's not just scared, she's downright terrified."

"Petrified," Surf added, earning him a scowl.

"Why are you so determined to believe the worst about her?" Arrow asked. There was no judgment in the other man's tone just genuine confusion and concern.

Because he had no other choice.

Didn't everyone get that?

His father was a vicious, ruthless man, and as the oldest of Konstantin's two sons, he was supposed to be the heir to the Mikhailov billions, the heir to the Mikhailov Bratva. Instead, he was the heir that threw it all away and left the family. Proof that his father had been the one to order Rosie's torture and murder was the only thing that had kept him alive this along. Alive and free.

But he'd always known his father wouldn't wait forever for him to return to the family fold.

Only that was never happening.

Konstantin must have realized he was never coming back and decided to try to force his hand. But why use Julia to do it? How did she fit into all of this?

"I believe what the evidence tells us," Domino answered smoothly.

"Bull," Surf muttered angrily. "You're trying and convicting her in your mind without having anything close to all the facts. You've read her papers. You know the kind of person she is, you know she's partially responsible for us being able to save Piper. Julia Garamond wouldn't betray her country any more than any of us would."

"So, what scared her into leaving?" Brick asked.

What indeed.

If she hadn't left because she'd completed whatever her mission was then she really had left because she was afraid, and the only thing she could have been afraid of was him because he was the only other person here.

Somehow the thought of her running because she was scared of him scorched his insides more thoroughly than her leaving because she had betrayed him.

* * * * *

October 7th
9:55 A.M.

Exhaustion weighed heavily upon her.

Still, Julia had no choice but to keep going on.

Moving forward slowly took so long, but she kept putting one foot in front of the other.

At least she was almost there now.

When she'd run, she hadn't taken her purse or cell phone, so she had no money, no credit cards, and no way to call someone for help. Hitchhiking had been her only option.

The Mikhailov Bratva were ruthless, and they had people everywhere. When she'd finally reached a road, she had been terrified that the first person to stop would be someone who worked for them. It was crazy because what were the chances? But these last few days had been crazy, and she'd known she was taking a huge risk.

Luckily the first people to stop were a couple of college guys who had taken pity on her and offered to take her wherever she needed to go.

Of course, she'd told them a sob story about how her boyfriend had assaulted her, and she'd run without her belongings, so it was no wonder they felt bad for her. And really it wasn't all that far from the truth. Domino might not be her boyfriend, but she had been falling for him, and in a way he had assaulted her. Perhaps not physically but her heart would never be the same again.

She'd had them drop her off near her place but a couple of streets over. It wasn't a smart move to be this close to her apartment because Prey had her address which meant Domino did too, which meant it was almost guaranteed that the Mikhailov's would be watching it, waiting for her to return.

But she had a friend here, someone she trusted, someone who would help her. As much as she didn't want to bring them into this mess, she didn't have a lot of options.

She could not trust Prey knowing that Domino had infiltrated the company. Maybe the rest of his teammates were oblivious to his true identity or maybe they weren't. She couldn't risk her life to find out. As much as she had liked Piper, even if the other woman wasn't involved, her loyalty lay with her boyfriend, and if Arrow knew who Domino was and was working with him or protecting him then reaching out to the psychiatrist would be signing her own death warrant.

Stuck.

Julia was completely stuck in a situation that right now she could see zero way out of.

Panic began to claw at her.

That same darkness she'd felt when she was trapped in the rubble after the explosion began to creep inside her. The terror of being trapped in a small dark space not knowing if she would ever get out or if she was doomed to an excruciatingly long and slow death. Now she was trapped in a situation not a place, but the fear was the same as was the sense of claustrophobia.

"Calm down, Julia, you can do this. It's not the worst situation you've ever found yourself in. Close, but no cigar," she muttered, trying not to draw the attention of anyone on the streets.

Any one of them could be an enemy.

The Mikhailov family had people everywhere, in law

enforcement, in the government, with a target from them on her back nowhere was safe. Having Prey on her side would have been a huge mark in her favor. It would have given her a chance at holding on to her life.

Because she was under no doubts that was exactly what she was fighting for.

Her very life.

As though to mock her, her bruised leg chose that exact moment to give out, sending her sprawling onto the pavement.

For a second, the urge to give up nearly overwhelmed her. What was the point in fighting what was almost definitely a losing battle?

She should just give up. Let the Bratva have her. Eventually, they would realize that she wasn't giving up anything she had on them and then they'd just kill her. Whatever pain they inflicted on her couldn't be any worse than Domino ripping her heart right out of her chest.

Anger began to trickle in.

Was she really going to give up just because some man had hurt her feelings?

So what if she'd been falling for him. That had been a mistake, one she could see now and would never be stupid enough to repeat.

Did she want to let him win?

If she just gave up that was exactly what she would be doing.

Never before had she given up even when the odds were stacked against her.

She wasn't a coward.

Nope.

No way.

She'd had her little meltdown moment, and now she was getting angrier with each pulse of pain in her leg. It wasn't fun being used the way Domino had played her. Hurting her was one thing, but sleeping with her? That cut really deep. It made her feel cheap and dirty, didn't help either that it had by far been the best sex of her life.

Well, screw him. He'd go down along with the rest of his evil family who thought they could buy and intimidate people into doing their bidding.

Julia would fight to her dying breath to take down the Mikhailov family.

"You got this, you totally do, and you know it," she said, infusing some confidence into her tone.

"Ma'am, are you okay?" A man crouched beside her. He had strawberry blond curls, a pair of bright green eyes similar in color to her own, and a scar that ran from his temple down along his right cheek, stopping millimeters away from the corner of his mouth.

Her cheeks heated in embarrassment. Julia had totally forgotten she was on a busy sidewalk, too distracted by her situation, anger, and hurt over Domino to pay much attention to anything else. That was something she would have to get a handle on because she was literally in the middle of a fight for her life. One moment of distraction was all it would take for the Mikhailovs to get her.

"Oh, yes, sorry, I'm fine. I just hurt my leg and it chose right now to give up on me."

"Here, let me help." A large hand cupped her elbow and gently helped her onto her feet. Instead of pulling away once she was standing, it lingered, the heat of it seeping into her chilled body, and for a moment Julia wished she had someone who cared about her at her side.

She had plenty of friends, people she loved and cared about, but right now, she had no one who would truly miss her if she was gone. No one who would call the cops because she'd disappeared, no one who would fight for her to be found, no one who would grieve her loss for very long. Because she was away working a story more than she was home, her friends were used to her not being an active part of their lives.

For the first time ever, she wished she'd put down roots.

Why did roots make her think of Domino?

The man had betrayed her. She had to stop thinking of him as someone she cared about. He wasn't. He was her enemy, and not seeing him as such could lead to her downfall.

"Thanks for your help," she said, shooting the man with the scar a polite smile as she tried to move out of his grip. If he thought helping her meant she'd say yes to a date he was sorely mistaken. Right now, she had much bigger fish to fry than worrying about her love life. It was her love life that was part of the problem.

Instead of loosening, the man's grip on her elbow tightened and he leaned in, provoking a stab of fear inside her. "Try anything stupid, and I'll start shooting innocent bystanders." To prove his point, she felt something cold press against her side. "I know a woman like you wouldn't want innocent lives on her conscience."

"Who are you?"

"I'm your worst nightmare, *moya dorogava.*"

She knew those words.

My dear.

In Russian.

Which meant the man with the scar was one of Mikhailovs.

"Catching on there I see. You have been a thorn in our side for too long, but one that is about to be removed. You will walk with me to the car and get in without making a scene. If you do not, I will start shooting. In case you need any additional motivation, I will start with the children." His head inclined to where a couple of mothers were walking with their kids, two strollers, and three preschoolers.

There was no other option.

Julia couldn't allow anyone, especially children, to be killed because of her, and besides it wouldn't change the outcome.

Her luck had run out, and now she was in the hands of the people who had put out a hit on her.

No one was going to come running to her rescue, she was on her own, and she had absolutely zero ideas how she was going to get out of this alive.

CHAPTER ELEVEN

October 7th
12:33 P.M.

"I don't like this."

"I know," Domino snapped at Arrow. "You've said it at least a dozen times already."

Between Arrow and the rest of his team, they'd had the same argument in a near continuous loop for the last several hours.

The guys didn't think they should wait to go in and grab Julia. He wanted to wait and see where she went and who she met up with.

"If you're wrong about her, and we all think that you are, then you're giving them time to hurt her," Mouse growled, his frustration evident.

Whether it was intentional or not, his friend's words cut deep.

Mouse wasn't wrong.

If Julia hadn't run because she was working with his father, then he was leaving her in a dangerous situation. A deadly one.

Julia was stubborn, she wouldn't back down, and wouldn't share what she knew about the Bratva. The woman would rather undergo torture herself than give up her source.

And she'd actually found a source.

Someone willing to share what they knew about his family and their criminal activities.

He had no idea how she'd managed to make the connection between his family and a bank, but somehow, she'd figured out which bank they used, and she'd found someone there willing to talk. She didn't know a lot, but his family used the safety deposit

119

boxes there, and Julia had gotten access to them. Inside, she'd found proof that his father was blackmailing several people. The ledger was in code, but given enough time, she would find someone to help her crack that code. If she sent it to the media, it was enough that his father could be ruined. If that happened, the people his father ruled through fear might very well revolt and his father could find himself in prison.

Either way it wasn't a risk Konstantin Mikhailov would take.

Julia was a threat that would be tortured and eliminated.

If she was really who she said she was.

If she wasn't, she might have gone to his father with what she knew and made a deal. Just because Julia didn't seem like the kind of woman who cared about wealth and power, it didn't mean that she wasn't. If nothing else, Konstantin was an astute businessman, and making deals was how he had become so powerful.

But he never made a deal that didn't keep him in top spot.

Any deal he made with Julia would involve her doing something illegal that he could hold over her head. Was that why she had decided to target him? Would his father see this as an opportunity to send in a pretty woman to do what his thugs couldn't?

"I'm not wrong about her," he said. "Why would she run if she had nothing to hide?"

"Why pretend she needed us at all?" Surf asked. Since his team didn't know who he really was, they had no idea that his father might have sent Julia in to drag him back into the life he had fought so hard to escape, and he wasn't going to tell them.

"She gave us a whole lot more than we gave her," Mouse said.

"And she was shot at twice," Arrow added.

"Shot at but not hit," he reminded them. Did they think he liked thinking this way about Julia? The woman had gotten to him, big time, in a way no one else ever had. He'd been stupid enough to think that it was mutual and that she was affected too. Now he knew she'd simply been playing him.

"So, you think she set up the shootings?" Brick asked with a snort. An actual snort.

"She didn't even have access to a phone," Bear said.

"Doesn't mean she's not involved."

"Look, brother, we know you slept with her, we get that you like her and that you're emotionally involved. You're not thinking clearly, you're acting like a jilted lover instead of the highly trained, intelligent special forces operator that you are," Arrow said.

"Which is the only reason we've gone along with you so far," Surf added. "But this has to stop. We're playing with a woman's life here. None of us are going to just sit back and wait any longer. We have to move in and get her out. Once we do, you can ask your questions and find out why she ran."

Oh, he'd be asking questions all right.

If she was working with his father, she'd tell him, and then he'd use her to get the revenge he had wanted on his father since he was a teenager.

Rosie deserved justice, so did his mother and all the other people his father had hurt in his lifetime. If Julia could get him that, he wouldn't hesitate to use her however he had to.

For the greater good.

And if it ripped out his heart in the process then it was a small price to pay.

"They stopped," Brick announced.

When Julia had stopped moving in slow motion through the woods surrounding the safehouse, and they knew she'd made it to a road and found someone to give her a ride they had hopped into their vehicles and followed. Other than a very brief pause close to her apartment, she'd been moving in a vehicle ever since.

Because they didn't need to remain within visual distance, they were several klicks behind whatever vehicle she was in. They were close enough to get to her quickly if it turned out she really was innocent and in over her head.

Contrary to what his teammates seemed to think of him, he wasn't really going to stand by and allow Julia to be hurt when he didn't have the whole story. That was his anger talking. But he was a better man than that, a better man than his father.

No matter how angry he was at Julia for running off like she had, if she had betrayed him and her country, she would pay by spending the rest of her life behind bars, not in blood.

"Where?" he asked, reaching for the tablet where they had been following her every move.

"Warehouse down by the docks," Brick replied.

A single glance at the tablet told him all he needed to know. Domino was intimately acquainted with this area of the docks. It was where his father ran his businesses. Everything from legal imports and exports to trafficking of valuable antiquities and art, weapons, drugs, and people. There wasn't a market around that his father didn't dabble in if he thought he could add to his mountain of money.

"Area is rumored to be associated with the Russian mafia," Bear said.

Not rumored, it was.

"Mikhailov family must have gotten their hands on her," Arrow said.

But by Julia's choice or not?

That was the only question he cared about.

She hadn't been out of a vehicle very long, they assumed she'd hitched a ride back into the city, but had she had something lined up for when she got there? She had to know that going anywhere near her apartment was stupid. The Bratva had a hit out on her and would be watching her place, so why had she gone so close? Did she have a friend in the area she'd been going to go to for help, or had she wanted the Bratva to pick her up?

"You have to decide now," Bear said as Surf sped to catch up to the vehicle transporting Julia. "I get that trust issues can be hard to overcome, believe me I do, but you have to make a

122

choice. Are you team Julia or not?"

Unfortunately, he couldn't make that decision without all the facts.

It would be great if he could, but he had been betrayed too many times before and his team had no idea who they were really dealing with. They thought they understood Konstantin Mikhailov. Thought that he was just like any other mobster, but the man was pure evil personified.

Konstantin wasn't crazy, he wasn't delusional, he was just a sick, twisted monster who cared about no one but himself.

If that was who Julia had decided to align herself with then there was no saving her. She would have to suffer the consequences of her actions.

Meeting his team leader's gaze head-on, he gave the only answer he could—the truth. "I want to know what's really going on here. I'm sorry, that's the best I can give you."

Bear studied him for what felt like an eternity, searching for something Domino wasn't sure he was able to give. Julia meant something to him, there was no way he could deny it, but that only made him more determined to see her pay if it turned out she was in bed with the Mikhailov Bratva.

"Julia is the primary target; we get her out. If we can we take them alive, but if they are Mikhailov's men they'd rather die than give up any intel. They know if they turn, Mikhailov will make them wish for death," Bear said.

That couldn't be more true. He'd seen up close and personal just how his father worked.

Which meant he knew what Julia was in store for if she was innocent.

If she was, and he hadn't stepped in sooner to get to her, then his soul deserved to burn in Hell for all eternity for damning hers.

* * * * *

October 7th
1:00 P.M.

She could do this.

She was a tough girl.

Julia hid a shudder as best as she could but was pretty sure that Scar felt it. After all, he was sitting close enough beside her in the car's back seat that they were touching from shoulder to knee.

The man was terrifying.

Intentionally so. He didn't try to hide the fact that he was basically dead inside. His eyes didn't hold a single spark of life. How had she not seen that the second she looked at him back near her apartment?

It had been a mistake to even get that close to her place. She'd thought that if anyone was watching her building, they would be right there, watching her building. Not watching the whole neighborhood. She'd thought her friend's house was far enough away that she would be safe, but obviously, the Mikhailovs were more determined to get to her than she had thought.

Another mistake.

Scar chattered away in Russian to the driver and the man in the front passenger seat. She could pick out the occasional word because of the research she had been doing into the Bratva, but nowhere near enough to even have a chance at figuring out what they were talking about.

They were heading down toward the docks, and the fear she felt grew by the second. She knew that the Mikhailovs used the docks to transport both their legitimate goods and their not so legal ones. Was that her destiny?

Were they going to sell her?

It would get rid of her just as effectively as killing her would, and if the Mikhailovs wanted payback that would mean she spent the rest of her life—however long that wound up being—suffering horrendously.

Nothing about her future looked good.

The car stopped, and nobody bothered to say anything to her. Scar pulled her out along with him and began to lead her through high towers of shipping containers. Even if she was able to break free of the crushing grip he had on her arm and wasn't shot in the process, it was unlikely she would manage to find her way out of this maze.

Finally, they stopped outside one particular container, and one of the two goons unlocked the door. Just as she was shoved inside Julia heard the unmistakable sound of gunshots.

Someone was coming for her.

No.

That was stupid.

Who would come for her?

No one even knew that she was in trouble. As far as her friends all knew, she was still in Somalia hunting for leads on the traffickers involved in the explosions. Domino would know that she was gone, but he was in on this, working with his family, so he wasn't going to come in after her with guns blazing.

Alpha team maybe?

No, that made no sense. Even if they didn't know Domino was a Mikhailov, they would believe whatever story he cooked up about why she had disappeared. They wouldn't be coming in to rescue her either.

Julia had to face facts, she was in this alone.

"Don't get any ideas. Even if they're here for you they'll never find you in here," Scar told her as he handed her off to the other two men who manhandled her onto the floor of the shipping container.

This was obviously some sort of torture room because there were metal cuffs in the floor.

She couldn't make this easy for them.

There was no way she was going down without a fight.

Better to get shot and die now than endure whatever they had planned for her and then be killed. Scar had shut the door behind them, this space was small and enclosed, and shooting a gun in here wasn't a good idea. Maybe they wouldn't risk it.

Before one of the men snapped a metal cuff around her wrist, Julia shot her hand out, reaching for anything she could connect with.

It turned out to be one of the men's faces, and she gouged her fingers down his cheek.

The man howled in pain and swung a fist at her. It connected with the side of her head and made her see stars.

"I should kill you right now for that," Scar informed his man in a monotone voice. "Get the girl under control. Now."

Julia thrashed, kicked, and clawed at anything she could, but between the two men, they easily got her locked into the cuffs on the floor. Bound on her stomach, cuffed at the wrists and ankles, she had never felt more vulnerable in her life.

At least she thought that.

Until one of the men knelt beside her and cut her clothes from her body leaving her bound and naked.

Tears threatened to spill out, but she shoved them back. There was still a chance she could survive this. In the past she'd been lucky, that luck could still hold. It wasn't impossible.

Improbable but not impossible.

A knight in shining armor could still appear. An undercover cop, a rival family, Prey.

No.

She had to stop thinking that. Because no one was coming and the quicker she accepted her fate the easier she could do what she had to do.

Which was keep her mouth shut.

There was no way she could give up sweet old Mr. Popov. The man had risked everything for her, and he was so nice. He reminded her of her grandfather, her mom's dad, he had died when she was really young, but she always loved when they went to visit with him.

No matter what Scar did to her, she couldn't allow herself to give up how she'd learned so much about the Mikhailovs.

"They all think they're tough at first," Scar said, standing above her.

The sound of something flying through the air was her only warning before pain sliced through her back.

A whip.

He was going to strike her for each answer she refused to give.

Since she had no plans of providing any answers this was going to suck a whole lot.

"You were lucky last time, you were rescued. That won't be happening this time." Scar stood before her, the whip in his hand, that dead look on his face. The man was the epitome of the bogeyman that haunted your nightmares.

Another strike hit her, this time across her backside, and she clenched her jaw together so she didn't cry out.

She wouldn't give him the satisfaction.

"You have been looking into things that are none of your business," Scar said. "What did you learn?"

When she gave no answer a series of strikes rained down across her back. The pain seemed to get worse with each hit, she could feel her skin growing wet as blood was shed.

"Someone talked to you," Scar said. "I want a name."

She could never give him that.

If she did, she wouldn't be the person she was, the person she wanted to be, and the person her parents raised her to be. It would be like a betrayal of their memory, and the last thing she wanted was for her parents to be disappointed in her.

"Need a little more motivation?"

More blows came, one after another until it felt like her back was on fire.

"Give me a name and the pain stops."

Tears trickled down her cheeks and pain burned through her

body, but she couldn't do that. She wouldn't. Not for anything, not even to save herself.

Before Scar could start whipping her again voices sounded from outside the shipping container.

Someone was out there.

More of Mikhailov's men?

Whoever it was, they were trying to get inside the container. Scar must have locked it while the men were cuffing her to the floor because the men outside were shaking the door, trying to get in.

If they were Mikhailov's men, why didn't Scar let them in?

It didn't make sense, and the blinding pain coursing through her body made it difficult for her to think.

The next thing she knew, there was a large bang, and then more people flooded into the container.

Hard voices shouted out orders, but she was too tired to even attempt to figure out what they were saying.

Hands touched her, and she shied away from them.

No.

No more pain.

Her plea to the universe was promptly ignored as she was turned over, and this time, she couldn't help crying out loud at the shooting pain consuming her alive.

Dark eyes looked down at her.

Domino's eyes.

Only this time there was no softness in them. There was no fluttering in her heart at his presence, even in the car that first day she'd felt something deep inside that had told her the man wasn't a threat to her.

Whatever that was it wasn't there now.

Domino was absolutely a threat to her.

Scar must be working against the Mikhailovs, and now Domino was here to take over.

Julia felt her mind snapping, something feral taking over. She couldn't let him touch her. She would do anything to get away from him.

With a scream that sounded more animal than human, she began to fight with everything her weak, bleeding body still had left to give.

It wasn't until something sharp pierced her skin and fuzziness invaded her mind that she finally gave into the calling darkness and surrendered to unconsciousness.

CHAPTER TWELVE

October 7th
12:31 P.M.

This was his fault.

No one else in the shipping container said it, but Domino knew it was what they were all thinking.

Maybe he wasn't any better than his father after all.

Part of him had wanted Julia to suffer for betraying him. So much of his life had been splattered with blood, physically and metaphorically, and Julia may as well have taken a knife to his chest and carved his heart from his body when she disappeared without a word right after he'd allowed himself to be vulnerable to her.

If she was guilty, she deserved it.

If she wasn't … he deserved to pay with his soul.

"Is she out?" Arrow asked, dropping to his knees beside Domino.

When they'd eliminated the muscle and tracked Julia to this shipping container, he'd known whatever they would find inside would be bad.

Still, nothing could have prepared him for the sight of the woman who had managed to find a foothold in the heart he hadn't believed he possessed lying chained to the floor, naked and bleeding.

Her cries of pain and terror as he and Arrow got her free would forever haunt him.

Whether she had known it was him and Alpha team or not, she had fought for her life. Even when he'd called her name over and over, assuring her that she was safe now, that he wasn't going to hurt her, she hadn't calmed.

And so help him, he wasn't.

Even if she was guilty.

Even if it meant no one ever paid for Rosie's death, he didn't think he could ever allow Julia to suffer for any bad choices she might have made.

If that made him a sucker then so be it. He'd fallen too hard and too fast for a woman he knew next to nothing about. A woman who from the very beginning they had suspected could be a threat.

"She's out," he answered, and thank goodness for that. Because listening to a second more of her petrified screams would have destroyed him.

"I need to check her wounds," Arrow said gently when Domino made no move to release his hold on the woman who had him completely tied up in knots.

He tried to let go, lay her out on the floor so she could be evaluated and her injuries tended to, then they could decide what they were going to do with her, but for some reason, he couldn't make himself do it.

They were as different as night and day. She may or may not be involved in a terrorist plot to overthrow the government. She had possibly been sent specifically to spy on him by his father, there should be no reason he'd fallen for her.

Yet he had.

And now he couldn't think straight.

"Why don't you hold her in your lap, drape her across your chest, that way I can see her back," Arrow offered when it became clear he couldn't bear to let go of her.

The medic helped him maneuver Julia so that he had access to her wounds, and even drugged unconscious her warm body seemed to sink into his as though she needed him.

His heart clenched.

He should let go of her, hand her off to his team, ask Eagle to assign another team to this mission, and walk away now before she completely shredded him. But even as he had the thought, he knew he wouldn't do it. Couldn't do it.

Arrow whistled in dismay as he surveyed her wounds. "They worked her over hard."

"Bet she didn't tell them a single thing," Surf said, clear pride in his tone. "She didn't even scream."

"She's a tough cookie," Mouse agreed.

"None of the wounds are deep enough to need stitches, but I am worried about infection," Arrow said. "I'll clean them, then I'll give her a shot of antibiotics. Painkillers too. And maybe some fluids," he added as he lifted her wrist and checked her pulse. "There's blood and skin under her fingernails."

"I think it comes from this guy." Bear pointed to a body propping open a second door in the back of the shipping container. The man's throat had been sliced, and he'd been left behind to bleed out, likely because of the fact that he had allowed a Mikhailov prisoner to scratch him. "He has scratches down his face and one of his eyes is bloody."

"She fought back," Surf said, still sounding proud.

"Tough cookie," Mouse said again.

The toughest.

It made no sense that his father would order her torture if she was working for them, unless maybe Julia had refused to turn him in, but still his mind clung to the notion. Betrayal in the world he had been raised was a part of life. It was hard to believe that there were truly good innocent people in the world even if he had met several of them.

Until he had definitive proof that Julia Garamond was exactly who she said she was, it was safer to believe the worst. Better to be wrong than dead.

That had always been his motto, but for some reason now it felt empty.

What good was being alive if it meant he was the one who had betrayed Julia? If he lost her and had to go on without her bright shining light in his life, was he really living at all?

Even though they'd had to sedate her so she didn't hurt herself further, her body seemed to flinch with each swipe at her wounds Arrow made as he carefully cleaned each one.

Each time her limp body tightened, Domino felt the anger inside him grow. His father had to pay for Julia's pain.

That was not up for debate.

For too long he'd allowed Konstantin to go unpunished because doing something to stop him meant revealing to the world, to Prey, and to his team who he really was.

Cowardly.

While Julia fought for everything she believed in, putting herself in the line of fire and taking risks, he had hidden because he was ashamed for anyone to know that he was the son of one of Russia's most notorious mafia families.

"Done," Arrow said as he wiped Julia's thigh with an alcohol wipe and administered a shot of antibiotics. "Once we get her settled, I'll set up an IV. She'll likely be out for a few hours still, so we should get her moved now."

"Where are we taking her?" Brick asked.

All eyes turned to him.

How should he know?

"My place." The words came out of Domino's mouth before he could stop them, but they felt right. That was where Julia should be right now. His place was about an hour outside the city, although he had an apartment he rented close to Prey's offices for when he needed it. It was quiet and secluded, she'd be safe there. While his apartment was in his name, the house wasn't, so his family didn't know he owned it.

No one argued with that idea.

"Here." Arrow held out a soft cotton blanket, and Domino carefully tucked it around Julia's naked body. She didn't stir when he stood, keeping her held chest to chest so he didn't put unnecessary pressure on the wounds on her back.

He cared about her pain.

Would take it from her if it were possible.

"Domino and Arrow, you two take Julia to Domino's place, get her settled, medicated, and the rest of us will wrap things up here then come and join you," Bear said.

"No. I can handle this on my own. Arrow can get the IV set up, but then he can leave." What he needed was time alone with Julia so he could find out what was really going on. The woman he'd been getting to know didn't fit the profile of someone who would work for either Storm Gallagher or Konstantin Mikhailov, and yet she was somehow all mixed up in this, and he couldn't move forward until he got this mess straightened out.

The guys exchanged concerned glances, and Domino felt his blood freeze in his body.

They were worried about leaving Julia alone with him.

Acting as though they believed he was a threat to the woman he cradled so gently in his arms.

The knowledge settled like a lead balloon in his gut.

His own team believed he was capable of hurting a woman just because he was angry. Yes, he knew that they knew his anger had been simmering almost out of control ever since Somalia, but he also thought they knew he would never actually hurt anyone.

That was exactly why he'd been so angry these last few months. The angrier he got the more he felt like he was becoming his father, becoming the man he had strived for a lifetime never to be, which made him angrier still. A vicious cycle he hadn't seen a way out of and yet never once had he laid a hand on anyone even in the darkest of his rages.

If his team thought he was the kind of man who would inflict pain on an already vulnerable and injured woman just because she'd broken his heart then they didn't know him at all.

Without another word, he turned his back on them. "I'll set up the IV myself, handle all of it myself." Then once Konstantin Mikhailov was destroyed, he'd walk away from Prey and the team who had just betrayed him.

Domino thought he knew pain, thought he knew betrayal, but the universe seemed determined to show him he knew nothing.

However bad things were, they could always get worse.

* * * * *

October 8th
6:12 A.M.

Julia surfaced slowly.

Her head felt like it was stuffed with cotton wool, but her memories were still intact.

Finding out Domino was the son of the head of the mafia who put a hit out on her, running through the woods, getting close to her friend's house only to be snatched off the street. The gun in her side, the hard floor beneath her, the cold cuffs pinning her in place, burning pain in her back, and then Domino's angry eyes above her.

After that everything was blank.

She had no idea where she was or if she'd been hurt while unconscious, and the unknowing left her feeling completely ripped open and vulnerable.

Doing her very best to shove away her fear, Julia tried to take stock of her body and surroundings. The pain in her back had subsided dramatically. She was on her stomach lying on something soft. It felt like a bed, and the thought sent a new wave of terror rushing through her.

Had she been violated?

It didn't feel like she had any clothes on, she could feel air whispering across her bare skin, her legs and bottom covered by what felt like a sheet. There was no pain between her legs so she prayed that meant no one had touched her there, but even if they hadn't it didn't mean they wouldn't.

Maybe they wanted her to be awake when they raped her.

Panic had her automatically trying to curl in on herself, but when she tried, she found her left wrist wouldn't move.

When she lifted her head, Julia saw it was handcuffed to the bedpost. Whoever had done it and left her here had wrapped strips of material around the metal cuff as though to protect her wrist which was already bruised from her body jerking against her restraints when Scar had been torturing her.

Why would they do that?

It seemed so incongruent with everything she thought she knew about her situation. After all, she had been drugged and brought here against her will. She was obviously a prisoner since she had been cuffed to the bed, so why would they care whether or not she was in pain?

Domino had to be the one who had taken her. He'd been there right before she'd been knocked out. Was he trying to mess with her head? Because that's exactly what he'd been doing ever since she met him.

Her poor heart couldn't take more of this.

It knew Domino was the enemy, but it struggled to remember that fact. It wanted to believe that everything they had shared was real.

But it wasn't.

It was lies.

Manipulation.

He was toying with her like a cat with a mouse, and sooner or later, he was going to pounce and devour her.

Julia whimpered as her heart rate accelerated and her pulse drummed a racing beat that felt like it reverberated through her entire body.

She couldn't breathe.

Oxygen seemed to drain out of the room.

The fact that she couldn't move made her feel claustrophobic.

Images flashed through her mind of being trapped in the rubble of the first explosion. Alone, scared, and hurt. Those images overlaid with the second explosion in Somalia. Pinned with her arm cuffed to a pipe, just like she was cuffed to the bed now. Domino had been there that second time and his presence had soothed her, but now knowing he was likely the cause of her current predicament it only made her more afraid.

Black dots began to dance in her vision.

The sound of her gasped breaths echoed in her ears.

"You're okay, Julia. Calm down."

The voice came out of nowhere, and even in the middle of a hyperventilating panic attack she recognized it.

Domino.

Here.

Any hope she might have clung to that she had imagined seeing him in the shipping container shattered beneath her.

He was here.

He'd drugged her and chained her up, still naked.

What was he going to do next?

Turning her head, she saw him standing in the doorway.

No, not standing.

He was walking toward her.

"No!" she shrieked. "Don't come near me!"

Of course, the arrogant man ignored her.

Tears tumbled down her cheeks, and even though she knew the cuff around her wrist prevented it, Julia tried to wrench her hand free so she could flee.

"Stop," Domino commanded as she flung herself off the bed almost wrenching her shoulder from its socket in the process.

Never before had she hated being small like she did in this moment. With complete ease, Domino maneuvered her back so she was lying on her stomach on the bed, one hand on her shoulder, the other curled around her hip, using his size to hold her down.

"Don't, please. Please don't rape me." She didn't want to beg and shouldn't be letting him know how scared she was, it gave him something else to use against her, but the thought of the man she had willingly given her body to now taking something from her she didn't want to give almost destroyed her.

"Hell, Julia, is that really what you think I'm going to do?"

The anger in his voice was what she expected, but she wasn't prepared for the hint of pain.

It was that pain that made her stop fighting and go completely still.

Why did he sound hurt? What did he expect her to think when he drugged and left her naked and cuffed to a bed? Surely he couldn't have thought she would think anything but that he intended to sexually assault her.

"Your wounds were starting to heal nicely. I hope you haven't ripped them open thrashing about like that." There was still controlled anger in Domino's voice, along with a little bit of lingering hurt, but there was nothing that made her feel like he was going to hurt her.

Was she just hearing what she wanted to hear, or was there another explanation for everything that was going on?

"W-why did you leave me n-naked?" As hard as Julia tried to control the wobble in her voice and sound strong when she felt anything but, she failed. Her fear was a palpable thing, filling the room, there was no way Domino couldn't feel it.

"So nothing would stick to your wounds while they were still weeping, pulling clothes or sheets off would have ripped the skin and reopened the wounds," he replied like it was obvious.

"That's why I'm on my stomach?"

"Yes."

He'd been worried about her? That was the only reason he would care about trying to make sure nothing got stuck in her wounds and caused her pain. Right?

Julia was so confused.

"Why did you cuff me?"

"Thought it would keep you in place if you woke up and I wasn't in the room so you wouldn't rip those wounds open. Guess that didn't work out. Arrow left some antibiotic cream, I'll put some more on."

She heard him moving about, and then he perched on the edge of the bed beside her. Something cool smoothed across her back, and Julia sucked in a breath, not because it was painful but because Domino's gentle touch did things to her insides that could only be described as sensual. What she should be feeling was fear. Despite his words, she was still a prisoner here as long as she was cuffed to the bed.

"Sorry," he murmured, obviously thinking she was in pain.

"It's okay," she whispered back. As he continued to attend to each one of her wounds, Julia tried to hold herself perfectly still. Letting him know how much he was affecting her by being so very gentle was a bad idea.

"Why did you leave, Julia?"

The question confused her even more. "You know why, Domino."

"Then it's true." There was resignation in his tone instead of anger like she would have expected.

Julia turned her head so she could look at him. He looked sad and dejected, not like the angry man she had first met, or the one she had been getting to know at the safehouse.

"Convince me," he said, standing abruptly and raking his fingers through his hair. "Convince me that you aren't working with the terrorists. Convince me that you aren't working for the Mikhailovs."

It felt like her heart was literally breaking in her chest.

"I can't do that, Domino. I can't do that because you *want* to believe that I'm evil, wicked, a betrayer." She didn't know why but she knew it was true. There was nothing she could say to convince him otherwise because he had already made up his mind.

"Or you can't do it because it's true," he growled, stalking around the room.

Feeling completely depleted, Julia closed her eyes and let her head sink into the surprisingly soft pillow. "I don't know why you're so determined to believe the worst of me. I haven't done anything to earn your distrust. Not a single thing. If you want to think I betrayed you then I can't stop you. Just do to me whatever you brought me here to do."

"I'm not going to hurt you," he roared. "Is that who you think I am?"

Tears trickled from her closed eyes. "I don't know who you are. All I know is that for some reason you seem to hate me."

"I don't hate you," Domino's anguished voice yelled. "But at least if you betrayed me you won't wind up tortured and murdered like Rosie."

CHAPTER THIRTEEN

October 8th
6:40 A.M.

Why had he said that?

The moment the words were out of his mouth Domino wanted to snatch them back.

He'd had no intention of doing anything but making sure Julia's wounds healed and then getting the answers he needed.

That all changed when she'd begged him not to rape her.

The raw fear on her face and laced into every word sent an arrow straight through his heart.

It was in that moment, he realized she was truly terrified of him. His head said it was because she knew she had betrayed him and feared reprisal, but his traitorous heart insisted it was because she knew who he really was.

The tattoo.

Julia had to have seen it, and since she had been researching the Mikhailov family it was likely she knew exactly what it meant.

"You need rest," he said, reaching out to spread the sheet back over the lower half of her body. Domino hated that his trying to protect her from the pain of her weeping wounds sticking to clothes or sheets and then being pulled away had actually made her think he wanted to sexually assault her.

"Don't. Don't walk away. Not now. Not when you're right on the edge of opening up to me. Who is Rosie?"

The name falling from Julia's lips should make him angry. Rosie was sweet, innocent, and everything that was good, and Julia was ... the same.

Everything in him but his need to protect himself from further pain knew the truth.

Had always known the truth.

Julia was exactly who she seemed to be. A strong, brave, stubborn woman who wouldn't blink at putting herself in danger to get to the truth of a story. Who had committed herself to helping dismantle the group that wanted to destroy the government even knowing there was a hit out on her.

If he hadn't known she was one hundred percent trustworthy, he never would have let her touch him during sex. But then she'd run, and he knew in his gut—even though he couldn't bring himself to acknowledge it—that she had run because she knew he was Konstantin Mikhailov's son and thought he was like his father.

"She's why you have the tattoo of a rose on your back. You loved her."

There was no jealousy in Julia's voice, just gentle curiosity, and for the first time he found himself wanting to tell her.

Sitting on the edge of the bed beside her, his hand automatically reached for her, stroking down her fiery mane. "Rosie was my father's driver's granddaughter." There was no point denying who he was or pretending he wasn't, Julia knew, and it was almost a relief.

"You knew her as a child?"

"My father was too paranoid to send me and my brother to school, so we had tutors. I was rarely allowed to leave the estate. I didn't have friends because my father was trying to mold me into his image. Rosie was this tiny little thing. Despite the darkness of our world, she was made of sunshine, she was always laughing, and even though I tried to stop it she wouldn't give up until she made me a friend."

"She knew you needed a little light in your life."

"Like you," he said softly. "I should have pushed Rosie away, should never have allowed her to get close to me, or fallen for her. It was like painting a bullseye right on her back. One my father didn't hesitate to use." The person most to blame for what happened to Rosie was him. He'd known spending time with her would wind up getting her hurt, but he'd been selfish. Like a dog starved for attention, he'd been unable to push her away.

"Your father is an evil man, Domino, but that doesn't mean that you are."

The words coming from Julia, who he'd drugged, brought here, and chained to the bed, sounded ridiculous.

"Make no mistake about it, Julia. I am my father's son. I have a lot of anger inside me, anger that let you get hurt. We knew where you were the whole time. I put a tracker in you on the way to the safehouse. I allowed you to stay with those men, knowing they might hurt you." Domino paused and blew out a breath. "Knowing they *would* hurt you I let you stay because I needed proof that you were working with my father or that you weren't."

"You weren't going to let me get hurt."

"You *did* get hurt."

"I heard the gunshots before they took me into that shipping container, you were already coming for me."

"Did you miss the part where I put a tracker inside you without your permission?" There was no way this woman was going to let that violation slide.

"Nope. I can assure you that I did not. I can also assure you that we will be having a long discussion about boundaries and how you're going to grovel to make that up to me. But, Domino, there is nothing I can say to give you the proof you want. You have to either believe me or not. That's your choice."

The urge to stand and move away, put some distance between them was strong, but he resisted. Julia was right, he was choosing to believe the worst of her to protect himself, she didn't deserve that.

"My father bought my mother. She was a trafficking victim, he bought her, kept her in his basement until she was broken, then made her his wife. After I was born, she wasn't allowed to have much to do with me. I was raised by nannies and tutors. I usually only saw her each night at dinner. There was no softness in my house. If I fell and skinned my knee I wasn't kissed and cuddled, I was punished for crying. My days were filled with school lessons in the morning and then my father's own brand of learning in the afternoons. I witnessed my first murder when I was five. It was my mother."

"Oh, Dom." Julia's voice sounded like it was filled with tears, and since she couldn't reach him the way she was lying on her stomach, she inched her body closer until it was pressed against him.

"It wasn't the last. My father thought immersing me in his world was the best way to mold me into a mini him, but it wasn't. All it did was make me hate him more."

"It made you know you didn't want to become him. And you haven't, Dom. You joined the military, became one of the elite Delta Force, and now you work for the best security firm in the world. You have more than proved you're not Konstantin Mikhailov's son in any way but blood."

"Rosie was the price I paid for my freedom."

"Tell me, Dom, you need to tell someone and I'm right here. I want to be there for you, all you have to do is let me."

Julia's words were soft, soothing, and infused with genuine care, and again he felt a need to unburden his soul and confess his deepest sins. Maybe it was so he could push Julia away or maybe it was because he needed absolution from the second woman to have claimed his heart.

"The night of my eighteenth birthday, I snuck out of the party my father had organized. It wasn't really a birthday party it was more an audition for the families my father was considering choosing a wife for me from. I didn't want to be my father's puppet. I never did. Earned myself more punishments than my brother ever did. Kristoff was always jealous of me. He was the younger brother, I was the heir, only I didn't want to be. My father was always evil, he made sure I saw everything he did. I was eight the first time I witnessed some of his men roughing up a traitor, ten the first time I witnessed a hit, twelve the first time I saw a shipment of terrified trafficked women, thirteen when he made me have sex with one of his slaves for the first time. I wanted out. I always wanted out."

Unable to keep touching Julia now that she knew what a monster he was, he strode to the other side of the room. His father had been grooming him from birth to become the next leader of the Mikhailov family. He'd never cared what Domino wanted, never cared who he hurt, including his own son, so long as he got what he wanted.

"As bad as my father was, my brother was worse. Kristoff had no soul. He thrived on pain and suffering, he was everything my father wanted me to be. He noticed me sneak away from the party and saw me with Rosie. That night was the first time I'd ever willingly had sex, and everything with the woman I had fallen in love with was perfect. The next morning, I went to a recruiting office and signed up. The plan was for me and Rosie to stay near base. Once I signed the paperwork it was a done deal, there was nothing my father could do to undo it. While I was gone Kristoff took Rosie, tortured her, then killed her, had her body left outside the apartment we'd rented, the place that was supposed to be our home. That was when I vowed that nothing would stop me from destroying my family."

"Unlock the handcuff, Domino," Julia said.

He should have done that earlier. Actually, he never should have cuffed her, he just couldn't bear the thought of her running from him again.

Selfish.

Cruel.

Konstantin would have been proud.

Numb, he pulled the key from his pocket and crossed to the

bed. Of course she didn't want to be in the same room as him now she knew who he really was. He'd call in his team, hand Julia off to them, then do whatever it took to destroy his family.

The second Julia was free, she launched herself at him, wrapping her arms around his neck, her legs around his hips. Her face as she buried it against his neck was already wet with tears. Tears that continued to flow as she held onto him, sharing his pain with him.

For a moment, his arms hung limply at his sides, this wasn't the reaction he had been expecting, but then he slowly lifted them and carefully held her, mindful of her wounds.

"Hold me properly," Julia ordered.

"Don't want to hurt you."

"Hold me properly. I'm sorry I ran. Saw the tattoo, knew what it meant, and panicked. I should have trusted my gut, it told me you were a good man."

Wrapping his arms around he, he held her tightly, burying his face in her soft hair. How could she still be here? She knew who he was, the things he'd been made to do, and knew that the last woman he'd loved had been given a brutal death. She should be running as fast and as far as she could get from him.

Whatever happened next, Domino would be forever grateful for this moment.

A moment he didn't want to end.

Carrying Julia to the bed, he laid down, draping her across his chest so she wasn't putting pressure on her wounds, then covered them both with the sheets. Sharing a little of his past with Julia had drained him, on top of everything that had been going on the last few days, he'd barely slept.

Julia was warm and soft against him, her breath on his neck was soothing, and her fingertips stroking lightly across his chest lulled him off.

Domino's last conscious thought was that for only the second time in his life he'd found someone he could trust.

Someone he could love.

* * * * *

October 8th
4:11 P.M.

With every breath Domino took, her head lifted along with his chest. The small, even movement couldn't not make Julia smile. Domino was completely relaxed, buried deep in sleep, which meant he had finally decided to trust her.

Not an easy feat for a man who had been through what Dom had.

His entire life had been one torturous ordeal after another. There had been no safe place for him to rest. While she had lost her parents far too soon, and in a very traumatic way, sending her entire life into a tailspin, she'd at least had fourteen years of their loving and steady presence. She'd learned from them, been loved and treasured, and begun to build a foundation for the rest of her life.

But Domino hadn't had that.

He'd had to fight just to survive.

Domino trusted his team because they had earned his trust by protecting his back. That bond had been forged in blood and bullets. Unless you proved to him that he could believe in you, Domino wasn't prepared to offer you the precious gift of trust, and her running—even though at the time she had believed he was working with his father—had convinced him she was an enemy.

One of many in his life.

But something had shifted between them. It started when she'd begged him not to rape her, that was the first crack in his armor. He'd been unprepared for her to say that and had realized she'd run out of fear not because she was working against him.

Then he had ripped himself wide open by admitting just how horrible his life had been, the betrayals, the grief, the suffering. Domino had been through so much, and it was in that moment, when he didn't hold back but allowed her to see inside his dark, damaged heart, that she realized she was falling in love with him.

Julia wanted to bring light into his life. He had lost so much, been so badly hurt, he had shut his heart and his emotions down, been drowning in anger, and she wanted so very badly to save him.

It could leave her with a broken heart, Domino was trying, but he could change his mind and push her away at any moment. If he tried, she'd fight for them, for him, but in the end, she couldn't make him do anything he didn't want to do.

All she could do was hope.

Hope that he would trust her more with each passing day, continue to allow her glimpses of the real Domino, the one he hid from the rest of the world, and hope that he wanted a future with her, that maybe he would fall in love with her too.

Was that too much to hope for?

She feared it was but knew she was already a lost cause. Whether he reciprocated her feelings or ever would, Julia knew he cared and knew that she was helpless to do anything other than fall deeper and deeper for this complicated man.

Propping her chin on his chest she watched him, enjoying seeing him calm and relaxed in sleep. Julia had dozed off and on for the last few hours, but she'd spent more time watching Dom than she had asleep.

He looked so peaceful like this, and she wished she could wipe away all the horrors he had been forced to endure.

Horrors she couldn't even begin to imagine.

If he let her, she'd do her very best to make sure no one ever hurt him again.

Domino stirred, blinking open his eyes and offering her a small smile. "How are you feeling?"

"How are *you* feeling?" He was the one who had cut himself open and bled in front of her, allowing her to see him vulnerable by sharing his deepest, darkest secrets.

"I'm not the one who was hurt."

When he went to move her off him, Julia shoved his hands away. "You might not have been hurt physically, but that doesn't mean you're okay. When they hurt me, they hurt you too. I hurt you when I ran. I saw the tattoo and I panicked. I should have known better. There's no way you would ever hurt me."

"Julia, I …"

She crushed her mouth to his, cutting him off with a kiss that quickly grew steamy. "Don't you ever think that again. Even when you were angry with me, when you weren't sure you trusted me, you made sure not to hurt me. You wrapped material around the handcuff so it wouldn't hurt my already bruised wrists, only a man who cares does that, Domino, you have to know that. You are not your father. Do you understand that?" Julia wasn't sure that he did or how to convince him of it.

Instead of answering, he used his size against her by picking her up and setting her on the bed. The movement tugged on the wounds on her back, but they were more annoying than painful.

He tried to climb off the bed, but she wasn't having any of that. Running hadn't solved anything. It had just made things so much worse. No way they were doing that again.

"Don't run from this, Dom. You need to be reminded that you're not your father. I will remind you of that every single day." Julia dodged around him and blocked the door.

Domino didn't reply, just picked her up, holding her carefully draped across his chest, his arms careful to avoid her wounds. And he thought he was like Konstantin Mikhailov. There wasn't a single similarity between the two of them. They might share DNA but that was it. Domino had a lot of anger, but anyone who had grown up the way he had would, that didn't mean he was his father's son.

"You're doing it right now."

"Doing what?" Domino asked.

"Taking care of me. It's so natural you don't even register you're doing it. Look how your arms are so careful not to touch my wounds. You're a good man, Dominick Tanner. A good, kind, brave man who fought hard to get out of the darkness. You have a sexy little butt too," she teased to lighten the mood. Julia shifted so her bare center pressed against his hardening length. "You also gave me the best sex of my life."

"Julia," he warned.

"Hmm?" Shifting to get a better angle, she rolled her hips, moaning as the friction sent a wave of pleasure flowing through her.

"We can't." Domino tried to set her down, but she tightened her hold on him.

"We can."

"Your wounds."

"So, we don't do this with me on my back." The last day had been rough, running from Domino, Scar hitting her with the whip, and Domino opening himself up to her. Her emotions had see-sawed from incredible, to terrified, to devastated, it was time to go back to incredible.

"I'm not having sex with you while you're hurt."

Damn him and his stubborn streak. "Please."

"Are you begging, sweetheart?" A sexy smirk curled his lips into a rare smile, and he looked so impossibly, handsomely delicious that she kissed him again, nibbling at his bottom lip.

"If I said I was begging, would it get me what I wanted?"

His hand shifted so he could drag a finger across her core. "I don't want to reopen any of your cuts."

"Then be careful," she whispered against his lips before kissing him again. The kiss quickly turned into a moan when he sat on the edge of the bed, her legs straddling his, opening her up to him.

He took advantage by slipping a finger inside her. It was one

152

touch, and yet her insides were already quivering.

"You close already, little flame?"

"When you're near me? Always."

Domino added another finger, stroking deep, making her body shiver in delightful anticipation. Their lips found each other's, and Dom's thumb found her hard little bundle of nerves, working it with his thumb while his fingers curled inside her, hitting a spot that made her entire body tremble.

"Come, little flame," he ordered as his thumb increased the pressure on her bud. "Now."

The command uttered in his too-sexy-for-his-own-good voice was all it took to give her that final shove she needed to explode into a fiery mess of pleasure.

As she floated back down, she rested against Domino, tucking her face against his neck. Everything felt so perfect, almost too perfect like she was afraid to believe in it in case the bottom dropped out of their world all over again.

"Are you crying?" Domino sounded worried, and she giggled.

"I'm happy, Dom, I promise you I am. That was amazing, and I can't wait to do it again, but there's just this ... feeling I have. I can't shake it. It feels like the worst is still to come."

His large hands grasped her shoulders, and he eased her back. "I swear to you that I will never let my family hurt you again. Ever. If it is the last thing I ever do, I will destroy them."

The problem was Julia did believe him.

She believed that Domino would do whatever it took to make his family pay for killing Rosie, that he would risk anything to make it happen.

Including his life.

CHAPTER FOURTEEN

October 9th
10:23 A.M.

"You okay?" Domino asked Julia who was flitting around the kitchen like an energizer bunny. She'd been wired ever since they got up this morning although she had yet to tell him what had her so nervous.

"Nothing. I mean, fine," she said, not glancing his way.

"You should be resting not tornadoing around the kitchen. Your wounds are still healing." They were looking clean with no signs of infection, and already beginning to heal, but there were close to two dozen gashes, some deep enough to leave scars. Her body needed time to rest and heal.

"I said I was fine. I'm sick of lying down, it's been almost forty-eight hours since you found me, and I've spent almost that entire time in bed. I want to get up, I need to be doing something."

There was a hint of desperation in her voice, and he was filled with a need to soothe it away.

Not a feeling he was accustomed to.

Having no idea of the best way to handle Julia and her currently overflowing emotions, Domino did the only thing he could. Trust his instincts.

"Come here," he murmured as he reached for her, pulling her into his arms. She stood stiffly for a moment before sinking down to rest upon his chest.

"I'm embarrassed," she said, her voice muffled.

"About ...?"

"All your friends saw me naked."

Okay, not what he'd expected her to say but a valid concern. "Julia, no one looked inappropriately. We were more worried about making sure all threats were eliminated and getting you the medical attention you needed."

"Do they think I'm working with the Bratva?"

So, she was battling more than one fear this morning. "No, little flame. They thought you ran because you were afraid, and they wanted to move in earlier as soon as we believed you had changed vehicles. They weren't happy with me for insisting we wait to see where you ended up."

He owed her an apology for that.

Actually, he owed her a whole lot more than an apology.

"Do you think you can forgive me for letting you get hurt?" Domino asked as he feathered his fingertips across her back. Part of him wanted to order her to forgive him, the other part—the larger part—knew he would do whatever it took to earn that forgiveness.

Forgiveness he didn't deserve.

Forgiveness he would take in a heartbeat regardless.

"Dom, I understand that you were raised in hell and don't know how to trust anyone who hasn't earned it. I also understand I made you think you couldn't trust me when I ran. I'll admit at first I was scared, I saw the tattoo and panicked. Some of what happened is on me, a little on you, but most of it is on the Mikhailov Bratva. You aren't the one who held a gun on me, chained me to the ground, and whipped me."

"But—"

Julia stood on her tiptoes and crushed a fiery kiss to his lips. "No buts. I wish you'd had more faith in me—I also wish I'd had more faith in you—but I don't blame you and this is something we can get through."

He wanted to argue and remind her all over again who he was and where he'd come from, but instead, he took a deep breath and nodded. Whispering his lips across hers, he held her a little tighter than necessary, needing to absorb some of her goodness.

"Hey," Surf called out, announcing the guys' arrival before they appeared in his kitchen. "Whoa, who's been on a cooking binge?"

"That would be Julia." Since he knew she was anxious about seeing his team again, Domino placed his hands on her shoulders, kneading lightly. This was the first time he'd seen them since walking away from the shipping container with Julia in his arms, but the anger he'd felt about them believing he was a threat to Julia had faded. He'd deserved their suspicion after the way he'd been acting.

Her hands lifted to cover his, and since he was touching her, he felt her physically pull herself together. She straightened her spine and took a step away, facing her fears on her own, refusing to let embarrassment overwhelm her. "I know how much you guys love to eat."

"You are my new favorite of all the significant others," Surf said, shooting her one of his trademark grins before he picked up a plate and began to fill it.

"I want to check your wounds before we go," Arrow informed her as he reached around Surf and grabbed a plate. "Oh, and Piper says hi. She wanted to come today but had work she had to do at Prey."

"Phoebe is anxious to meet you. As soon as things are safe for you to leave, she's planning a get-together at our place," Mouse said.

"Mackenzie is in on the planning," Bear added.

"Thanks for the food," Brick said.

"Told you," he whispered in her ear, "nothing to be embarrassed about."

Julia rolled her eyes but touched a quick kiss to his cheek before she joined the guys at the table. They'd both eaten earlier, but Domino was a big guy and needed a lot of fuel, so he filled his plate and then took the seat beside Julia, which the guys had left empty for him.

It was the first time he'd had everyone over at his place. This was his sanctuary, a place just for him to come and relax, unwind, and try to forget who he was and the noose that would always be hanging around his neck, waiting for his father to tighten it. Bringing Julia here had felt like the right thing to do, the only thing to do. Now having his team here felt right too.

Maybe he was ready to share his home with the people in his life.

Maybe.

Because most of the people in his life didn't know who he really was.

Once they did, it would change everything.

"You ready to tell us about what happened, Jules?" Mouse asked.

"I'm ready," she replied. Her voice didn't even waver, and he was so proud of her.

"How did you get back into the city?" Arrow asked.

"Hitchhiked. I was kind of scared I'd run into someone from the Bratva. I know it's crazy, they didn't know where I was, but the Mikhailovs have people everywhere. I asked them to drop me off near a friend's house, I thought I was far enough away from my place, but obviously I was wrong. My leg was sore from walking for hours through the woods, and it kind of gave out on me. The next thing I knew there was this man there."

"Had you seen him before?" Surf asked.

"No. I thought he was just trying to help, but then he spoke Russian, pushed a gun into my side and told me he'd start shooting anyone around us if I didn't get into the car, so I did. We drove to the docks, and you guys know what happened after that. He knew there was a leak, that someone gave me intel, he wanted a name, but I couldn't give it to him."

"Did he tell you his name?" Bear asked.

"He told me to call him Scar."

Mouse stiffened, his hand frozen halfway between his plate and his mouth. "Describe him."

The harsh tone made Julia jump, but she quickly complied. "Blond curls, green eyes, my kind of green, really vivid. He looked really sweet, the kind of guy you would never suspect as being part of the mafia. At least until you looked into his eyes. They were dead. No emotion. You guys know who he is."

Not a question, but Mouse nodded tightly anyway. "He kidnapped Phoebe and Lolly earlier in the year. Phoebe had been dating a man who turned out to be involved in this plot and they wanted to know what she knew. Took my daughter to use as leverage. Both Phoebe and Lolly described their abductor as a man with green eyes and blond curls, with a scar running from his temple along his right cheek, stopping near the corner of mouth."

Julia shuddered. "That's him. So that proves the Mikhailov Bratva is involved in this. Do you think that Konstantin is the one who came up with the plot? Is he the one in charge?" Julia asked.

The guys began to voice theories, but all Domino could do was stare blankly into space.

It hadn't occurred to him after Phoebe and Lolly had been abducted that the man they could be looking for was his own brother. There had been no indication that the Bratva was involved. Neither Phoebe nor Lolly had mentioned hearing anyone speak Russian. Why would he think his brother was involved in a terrorist plot to take over the government? Besides, the last time he had seen Kristoff he hadn't had a scar. But blond curls, green eyes, and spoke Russian, who else could it be but Kristoff?

"Dom? You okay?" Julia rested a hand on his shoulder, drawing his attention out of his own head.

Without answering, he shoved his chair back and grabbed his laptop from the counter. While everyone watched him with concern, he opened it and navigated to the hidden folder where he kept a copy of the evidence he had on his family.

Bringing up the video, he fast-forwarded through it until there was a clear image of Kristoff's face.

He didn't want to do this, it was bad enough that Julia knew who he really was, but having his team know as well? It was too much. And yet there was no way around it. His family was involved. Kristoff had tortured Julia and would have killed her if they hadn't stopped him.

It was time to destroy his family once and for all.

To do it he just had to bare his secrets to his friends.

People who meant everything to him.

People he might be about to lose.

"Is this him?" he asked, tilting the screen so Julia could see it.

There was pain in her eyes when she looked at the image, realizing without him saying that the man who had tortured her didn't just work for the Mikhailovs he was one of Konstantin's sons.

His brother.

"He doesn't have the scar in that video, and he's a lot younger, but yeah, that's him," she said softly, taking his hand and entwining their fingers.

"You know him?" Brick asked, brow furrowed.

"His name is Kristoff Mikhailov, he's Konstantin's son. He's also my brother."

* * * * *

October 9th
10:45 A.M.

Shocked gasps echoed around the room.

"Your brother?" Mouse asked, sounding horrified.

"What do you mean?" Bear demanded.

"You knew who he was all along?" Arrow asked, looking

160

shocked.

"You're Konstantin Mikhailov's son?" Brick growled.

"You're part of the Bratva?" Surf asked.

With each question his team threw at him, Domino's pain grew. Julia could feel it like it was a living, breathing entity, feeding off the negative energy in the room.

Every word his teammates tossed so carelessly at him pierced Domino's heart. She could feel it happening, see it in the minute flinches, the tightening of his mouth, the pain flaring in his eyes. Each one of those wounds his friends inflicted would leave a scar. More to add to the litany his twisted father had already left behind.

As his hurt increased, so did her anger.

Why were they doing this to him?

Couldn't they see that every word they said was hurting him?

Didn't they care?

"So, you knew who abducted my daughter and the woman I love, and you didn't tell us?" Mouse sounded about ready to do some serious physical damage.

"I don't understand," Surf said, shaking his head. "Why wouldn't you say something?"

"It's been months since we knew Scar was involved. Why did you wait till now to say anything?" Bear asked.

Domino didn't utter a word in his own defense, he just stood there and took their cruel words as though he deserved every shot.

That did it.

"Stop!" she yelled.

All heads turned to stare at her, confusion on the faces of the guys, but it was the gratefulness on Domino's that made her tear up. She had a feeling no one had ever stood up for him before.

Well, that was about to change.

Now Domino had her, for as long as he wanted her—hopefully forever—she would be there for him. She would support him and stand up for him and love him with everything she had to give.

Moving so she was between Domino and the rest of his team, she fixed the guys with her fiercest glare. The fact that she had tears streaming down her cheeks probably made her seem pathetic to them, but the tears were a mixture of sadness that Domino thought he had so little value he deserved what his team was saying to him, and anger unlike anything she'd ever felt before because the man she was falling for was hurting.

"Back off," she growled. "You have no idea what his father did to him. If Dom knew that it was his brother who had kidnapped Phoebe and Lolly, he would have told you. He didn't figure it out until just now. What he needs is your support. You think this is easy for him? Telling you who he is is like baring his soul, and this is how you react? You're treating him like he's guilty of something. You know Dom, and frankly he deserves better than what you all just gave him. I thought you were good guys, but right now I'm doubting that. If that's how you treat a man who's like a brother to you, then I'm completely disappointed in all of you."

Julia felt Domino's warmth press against her back a moment before his large hands landed on her shoulders. In his touch she felt everything he couldn't say yet. She felt his respect, his trust, his appreciation, and even his love.

"She is going to make one hell of a mom one day. Best mom speech ever," Surf told her with a grin. "She's totally right, man. We were shocked, but we made it sound like you had done something wrong. Not cool." Surf stood and moved around her to slap Domino on the back.

"You should have told us who you really are. We're a team and we shouldn't have any secrets," Bear said, his face hard, but then it softened. "But I understand why you didn't. If I was the son of Konstantin Mikhailov, I wouldn't want anyone to know either."

"Not that you have anything to be ashamed about," Arrow

added. "You are not your father. Or your brother. It sucks that you didn't trust us enough to let us know because we would have worked with you to take them down."

"But we will take them down," Brick vowed. "We are going to destroy everyone involved in this plot. They've hurt enough innocent people. They've hurt us and the people we care about. None of us are going to stop until it's over and every last one of them is dead or in prison. We have your back."

The rest of the guys echoed that sentiment, all except for Mouse, who was still sitting at the table with his head in his hands. As much as this was personal to all of Alpha team, Mouse was the one whose family had been touched by Domino's brother specifically. From what she'd been told, the man hadn't just kidnapped Phoebe and Lolly, he'd had Phoebe beaten and tortured.

While she understood that Mouse was hurting and angry, he had to know that Domino hadn't been the one to inflict that pain. If he had realized his family was involved and his brother was the man called Scar, she knew he would have told his team no matter how much he didn't want them to know who he really was.

"If you can't accept Dom for who he is then you should leave," Julia said firmly. Domino deserved to have more than just her in his corner. These men had been a part of his life for years, it would devastate him if one of them couldn't accept him just because of his DNA.

Mouse's head lifted, and he gave her a one-sided smile before shifting his attention behind her to where Domino was standing. She knew Dom was nervous about what his friend was going to say because his hands tightened on her shoulders. Wanting to let him know that no matter what happened he always had her, she shifted so she was at his side, her arms wrapped around his waist, and her cheek pressed against his chest, right above his heart.

"I'm going to be honest," Mouse started, and Dom tensed further until he was like a marble sculpture beside her. "This is a lot to take in. I wish the description Phoebe gave us was enough for you to put this together sooner. But do I think that you're like him? No. Absolutely not. Like Bear said, do I wish you had told us this sooner because a team shouldn't have secrets? Heck, yeah. Arrow is right, it sucks that you didn't trust us. However, given our bad reaction maybe it was a good thing you didn't say anything until you had this little spitfire by your side."

"Right by his side and not going anywhere." She tightened her hold on him. It didn't matter that they hadn't known each other for very long or that they'd had the craziest of starts to a relationship. What she felt for him was real and it grew a little every day.

"Good. That's exactly what he needs, exactly what he deserves." Mouse fixed his gaze on Domino. "You deserve all the good things in the world. Just because your father is the head of the Russian Bratva doesn't mean that you don't deserve good things. I wish you had told us who you were sooner so we could have beaten that into your thick head because you're standing there looking at us like you believe you're less worthy."

That was exactly what Domino thought.

He believed he was undeserving because someone had to pay for his father's sins, and so far, Konstantin Mikhailov was running free, working on a plot to take over the government. But it wasn't Domino's job to pay for the things his father had done, he'd suffered enough at the man's hands.

"I didn't think I would ever say this, but I'm actually relieved you all know now," Domino admitted. "I didn't like hiding who I was, but life with my father was ... Hell. And I only got away because my father had my brother kill the woman I loved. I had proof, and it was enough to get Konstantin to keep his distance. I've lived the last sixteen years waiting for the day my father decided to make a move to force me back. I was supposed to be his heir. Kristoff wasn't happy with that. My father is an evil man, but my brother ... he's a monster."

Julia could vouch for that. Kristoff Mikhailov was barely human. He thrived on pain and suffering and had zero morals or empathy. He was basically a perfectly honed killing machine.

"We need to talk through everything you know, then pass it along to Prey and see if Raven and Olivia can use it to get us more information," Bear said.

When she went to move back toward her chair, Domino slipped an arm around her shoulders, stopping her. "Thank you," he murmured in her ear, then touched his lips to her temple and held them there for a long moment.

"You don't ever have to thank me for being on your side. That is where I am always going to be."

It was too early to add the until death do us part bit, but that was how she felt. Domino was it for her, she was falling in love with him, and she was sure he was falling for her too. Julia just hoped that death in the form of his insane brother and father didn't manage to sink its claws into them and steal what should be their happy ever after.

CHAPTER FIFTEEN

October 9th
9:50 P.M.

Scar's hand around the woman's neck tightened as he felt pleasure building inside him.

Her eyes bulged.

Her face turned red.

He could feel her internal muscles quivering around him.

She was every bit as sadistic as he was, sadistic and masochistic, a thrilling combination, but right now this wasn't about her and her pleasure. It was about him and his.

He was in control here.

He was always in control.

Money wasn't important to him, and he didn't care about power. Other people's feelings meant absolutely nothing to him. The only thing in his life that he cared about was control. He lived to be in control, everyone and anyone who came into his world he needed to control. Didn't matter who they were, everyone from his driver to the housecleaner to the woman currently tied spreadeagled to his bed, were puppets in his theatre. His to do with as he pleased.

To that end, he touched his lips to the woman's ear. "You come, and you'll be punished," he warned.

Of course she would come.

She always did.

And he would punish her.

He always did.

It wouldn't be pleasant, but she loved every second of the

167

torture he dished out because masochist.

Which he supposed meant it wasn't really much of a punishment. But that couldn't be helped, and she was his match in every way, his other half, two black hearts who had somehow managed to find each other and who were working out a plan to rule the world. She wanted the power and money, and he wanted only the control. Together they had the brains, the influence, and the resources to make it happen.

Scar tightened his hand further, digging his fingers into the fragile skin of her throat. His grip was hard enough that it would leave bruises, but she wore her wounds like a badge of honor.

A strangled sound escaped her crushed throat and the bubble of pleasure growing inside him burst as he came in a rush.

His orgasm was enough to spur her into her own, and he felt her muscles clench around him, spurring on his own pleasure.

By the time his head cleared enough to think again, he saw that her eyes had closed, and he released his grip on her neck, allowing her to breathe once again. He didn't want her dead. If he was capable of love, this woman he was still buried inside would be the only one who would capture his heart.

What he felt for her now was more like obsession. She was his, no one else was allowed to touch her, and there were no lengths he wouldn't go to protect her, burn the world down if that was what it took, but love? No, he didn't love her.

Still, as he pulled out of her and climbed off her still body, he did run a fingertip gently over the angry red marks on her neck. Soon they would turn the most divine shade of black. Black was his favorite color, it was the only color he could relate to, and he loved to see her body covered in his marks.

Dark eyelashes fluttered on her pale cheeks. With high cheekbones, a delicate nose, and naturally plump lips, the woman was perfection in a five-foot-nine package. With just the right amount of curves, legs that seemed to go for miles, and a seductive smile that could make anyone—man or woman—fall all over themselves to do her bidding, she turned heads wherever she went.

But no one else touched her.

No one but him.

Sliding a finger inside her, he stroked lightly against the spot he knew could reduce her to a sobbing, begging mess. Careful to keep his touch soft enough not to let her come, he brushed his thumb over her overly sensitive bud.

"You were a bad girl," he murmured, leaning over so his eyes were inches from hers, close enough to see every flare of pure, molten desire. "I told you not to come. You receive pleasure only when I decide. Did you forget that, *moya dorogava?*" Scar drew the word out as he increased the pressure of his touch ever so slightly.

With her wrists and ankles bound to the bedposts and a ball gag in her mouth, she couldn't beg him for mercy or get herself off. When he increased the pressure a little more, her hips came off the bed, silently begging for more as she tried to force him to increase the friction enough to let her come.

He wouldn't be doing that.

He would keep her in his bed, tied up and at his mercy, hovering on the edge of pleasure he would continue to deny until she remembered that he controlled everything including that pleasure.

When the sun rose, if he felt like it, he might take pity on her and allow her release or untie her and send her off home turned on and unfulfilled. Whatever he decided. Either way, she would leave—as she always did—fitted with the chastity belt he'd had made especially for her. Her babysitter slash bodyguard accompanied her at all times, and she was allowed bathroom breaks every few hours.

Supervised bathroom breaks.

By him not the babysitter.

The man would unlock the chastity belt and then set up a camera so Scar could watch her as she used the restroom to ensure she didn't touch herself.

Coming without permission was one thing, but she knew better than to tempt fate and pleasure herself without being ordered to. While she was definitely his obsession, which placed her in a category no other human being fell into, it didn't necessarily exempt her from the same fate as anyone else.

There was every possibility that one day he would kill her.

If he did, there would be no regret, no grief, no mourning. He would pick up and carry on with his life, although ... perhaps she would take a little piece of him with her.

Knowing she was close, Scar withdrew his hand. "I'll be back, *moya dorogava.*"

Not bothering to clothe himself, this was his house after all and his men guarding it, Scar strode out of his bedroom and down the hall. This was the house he had grown up in, watching from the sidelines as his older brother was groomed to take over the Mikhailov empire.

There had been no anger at the fact that Dominick was the heir, more a sense of confusion. Perhaps a little puzzlement as well. Dominick had no interest in following in their father's footsteps. Why did the man continue to insist that something as simple as birth order should dictate all of their futures?

Dominick lacked the ruthlessness needed to survive in the world of the Russian Bratva. The man had a heart, he cared, he believed in justice, righteousness, and in doing the right thing. He didn't have what it took to one day take over the Mikhailov empire.

But Scar did.

Did and had, and made it flourish in a way it never had when his father was at the helm.

Konstantin was a smart man, ruthless and cunning, he knew how to cultivate fear and use it to his advantage, but he lacked one important component that Scar did not.

The ability to operate without emotion.

Anger could be as much a weakness as love. Love left you with vulnerabilities that could be exploited but so did anger. Konstantin had been angry that Dominick, his firstborn son, had refused to take over the empire, had run and joined the military, had fallen in love with the daughter of a servant, and had gathered evidence that had forced him to keep his distance. That was what Scar had used to destroy him.

Stepping into his father's bedroom, he smiled as he approached the bed. Konstantin's eyes were open, and he tracked the movements of his youngest son. There was a flare of fear in the old man's eyes, and Scar felt a sense of ... satisfaction.

Contrary to what people thought of him, he didn't actually take pleasure in the suffering of others, he actually felt nothing.

Not a single thing, save perhaps for a rush of what he could only assume was pleasure at knowing he was in control of their fate.

So, he supposed he was capable of feeling something, just not in the normal human sense of the word.

"Good evening, *Otets*," he said as he stood beside his father's bed.

Anger replaced the fear as his father glared up at him, unable to speak, to move, or even to breathe on his own. For a man used to being in charge, he knew Konstantin hated being reduced to a lump in a bed kept alive only by the medical equipment standing guard around the bed.

"Don't worry, *Otets*, the empire you built is safe in the hands of the one best to run it. Dominick is too good, you are too evil, but I am the one who can turn it into a powerhouse that will soon be ruling the entire world. Soon you will have company, *Otets*, the Mikhailov family reunited once again." Scar nodded at the bed on the other side of the room, similarly surrounded by medical equipment.

A bed that would soon be occupied by his brother.

Scar had challenged his father for control of the empire and won when he broke his father's neck, rendering him completely paralyzed. The tube down his throat breathed for him, IVs kept him hydrated, tubes kept him nourished. All Scar had to do was say the word and all of that would be taken away and his father would die.

Already he was circling closer to Dominick, and soon the only other person who could challenge him for control of the Mikhailov empire would be likewise confined to a bed, paralyzed and reliant on Scar's goodwill to remain alive.

Control was life.

CHAPTER SIXTEEN

October 10th
6:32 A.M.

He never wanted to move.

Domino could quite happily stay like this forever.

In bed, with Julia draped all over him like the world's most beautiful blanket. She was peaceful in his arms, although she'd stirred a couple of times throughout the night, whimpering as though in the grips of a nightmare. His touch and his voice seemed to soothe her, and she'd settled right back down.

He'd done that.

Him.

Managed to soothe someone with words and touch.

Julia made him feel almost normal. Like he wasn't the son of a notorious crime family. Like he hadn't been raised completely without love and affection. Like he hadn't been groomed to be the next head of the family since birth, witnessing things no human, and certainly no small child should ever have to see.

He wasn't just falling in love with her, he'd already fallen.

Yesterday in his kitchen, when she had gotten angry on his behalf and then stepped between him and his team as though her tiny little five-foot-one frame could protect him from five highly trained men that outweighed her by over a hundred pounds each and had more than a foot of height on her, that was when it had happened.

That exact moment.

She'd been outraged and heartbroken for him, a thing of beauty as she put his team in their place. No one had ever been outraged or heartbroken for him before. No one except this gorgeous woman who seemed to see something in him that had been overlooked by everyone else.

Julia was his.

It was as simple as that.

They hadn't said the words, he wasn't sure if he even knew how to tell her that she was his everything, that he would love her forever, burn down the world to protect her, but he knew it with absolute certainty. She was his, and he was hers.

With her naked body lying atop his, his morning hard-on between her legs, pressed against her hot center Domino wanted her so badly it hurt. Not just hurt because he was literally as hard as he thought it was possible to be, but because there was this ache in his heart that pumped need through his body with each beat.

Slipping his hand between their bodies, he swiped a finger across her center then slid it inside her.

"Mmm," Julia moaned and shifted, lifting her head from his chest to give him a sleepy smile. "Woke up with sex on the brain, huh?"

"Not sex, you." He added another finger, and then a third, stretching her, enjoying the way her hips pressed down, taking him deeper.

"Perfect way to wake up."

When she began to rock against his hand, he withdrew it, her wounds were healing, but he was worried about her hurting herself.

"Huh, not fair at all." Julia propped her chin on his chest and pouted.

"Don't want to hurt you, little flame."

"Well, you can't start that and not finish, that would be mean."

Domino chuckled, laughing felt unfamiliar but not unpleasant. "I intend to finish, sweetheart, just carefully." He went to roll Julia onto her side but stopped when he noticed her pout had morphed into a huge smile. "What?"

"You called me sweetheart." If it was possible, her smile grew even bigger. "I just knew you were hiding this softer, sweet side underneath all the tough guy, closed-off attitude."

There was a moment of embarrassment at letting an endearment slip out, but it quickly passed. He had fallen in love with Julia. What she wanted, what she needed mattered to him, and he knew that what she needed was someone to fill the gap her parents had left behind. Someone to love her, make her feel special, safe, protected, and she needed to know that she wasn't alone anymore.

Touching a kiss to her forehead, Domino shifted her so she was spooned against him, his front to her back, but not pressed together so tightly he would cause her any pain. "You let me do all the work," he warned as his hand found its way back between her legs. She felt hot and tight, and she was already wet for him. Plunging two fingers inside her, his other hand claimed one of her breasts, playing with her nipple as he thrust in and out.

"Feels so good." Julia hummed her appreciation as his thumb grazed across her bundle of nerves with each thrust in. "More, faster, harder," she begged.

At her words, his length jerked like it had a mind of its own and was imagining how good it would feel when it was the one buried inside Julia instead of Domino's fingers. "Here you go, baby," he murmured, increasing his pace, giving her what she needed because what he needed was to watch her fall apart.

"Oh," she gasped. "That spot right there."

Hitting that spot with each thrust, he nibbled at her neck his own breathing accelerating as Julia began to pant, her hips following his hand each time he pulled out, a little breathy moan escaping her lips each time his fingers buried deep inside her.

She was close, he could feel it, her entire body wound tight, ready to unravel, she just needed one more tiny little push. Tweaking her nipple between his thumb and forefinger, he swirled the tip of his tongue on the sensitive spot behind her ear. "Come, baby, now."

At his command, she flew apart, and the sight of her head tossed back against his shoulder, her eyes closed, and an expression of euphoria on her face was utter perfection.

Loving someone was a lot easier than he had anticipated it would be.

Or maybe it was just that Julia made it so damn easy.

Before he could stop her, she had moved, taking him along with her, and was straddling his hips.

"Easy, honey, your back is still healing," he cautioned.

"Not made of glass, I'm not going to break, you have to stop worrying about me. No condom this time, I'm clean and on the pill," she said as she sank slowly down, taking him fully inside her.

"I'm clean too. But you have to understand I'm never going to stop worrying about you, little flame, not ever." Protecting was hardwired into his brain, much to his father's frustration, but Julia awakened a protective beast that would go to any lengths to save her from even the smallest amounts of pain. "I will always do whatever it takes to protect you."

"Right back at ya, tough guy." She grinned, and it was such an open, free smile, her love for him shining through as clearly as if she'd said the words.

"You're almost too good to be true." Domino palmed both her breasts, kneading the soft mounds.

"Don't put me on a pedestal, Dom, because that's a long way to fall and a lot of pressure I can never live up to."

"Nothing you could do to ever disappoint me, little flame." Gripping her hips so he was the one doing the work, he began to thrust into her.

Hard, fast, desperate.

Suddenly, he was filled with a deep-rooted need to possess every inch of this woman. Whatever spell those pretty green eyes of hers had cast on him had him consumed by Julia Garamond.

In just days she had become everything to him.

Everything he hadn't wanted, but everything he had needed.

"Touch yourself, sweetheart. I want to watch you come again."

Julia's gaze locked on his as she moved a hand to where their bodies were joined. Watching her bring herself to the edge of pleasure as he held onto her hips and plunged in and out of her was the sexiest thing he had ever witnessed in his life.

"Tell me to come," Julia said between pants.

So, his little flame liked to be ordered around in the bedroom. "Now, baby, let go."

As soon as the words were out of his mouth, he felt her orgasm hit, her internal muscles clamped around him, cutting the thin thread containing his own pleasure, and it slammed into him with the power of a storm.

A wild, beautiful storm that cleansed his soul, and watered the seeds of happiness Julia had somehow managed to plant in his heart.

"Best way ever to start the day." Julia sighed as she leaned forward to nestle her face in the crook of his shoulder. "I wish your friends weren't coming over this morning because I never want to move from this spot. You inside me, your arms around me, this is paradise right here. Who needs tropical islands when you can have a warm bed, hard muscles, and the most perfect man ever stroking your back."

They both knew he wasn't perfect.

Far from it.

While he might not be his father or his brother, he had killed, he had inflicted pain when it was the only way to get intel his team needed, he wasn't a warm and fuzzy guy, he struggled with emotion, and he had never experienced love.

But in this moment, he realized that there was no such thing as being perfect. Everyone had scars, everyone had a little bit of darkness inside them, but you could find the perfect person for you.

He'd found his perfect person.

"Just so you know, I'm never letting you go, little flame," he whispered in her ear.

"Good, because I don't want you to."

* * * * *

October 10th
9:03 A.M.

What would Dom do if she went and sat on his lap?

Julia glanced over at him as she and Surf made coffee. Domino looked deep in conversation with Bear, they were speaking softly so she couldn't hear what they were saying, but from the look on Domino's face, she wondered if they were talking about Eagle Oswald and how he had responded to Dom's bombshell. Since Domino looked upset but not overwhelmed, she didn't feel like she had to intervene. Alpha team had stepped up and had Dom's back, and from what she knew of Eagle, he would die for anyone who worked for him. He wouldn't turn on Domino, but she wanted Dom to know it, and she figured it would take him longer to get there than it had her.

He had a lot of people who cared about him. All he had to do was accept that.

Things had shifted between them yesterday, Julia was sure of it. It felt like Dom was no longer fighting against his feelings for her, and she had to hope that meant he wanted the same things she did. He hadn't hidden those feelings for her from his team, and she'd made it pretty obvious where she stood, but they hadn't been overt about their fledgling relationship. Mostly because it was so new, and tiny, and fragile.

"Here, I got it," Surf said when she loaded up a tray with coffee cups. "Go sit down."

Ignoring the empty chair beside Domino, she went straight to him and sat on his lap. For a second Domino stiffened, but then his hand moved to her hip, his fingers digging in just enough to make her feel like he needed her.

Surf grinned at them, Arrow looked satisfied, Mouse and Bear looked pleased, and even Brick appeared happy that she and Domino were together. She hoped knowing that his team was happy for him meant that he would feel more comfortable and not like he had to run from what was happening between them.

"I was just telling Domino that Eagle is giving us free rein to do whatever we have to to find and apprehend Kristoff Mikhailov," Bear informed them all. "Whatever we need, all we have to do is ask and we have it. He's got a couple of Raven's team on standby. If we have intel we need them to dig up for us they'll do it, we just have to let them know."

"We're going to get him, your father too," Mouse assured Domino. "Everyone involved in this whole plot will pay."

Domino's fingers dug further into her hip, his grip just shy of painful, then as though realizing he might be hurting her, his fingers began to knead. "I don't care about revenge, I just want to know that Julia is safe, that the threat hanging over her head is eliminated."

Julia frowned. "But Rosie, what they did to her, they have to pay for that."

Touching his lips to her temple, he held them there for a moment. "Rosie is gone, she wouldn't want me to prioritize revenge for her death over protecting you. She was everything that was good and bright in the world. She'd be pleased I found you."

"Aww." Those words melted her heart. She'd expected that taking down the Mikhailov Bratva was about punishing them for what his father had put him through when he was a child, and for torturing and murdering Rosie. Instead, he was making it about her and their future. "Bet you guys didn't know your boy here was such a sweetheart."

The guys all laughed. "Never underestimate the influence of love on a man's personality," Surf teased.

Love.

Did Domino love her?

He hadn't said the words, although neither had she because she was cautious of pushing too hard too soon. What he had told her was that he wasn't letting her go, which she took to be the tough guy, former Delta Force operator way of telling her he loved her. At some point, she was going to need the words, but for now, he was showing her with his actions that he cared about her a lot and that was enough.

Julia pressed a kiss to his cheek. "I'm definitely a good influence on Mr. Tough Guy here."

A small smile curled his lips up, however, the strain not just of the last few days but of an entire lifetime of living under the Mikhailov curse was evident in the shadows haunting his eyes. Shadows she wanted to banish. If it was up to her, no one would ever hurt Domino again. He probably wouldn't like her protectiveness, probably thought in all his alpha male wisdom that he was the protective caveman, and she was his woman.

But love wasn't like that.

Love meant she could be just as protective of him as she knew he would be of her. Especially when he said sweet stuff about putting her safety above all else.

It made her want to do the same for him.

To that end, Julia drew in a deep breath and braced herself for the fallout of what she was about to say.

"So …"

Domino tensed at just that one word. "What?" he asked, well not so much asked as growled out a demand.

The other guys were looking at her without a whole lot more confidence that whatever she was about to say was something they wanted to hear. Even though a part of her wanted to back up, they needed to end this, and she truly believed this was the best way to do that.

There were so many lives at risk, more than just hers even though it was sweet Domino wanted to put her first. The Mikhailov Bratva was mixed up in this plot to overthrow the government. They'd set multiple explosions off across the country, they were trying to cause panic, and they didn't care who they hurt or killed in the process. All they cared about was their own agenda, money, power, control, and whatever else they were after.

"Well, I was thinking I have an idea on how we can get to the Mikhailovs."

"And?" Bear prompted suspiciously.

"We need to get them thinking they have the upper hand but keep the ball firmly in our court," Julia continued.

"And?" Arrow was the one to ask this time.

"And I know a way we can do that."

"Which is?" Mouse asked.

"Me."

Six angry, overly protective faces glared at her. It was almost funny, except that she knew laughing would only make them angrier. She was no stranger to putting herself in danger for a story she was writing. Julia believed sharing the darker side of the world was the only possible way to shine light on it, and light was the only thing that could banish the dark.

This story was no different.

It needed to be told, those involved needed to be uncovered, and the truth had to be revealed. If she could do something to make that happen then she had to.

Domino felt like he had turned to stone beneath her, he seemed to be barely breathing, and the hand on her hip held her tight enough that it would likely leave bruises.

Still, Julia plowed on when no one else spoke. "They want me, I'm the one who has a hit out on them, I say we take advantage of that."

"You mean we dangle you in front of my brother and father like a nice, tasty piece of bait and wait for them to snatch you up, torture and kill you." Domino's voice was colder than ice, and harder than it had been that first day they met when he slipped into the back of her car.

But Julia had never been one to back down from a fight, especially one that was important to her. One where she knew she was in the right.

"Well, that's putting a bad spin on things," she aimed for levity, hoping to crack the glowers staring at her, but she didn't even make a dent in them. Julia sighed. "Look, I know it's not ideal, but right now we don't have anything much to go on. I have some intel on the Mikhailovs, and so does Domino, but with their power, influence, and connections it's not going to go anywhere. We need to know who else is involved in all of this, which means we need someone alive. This option gets us all of this. I still have the tracker Domino put in my arm. I go back home, wait for Kristoff to come for me, or send someone to get me, and you guys follow me."

She felt the rebuttal rumbling through his body before Domino exploded. "Absolutely not. I won't allow it."

Julia felt her eyes grow round. "You won't *allow* it."

"Correct."

"When did you become the boss of me, Domino?"

"When it became clear you have a death wish."

His words ripped through her heart, tearing open wounds that had never completely healed.

CHAPTER SEVENTEEN

October 10th
9:40 A.M.

The second the words were out of his mouth Domino wanted to take them back.

The light that shone so brightly from Julia's eyes suddenly extinguished.

His heart clenched knowing he was the one who had doused it, but there was no way he was backing down.

No way he could back down.

Allowing Julia to willingly put herself in danger wasn't going to happen.

It was as simple as that.

If that made him a controlling jerk, then so be it. He had already lost Rosie to his sadistic brother and father, there was no way he was going to sacrifice the woman he had fallen in love with. And not just sacrifice, but actually throw her to the wolves.

Yeah, wasn't happening.

Surely, he could make her understand how using her to play bait would destroy him. Mistakes happened, even with carefully planned missions undertaken by highly trained operatives. Just because he and the rest of Alpha team were amongst the best of the best, it didn't mean that something couldn't go wrong. And he knew that the men his father hired were all also highly trained. Konstantin prided himself on having a loyal and skilled army at his disposal. His money would still be on Alpha team, but it wouldn't be easy, and that meant there was room for error. Room for Julia to be hurt or even killed.

As though her body was wracked by physical pain, Julia moved slowly, haltingly off his lap.

Domino wanted to grab her, hold onto her, shake sense into her and make her see reason, but instead he let her go. Maybe they both needed a little space to see clearly right now. He knew he was blinded by his feelings for the stunning redhead, she was sweet, brave, and full of life.

How could she ask him to risk that?

To risk her?

Backing away from him like she was physically unable to be near him, Julia wrapped her arms around her waist in a display of self-comfort he hated. Not the gesture itself but her apparent need for it. He wanted to be the one to comfort her, but right now, he was the one causing her pain.

"We can't ask you to put yourself in danger like that, darlin'," Surf said, his tone gentle, soothing.

"You didn't ask, I offered," Julia replied. Her voice was so dull that it hurt him to hear it. She never sounded like that, it was like he had somehow pulled out the plug and all her emotions, her very lifeblood, had drained away, leaving an empty shell in its wake.

"It's too dangerous," Bear said.

"I've been in danger before." A flicker of annoyance sparked in her green eyes, and Domino thanked God for it. For a moment there he feared he'd killed her spirit. "I'm already not safe, they already know about me, they probably already know I'm here at Domino's place. That's something we can use to our advantage. Scar—Kristoff—wants to rule the Mikhailov family. If he thinks I'm someone important to Domino he's going to be even more determined to get his hands on me. We'd be stupid not to take advantage of that."

"Then we're stupid," he muttered.

Julia tossed a glare his way. "I'm not asking for permission you know."

"Domino could have worded it better, but none of us are going to be okay with using you as bait," Arrow told her.

"Why? Because I'm a woman?" Fire was returning to her expression and voice, and she unwrapped her arms from around her waist and planted her hands on her hips.

"These are dangerous men," Mouse reminded her without addressing her comment. No, he and the guys on his team weren't sexist, but yeah, they were protective, and it wasn't like Julia had any training. She was a journalist and she might have escaped some dangerous situations, but it wasn't because of skill on her part it was pure luck and other people getting her out.

"You think I've forgotten that in the few days since Kristoff Mikhailov had me chained to the floor, slicing a whip into my flesh and making me bleed?"

All six of them winced at her words.

None of them had forgotten that, and none of them wanted to see a repeat.

"You guys would be following me. You wouldn't let him hurt me."

While her confidence in them was nice, Domino couldn't not remind her. "We were following you last time, and last time you got hurt."

"Then this time you'll get to me quicker. I'm not going to live the rest of my life with an axe hanging over my head, ready to decapitate me at a moment's notice."

"Less talk about you being dead might be helpful when we're talking about risking your life, darlin'," Surf said with a rueful smile.

"I won't live like that, I can't. And I wasn't asking for anyone's permission." Julia moved her gaze from one man to the next until it finally settled on his. Anger and pain swirled in those green depths, but along with that was a healthy dose of defiance. "Not even yours."

"You're not doing it, Julia," he said firmly.

"You can't stop me."

"We can put you in protective custody until we have the threat eliminated," Bear told her.

Julia flinched, open betrayal on her face. "You'd do that? Lock me up like a prisoner? Take away my free will, my choice? That's no way to live, and neither is having a bounty on my head. I'm going to do whatever it takes to bring down the Mikhailov family, they're involved, and they've hurt too many people. They have to be stopped. If you guys don't want to work with me that's fine. I'll go to Eagle and ask to work with another one of Prey's teams."

If she was determined to toss her life away like it didn't mean anything, then he didn't have to be a part of it. "I'm out."

"You're what?" Julia asked, shock on her face.

For as long as Domino could remember, all he had dreamed about was destroying his family. Now that was hovering within his grasp, yet he was turning down what could be his one chance to actually do it.

He still wanted that, so very badly.

But not like this.

If anyone should be risking their life it should be him, not Julia. His family would meet with him no questions asked. He could infiltrate, destroy them from the inside out, find and expose their weaknesses, gather intel, then call in his team.

"I'm out. I refuse to sit by and watch another person I care about die at the hands of my family. I lost Rosie, I won't lose you as well. If you want to die so badly that you're determined to go through with this death wish of a plan, then you won't do it with me or my team by your side. I won't help you kill yourself because you feel guilty about your parents' deaths."

Words were spewing from his mouth without thought. Domino knew he was hurting her and was driving a wedge between them that probably could never be overcome, but he couldn't seem to stop.

Never before had he been this angry or this completely and

utterly terrified.

Losing Julia would kill him as surely as any bullet to the brain could.

It wasn't until he saw her backed against the counter, one arm locked around her stomach, her other hand pressed to her mouth, eyes wide as saucers and brimming with enough pain to fill the ocean, that his mouth finally snapped closed.

What was he doing?

Scared as he was to lose Julia, if he continued down this path he was going to lose her anyway. She put herself in dangerous situations because part of her believed she should have died that day when she was fourteen along with her parents, he knew she did.

Just like he knew that he couldn't be with a woman who lived to flaunt with death.

He had already lost so much, Rosie's death about killed him, but Julia's would shred the remaining humanity right out of his body. Domino didn't want to end up like Kristoff. He had spent his entire life fighting not to be like his brother, not to be the man his father wanted to create.

Dragging his fingers through his hair he met Julia's tear-drenched gaze. "Julia, I care about you, but I can't help you kill yourself."

"Stop, please, don't say another word," she begged.

When she turned and ran from the room, fleeing up the stairs, Domino ignored the concerned glances of his friends, grabbed his keys, and left. He needed space, time to process the whirlwind of emotions he'd flown through over the last eight days, ever since Julia Garamond barreled into his life.

Time to figure out if there was any salvaging of this thing that had been growing between them.

Domino knew better than most you couldn't save someone who didn't want to be saved. Was that Julia? Was she so weighed down by guilt that there was no saving her?

* * * * *

October 10th
4:17 P.M.

Her perfect day was no longer so perfect.

Julia felt like her heart had cracked into a million pieces.

Domino might not know it, but his words had cut her deep. Telling her that she had a death wish and throwing her guilt over her parents' deaths in her face was so cruel, so callous, so not the man she had been falling in love with.

What he didn't know was that she *had* battled horrific grief in those first few months, to the point where she had contemplated ending her own life.

She had been the one to insist that they go skydiving that day, she'd been so excited, and her parents usually indulged her, so she'd known if she begged they would say yes. They'd died because of her childish insistence that she wanted to fly through the air just like they had done.

Adding to her guilt and self-blame was the complete culture shock of moving to a suburban neighborhood, going to a regular school, and all the things she hadn't been prepared for at fourteen. She'd tried hard to be brave, strong, and confident, but she was odd, different than the other kids, and a couple of the other girls had decided she was the perfect target for their bullying.

They'd taunted her mercilessly, calling her a witch, saying her green eyes and red hair proved it and that she had killed her parents with her spells and dark magic. Even though she knew it was her selfishness and not magic that had gotten her parents killed, their relentlessness had taken a toll, and she'd gotten to the point where all she wanted was to be with her parents again.

If it hadn't been for the scrapbooks her mom had made, she

probably wouldn't be here right now.

Those scrapbooks had become her lifeline. A way to relive the amazing times she'd spent with her parents, a chronicle of her life, all the places they'd been, all the fun times they had shared. It was like having a piece of them still with her, and as she'd read through them and looked at the photos, she'd remembered all the things her parents had taught her.

You couldn't control other people, only yourself. Your emotions were what they were, they weren't right or wrong, feel them but don't let them control you. You are the only you that can ever be, so don't worry about what other people think, what they enjoy, what they like. Be true to yourself and be the very best you that you can be.

Julia had internalized those beliefs until they sunk in and became part of who she was. That was why she was now able to live every day as though it were her last, free and happy, looking for things to enjoy. It was also why she was able to put herself in dangerous situations. She wanted her life to mean something, wanted it to honor the parents who had given her everything she would ever want. So, she'd dedicated her time to shining light onto the darkest crevices of the world.

It might not be a lot, but it was her way of trying to make the world a better place the same way her parents had made her world a better place. It had absolutely nothing to do with having a death wish.

On the contrary, Julia didn't want to die, she wanted to live, wanted to live and make her parents proud. If Domino thought otherwise, then he didn't know her at all.

"Hey."

She looked up as Surf took the armchair on the other side of the fireplace. It wasn't really cold enough to have a fire going, but she loved sitting before a fire, watching the flames dance about, the warmth was soothing, and it reminded her of good times with her parents as a child.

"Hey," she replied, then returned her gaze to the fire. Not that she wanted to be rude, it was so nice of Surf to offer to let her move in with him—since she couldn't be around Domino right now—but she wasn't really in the mood for company right now.

"Domino is an idiot."

His words surprised a chuckle out of her, and she turned in her chair to look at him. "Aren't you supposed to be defending him? He's your friend after all."

"Which is why I'm qualified to make that determination." The man shot her one of his adorably charming smiles, and Julia couldn't not smile back. There was something about Christian "Surf" Bailey that just put you at ease.

"He's an idiot," she agreed.

Leaning toward her, Surf propped his elbows on his knees. "Doesn't mean he doesn't care about you though."

Julia shrugged, not sure what to say to that. This morning she would have agreed with Surf in a heartbeat, but now …

Now she was having doubts.

Major doubts.

Being upset with her plan to play bait was understandable, but he hadn't had to say those things about her having a death wish, he'd done it on purpose to push her away.

And it had worked.

"Domino's lack of emotion makes him a good soldier, but a hard person to care about. Me and the guys, we all love him like a brother, but our bonds have been tested through blood. You, you took to him right away. Somehow you just barreled your way through his walls and did something I didn't think was even possible. You made him human. Now that we know the truth about him, it makes sense that he is the way he is. He's protecting himself from being hurt again. He didn't have anyone to love him or teach him when he was a child. He reacted so badly because you're teaching him to love, and he's terrified of losing you."

"Then he could have talked to me about it. He didn't have to

190

be cruel."

"No. He didn't. And he deserves to be called out on it. But you're good for him, Julia."

She probably wouldn't argue with that. "Doesn't mean he's good for me."

As much as she liked him and had already fallen half in love with him, she couldn't allow herself to be put in a position where her feelings could be so easily disregarded. Julia got that feelings were new to Domino, that he'd locked them down as a child so he could survive, but he had to know it wasn't okay to lash out at her like that.

"Only you can decide that, Jules." Surf's green eyes—a darker shade of green than her own—were warm and sincere. "Either way, you have all of us as friends. We're here for you, okay?"

"Okay," she agreed. She liked all of Alpha team, but there was no way she intended to come between Domino and his team. He needed them, they were his support system, the only people he trusted, and no way was she going to take that away from him.

Surf rolled his eyes like he knew exactly what she was thinking. "I mean it, I hope things work out between you and Domino because I think you're a great couple, but even if they don't, you ever need anything and me and the guys are here."

"I appreciate that, I really do. And no matter what happens with me and Dom, I hope he can be happy. I hope he can learn to let people in and realize not everyone will hurt him."

"See, perfect for the man." Surf shot her a grin.

"You don't have to keep ignoring calls for me," she told him when he reached into his pocket and declined another call on his cell. He'd been doing it all afternoon, and she hated the idea she was keeping him from someone special.

"It's okay, she can wait."

"Your girlfriend?"

Julia never would have guessed it, but the man's cheeks actually pinked. "Actually, yeah."

"Your team doesn't know?" The guys all seemed close, and Bear and Mouse were married, Arrow involved. She wondered why he wouldn't have told them if he was seeing someone.

"It's new, and ..." Surf blew out a harsh breath. "After we were held captive in Somalia, we all struggled. I kind of found myself addicted to women."

"Sex?" she asked gently.

"Yeah. I needed that high, I can't explain it, just *needed* it."

Reaching out, she placed her hand on his knee. "It's okay, Surf, you don't have to explain yourself to me."

He gave her a tight smile. "It was a one-and-done thing, no emotion, no connection. I didn't need that, just the high. I wasn't supposed to get attached to any of them."

"But you did?"

"Yeah." His smile relaxed into a more genuine one. "Been seeing her for about a month. I know it's not long and I don't know if it's going to go anywhere, but ..."

"You should call her back. Go, I'm fine."

"You sure?"

"Positively." Julia infused as much confidence into her voice as she could. Just because her heart felt broken didn't mean Surf shouldn't go and talk to his girl.

"Call out if you need me, and help yourself to anything in the kitchen," he told her as he stood.

As soon as she was alone, she sunk back into the armchair, tucking her feet up beneath her, and wrapping her arms around her stomach. Given the amount of time she'd known Domino it shouldn't hurt this badly, and yet, for the first time since those early days after her parents' deaths, Julia felt completely and utterly alone in the world.

CHAPTER EIGHTEEN

October 10th
7:27 P.M.

Everything felt wrong.

Julia had been at his house for less than seventy-two hours, yet when Domino arrived back home after driving aimlessly for a while to find that she was gone it felt like she had left this giant hole behind.

This giant black hole that was sucking him down into its vortex.

A dangerous vortex. One that could lead him to do things he had vowed never to do like take a step closer to being the man his father always told him he was.

Had he been deluding himself all these years?

Was he really more like his father and brother than he wanted to admit?

Knowing Julia was gone because of him had the anger inside him that she had somehow managed to turn down to a simmer now on full boil. It was bubbling and steaming and desperate for an outlet.

It was stupid of him not to have expected that she would be gone by the time he got back. Domino had been too fired up with what he was feeling, his own suffocating fear that he wouldn't be able to protect her like he hadn't protected Rosie, to have given enough thought to what Julia might be feeling.

Surely, she understood what she was asking of him. It wasn't just about using her as bait and her being in danger. He knew his family, knew how ruthless they were. If his brother had even an inkling that Julia was important to him, Kristoff would do unspeakable things to her.

Why would she put him in the position of knowing that if one tiny thing went wrong then he would be responsible for that pain?

While he was grateful that Surf had stepped up and offered her a safe place to stay if she was no longer comfortable in his home, he hated the idea of her alone with another man. Especially a man who had been on a sex binge for the last several months, even if that man was a teammate and a friend and wouldn't make a single move on Julia.

Not having her close after spending almost every minute together for the last eight days felt like a part of himself had been amputated. How had he gotten so attached to her in such a short amount of time? It absolutely defied any and all logic, and the only way he could describe it was that the woman actually had managed to put some sort of spell on him.

Of course not a literal spell, Domino didn't believe in magic, but there was something about her charm, her genuine care for others, and her bravery that bordered on stupidity that sucked you right in. He might not have known it that first night in Somalia but falling for her had always been inevitable no matter how much he hadn't wanted to or how much it hurt right now knowing she was gone and he might not ever get her back.

"If you want to know how she is we have this magical little device called a phone," Arrow said.

Throwing a glare at his friend, Domino shoved out of his chair and stormed into the kitchen, opening the fridge with more force than necessary as he searched for something to drink.

"You ready to talk or you still sulking?" Mouse asked as the guys followed him from the living room.

"I don't sulk," he growled.

"Pouting then?" Arrow asked. "Moping? Fretting?"

"They all mean the same thing." Grabbing a can of soda, Domino slammed the fridge closed and yanked out a chair from the kitchen table, it wobbled for a moment but stayed upright, and he dropped down into it.

It wasn't until he went to open the can that he realized what he'd picked. It was some fruity concoction that was Julia's favorite. Wanting her to feel at home while she was staying with him, he'd asked her to make a list of some of her favorite foods, and the guys had picked them up for her.

This was one of the things on her list.

She'd been so excited when she'd seen it, squealing her thanks and throwing her arms around his neck to kiss him. At the time, he had thought it was adorable that she got so excited over the smallest and simplest things. Now he'd give anything to have her sitting at his table, chattering away about something, her smile engaging and irresistible.

But she wasn't here.

And if he called her, she might not answer.

Probably well deserved. If she'd packed up her few belongings she had here and left then it made sense that she didn't want him calling her.

Right?

To be honest, Domino had no idea what Julia wanted right now or what he was supposed to do about it. It was hard enough figuring out what he wanted right now let alone a woman he had known for a week.

Figuring out what his father and brother wanted had always been easy. His father wanted money as much of it as he could get. It mattered little that he was already a billionaire, that he had enough to own multiple properties around the world, acquire anything he desired, buy off anyone he wanted, pay for silence, and own his own army of men, it was never enough. His brother needed control like most people needed air and water and sustenance. Kristoff's entire life revolved around controlling everything he could in his environment.

On the other hand, Julia didn't care about money or power.

Nor was she fueled by rage like he was. Domino wasn't quite sure what motivated her. He'd thought it was guilt over her parents' deaths and a passive need to punish herself by flaunting with death. She would never take her own life, but she would put it in one dangerous situation after another until death came for her anyway.

What if he was wrong?

If he didn't even understand what made the woman he had fallen for tick, then what hope could there possibly be for any sort of future between them?

"Call her," Bear said in that growly way that could only sound like an order.

"I can't," he admitted. It was bad enough knowing that he'd pushed her out of his house, but calling her and having it confirmed that in doing so he'd also pushed her out of his life was more than he could handle right now.

"You can," Arrow contradicted. "You mean that you won't."

"Fine, I won't," he snapped.

"Do you even know what you did that made her so upset?" Mouse asked.

Of course he didn't.

If he knew how to fix this, he would. Wouldn't he?

Was he self-sabotaging here? Letting anyone in wasn't just a major step for him, it was doing what he thought was impossible. His heart had lost all its pieces through his childhood, each beating, each hit he witnessed, and each sex slave his father forced him to have sex with. Domino had truly believed there was nothing left. Falling in love hadn't even been on his radar. Then along came Julia with her fiery mane, her sparkling green eyes so full of life, love, and hope, and all of a sudden, he was feeling things besides anger.

It was terrifying.

Terrifying enough he might have pushed her away subconsciously at the first reminder of what he could lose.

Was he that much of a coward?

"She's angry that I wouldn't go along with her plan," he answered Mouse's question.

"Wrong," Mouse said so confidently that Domino's head snapped up to look at his friend.

"Then what?" He knew women were a mystery to most men, but he felt at an extra disadvantage because he rarely understood anyone who wasn't motivated by greed and selfishness.

"It was you telling her that you believed she had a death wish that hurt her," Mouse replied.

From where he was standing that appeared to be true.

"Maybe you touched a nerve," Arrow suggested. "Maybe that's something she's sensitive about because there was a time after her parents' deaths when that was true."

His gut clenched at the idea that there had been a time when Julia had had a death wish, and he'd thrown it in her face, used it as a weapon to push her away because he had prioritized his own fears and feelings over hers.

"You need to call her," Bear repeated.

"I don't think I can. Not yet." Domino hated admitting weakness, yet right now he was so tangled up inside. For a man used to feeling nothing but anger, suddenly having all these other emotions raging inside him was confusing. Before he could reach out to Julia, he needed to sort himself out, untangle himself.

"The longer you wait, the harder it will be," Bear said, no doubt speaking from personal experience. When Bear first met his now-wife, Mackenzie, he'd tried ignoring the connection he felt to her, and Mackenzie had almost died because of it.

"Surf won't let her do anything stupid, right?" he asked, needing the reassurance of knowing she was safe. Whatever happened that was all he really cared about, so long as Julia was alive and unharmed then he could deal with anything else. Including losing her.

"He's not going to let her go running off and play bait," Bear assured him.

"Good," he murmured. Standing, he took the can of Julia's favorite soda to the sink and poured it down the drain.

As he watched the pink liquid swirl around the sink and then fall down the drain, he couldn't help but feel like the same thing was happening with his relationship with Julia. It was draining away, running through his fingers, disappearing far too easily and he didn't know how to stop it.

* * * * *

October 10th
11:44 A.M.

"Are you sure it's safe?" Julia asked, glancing at Surf who was driving her to the house Bear and Mackenzie owned to meet the Alpha team wives and girlfriends. As much as she was looking forward to meeting Mackenzie and Phoebe—she'd already met Arrow's girlfriend, Piper—she didn't want to do anything to endanger them.

Mackenzie had been through a lot because of her half-brother, Storm, and was now finally happily married with a three-month-old son. And Phoebe had also been through too much, first at the hands of her abusive ex and then the Mikhailov family, and in addition to Mouse's daughter with his first wife they were now expecting a baby, Phoebe was four months pregnant.

Then there was Piper who'd had her own battle with the Mikhailov plot to overthrow the government, when a man she had tried to counsel had blamed her for losing his job with Prey Security and being confined to a psychiatric hospital.

These people had been through so much, and the absolute last thing she wanted to do was bring any more pain and danger right to their doorstep.

Didn't matter how lonely she felt. That she'd laid alone in the bed in Surf's guestroom and cried herself to sleep last night because the loneliness was so extreme it was like a physical ache in her chest. That she'd been plagued by nightmares and what little sleep she had gotten had been fitful at best. That all she wanted was the one thing she couldn't have.

No way would she allow others to be hurt because of her.

"Relax, Jules, none of us are going to let anything happen to you," Surf assured her.

"Not me I'm worried about."

"And that right there is why every single one of us will do whatever it takes to keep you safe."

She mustered up a smile because Surf had been so wonderful. Actually, all the guys on Alpha team had been so good to her, and she was very grateful for them and their support and protection. Even if things didn't work out with Domino—and given that he hadn't reached out to her she had to accept that they might not— she hoped she might be able to keep some sort of relationship with the other guys.

"Here we go," he said a couple of minutes later when they pulled up outside a cute little brick house. It was two stories, with a couple of large trees in the front yard and some flower beds along the front of the house that she was sure in the spring and summer would be a riot of color. "They only just moved in a couple of weeks before we found you in Somalia."

"It's a great-looking house, a perfect place to raise a family. I bet they're going to be so happy here."

Even though her childhood had been so unusual, she found herself intrigued by the idea of putting down roots like Bear and Mackenzie were, like normal people did. A home with a community around you, people who you saw on a regular basis, hobbies and activities you went to, traditions you built. It was so very different than her life, but it definitely held appeal, it would be nice to rest her wandering feet and stay in one place. Build a real home with furniture and possessions, a place that would be filled with memories forever. Little feet running up the stairs, marks on the wall measuring a child's growth, a swing in the yard, a vegetable garden, and a huge Christmas tree and decorations in every room. It made her long for what Mackenzie and Bear were building.

As though he knew what she'd been thinking, Surf reached over and squeezed her hand before they both climbed out of the car. Surf kept her in front of him as they walked through the front gate and up the path to the door. He knocked once, and a moment later, it was thrown open by a stunning woman with big brown eyes, smooth cocoa skin, and wild corkscrew curls.

"You must be Mackenzie. I'm so excited to meet you," Julia said, shoving away her loneliness, determined to have a great day.

"Ditto. Piper has been telling us so many wonderful things about you. I feel like I already know you." Mackenzie's smile was warm and welcoming, and she stepped back to allow Julia and Surf to enter. "Come on in, we're in the kitchen. It's the middle door."

The front part of the house was a large living and dining room with a staircase in the back right corner and three doors in the far wall. Surf hugged Mackenzie, then the three of them headed for the kitchen.

It was a bright sunny yellow, with white kitchen cabinets and light gray granite countertops. A gorgeous blonde with a tiny baby bump was sitting at the table, big double glass doors opened onto a backyard, and a blanket was spread out in the sunshine that flooded the floor, with the most adorable baby resting in a baby bouncer.

"Hi, I'm Julia," she introduced herself as she headed straight for Phoebe.

"I'm Phoebe. We've heard so much about you from Piper and the guys, they all think you're amazing. Lolly is so disappointed that she's at school and didn't get to meet you today."

"Hopefully next time, I love kids so I can't wait to meet her.

And I love babies too." Walking over to little Mikey, Julia knelt beside him and smoothed a hand over his soft little head. "Oh, Mackenzie, he's just adorable. Can I hold him? He's asleep, and I don't want to disturb him or ruin his schedule, but I could really do with baby cuddles today."

Mackenzie laughed. "Don't worry about waking him up. That kid could sleep through anything. Go ahead and pick him up. I was just about to get a bottle ready, so you can feed him too if you want."

"I would love to." Gently gathering the baby into her arms, she stood and carried him to the table, sitting in the chair Surf pulled out for her. "Thanks so much for inviting me over today. Piper talked you guys up to the point where I was nervous about meeting you both."

"There is absolutely nothing to be nervous about. We already think you're great. Piper and Arrow are coming, they got held up with something at Prey that Piper has been working on, but they should be here within the hour," Mackenzie told her as she bustled about the kitchen.

"Are Bear and Mouse coming?" Julia asked. Surf had been kind of hazy on the details, and she was sure it was because he was trying not to bring up Domino again after their talk last night. Of course she was thinking about him constantly anyway regardless of whether they talked about him or not.

"They're stopping by to say hi, but I don't think they're staying," Phoebe replied, tossing a quick glance Mackenzie's way. "I think Arrow is just dropping Piper off and then leaving too."

It was obvious everyone was trying to tiptoe around the issue of Domino, but it wasn't like she couldn't handle talking about him. She'd never been one to shy away from things that were hard, and it wasn't like she didn't understand Domino. He had worked hard to shut down his emotions, and she'd reawakened them. He'd panicked and shoved her away because in his mind, it was easier than losing her to his family the same way he'd lost

Rosie.

She might understand, but that didn't mean she was willing to allow him to treat her that way.

Julia had seen true love. Her parents had the kind of love that songs, movies, and romance novels told of. If she was going to share her life with a man, then it had to be one who would love her the same way her mom and dad had loved one another. To have that, Domino had to meet her halfway, not even half, all he had to do was take a step toward her. Scratch that, she'd take him just holding out his hand to her, anything to show her that he understood that hurting her to push her away wasn't okay.

Domino was the only one who could make that decision. This wasn't something she could do for him, and it wasn't the kind of thing his team could force him to do. He had to be willing to allow himself to be vulnerable to her. He had done it before, so she knew he could do it again, but it didn't matter what she knew, he had to know it too.

"Uh-oh," Mackenzie said as she carried a bottle over to the table. "I know that look."

"Me too," Phoebe agreed. "I remember seeing it on Mouse's face when he tried to convince me to take a chance on him and I was too scared."

"I remember it from Bear's face when I wanted him to give me a chance, and he was too scared," Mackenzie added. Turning to Surf she said, "Okay, you, out. Go wait for your team in the other room. We need girl time in here."

"You kicking me out, darlin'?" Surf asked, amusement dancing in his green eyes.

"Yep, you gonna make me fight you?" Mackenzie asked.

Surf threw his head back and laughed. "Fight *you?*" he asked in mock horror. "Wouldn't dream of it."

Mackenzie laughed too and went to grab a bag of chips from the cupboard, tossing it to Surf. "Here, your favorite, now be a good little soldier and go wait in the other room."

"You keep feeding me these and I'll do anything you want," Surf said.

"I'll keep that in mind. Now shoo." Mackenzie ushered him out of the room and then joined Julia and Phoebe at the table. "Okay, Julia, now that he's gone, spill, what is going on with you and Domino?"

"That's actually the problem," Julia admitted. "I don't know if we even have a me and Domino anymore, or if there ever will be."

CHAPTER NINETEEN

October 11th
12:56 P.M.

Maybe if he kept running until his body gave out, he could pass out into blissful slumber where he wouldn't be tormented by constant thoughts of his little flame, whose light had now been extinguished from his life.

Domino had barely slept last night. All he could do was lie in his cold, empty bed and miss Julia's warm, comforting presence. The last couple of nights she'd slept draped all over him, her heat soaking into him not just in a physical sense but thawing him out, helping him become used to another person's touch. As a child, the only time he received physical contact was in the form of beating and torture, meant to make him into a man. Or at least the kind of man his father fantasized about having as a son.

But Julia's touch didn't hurt, it healed.

And now it was gone.

Wiping swept from his brow, he ignored Brick, who had been a constant hovering presence since he'd returned to his house yesterday to find Julia had left with Surf. Domino didn't know whether his team thought he was likely to do something stupid—and to be honest, he wasn't far off from that—or if they just wanted to annoy him, but he was getting sick of having a babysitter following him around.

Opening his back door, he slammed it closed before Brick could follow him inside. Childish, he acknowledged that, but he was teetering on the edge right now. All that anger he had been battling since Somalia, which had dimmed while spending time in

Julia's presence, was now back with a vengeance, and it had grown tenfold.

He came up short when he saw he wasn't alone in the room.

The rest of Alpha team, minus Bear, were sitting at his kitchen table, an open box of pizza in the middle of the table.

"What is this? Some kind of intervention?" he snapped, heading for the fridge to grab a bottle of water. That was the last thing he wanted. Was it too much to ask to just be left alone to wallow in self-pity?

Okay, so that wasn't very productive, but he was spiraling here, and their presence only made things worse.

"Actually, yeah, it is," Surf replied, a spark of anger in his usually calm and cheerful green eyes.

"Well, I'm not in the mood."

"Too bad," Surf growled. Unused to a sound like that coming from the lighthearted one on their team, Domino took a mental step back. Things had to be bad if Surf was this angry and agitated.

"Is something wrong? Did something happen with Julia?" he demanded. He thought it was implied that if anything had gone down, he wanted to be informed about it.

"Julia is fine. She's hanging at Bear and Mackenzie's. I was supposed to stay with them, but I asked Bear to stay instead because I needed to be here for this," Surf said.

"What is this exactly?" Interventions were for drug addicts or alcoholics, a family pulling together to try to help someone who was struggling. What did his team hope to achieve by this little meeting? Did they think he was going to magically learn how to use and understand emotions like a normal person? You couldn't just click your fingers and unlearn a lifetime of behavior.

Although Julia made him want to.

She made him want to be the kind of man she deserved. One who would know what to say to her and when to say it, who would comfort her when she was sad, and make things better when she was afraid. One who would spoil her with gifts and romantic gestures, who would be a partner in the complete sense of the word.

In other words, the opposite of who he was now.

"Don't do that, man," Arrow said. "I can tell what you're thinking."

"Do what?"

"Put yourself down like that. I hate to see you do it," Arrow replied.

"I am what I am. I've accepted that." At least, he thought he had until Julia came along and opened up a whole new world to him.

"You're more than you give yourself credit for," Arrow said. "I remember how you were with Piper when she was being stalked. She felt safe with you, and more than that, she felt comfortable. You made her feel like you cared, and I know you did. I know you still care about her. Her, and all of us, and Mackenzie, Phoebe, Lolly, and Mikey. You might have closed yourself off to protect yourself from pain, but you have always been a man who cares about the people in his life."

If that were true, he wouldn't be sitting here with his team right now. He'd have Julia here, she would have spent the night in his arms, and they would have started the day by making love. They'd be planning a way to take down the Mikhailov empire together, one that didn't involve her putting her life on the line.

"I hate that you don't believe that," Mouse said when Domino didn't comment.

"It is what it is." Domino shrugged then went to take a seat at the table, snagging a slice of pizza. Brick must have followed him inside while his attention was on the guys at the table because he also pulled up a chair at the table and took a slice of pizza.

"No, it's not," Surf growled. "You're giving yourself an easy out because it hurts less. You lived through hell, man, no one is denying that. And no one faults you for doing what you had to do to survive. But you did survive. You're free of your father, have been all your adult life. You joined the military, made Delta, work for Prey, and your whole life is about protecting innocents. Doing good. That's why it's so frustrating to see you throw away this chance at happiness because you don't think you deserve it."

As far as Domino was concerned, he didn't deserve to be happy.

Instead of focusing his energy on dismantling his father's empire, he'd run away and joined the military. Protected himself instead of doing whatever it took to take down his father and protect the innocents that would be destroyed so his father could gather more unneeded wealth.

There had been no justice for his mother, none for Rosie, and now he was pushing away Julia and all but ensuring there would be no justice for her either. Or the countless other people his family had hurt.

"You did something I didn't think could be done," Surf continued. "You doused her bright, shining light. She's trying to hold on, keep it alive, but I can see it fading. You hurt her, made her rethink everything, and have her thinking that while she might be good for you, you might not be good for her."

It hurt to hear those words said aloud, but they were true.

"She's probably right. I'm not good for her."

Instead of answering, Mouse reached over and smacked the back of his head. "Would you stop saying garbage like that?"

"If you believe it, you'll make it happen. It's like a self-fulfilling prophecy. You believe you aren't worthy of the girl, so you make sure you push her away to show her that she deserves better than you. Stop it. Now," Arrow ordered.

"Everyone has stuff in their past that hurts them, you know that. What you can't do is use it against them like you did with Julia and her parents' deaths. Not cool, dude," Surf said.

"Julia cares about you. A lot. She gets your past and she's not holding it against you. She's trying to help you find a path to work your way through it. You have to make the decision to take her hand and let her help you. It's not easy, especially when you're afraid of hurting the person you're falling in love with." Arrow's face got sad, and he knew his friend was thinking about when he'd almost killed Piper while trapped in the grips of a nightmare.

"Seems to me if you continue down this path then your father got what he wanted after all," Brick said, speaking up for the first time. "He wanted a son not ruled by emotion, alone with no love in his life. Angry and hurting. That's the man you are without Julia. Be careful of your next step, and don't lash out and inflict wounds because some of those wounds can never be healed." From the tone of his voice, it sounded like Brick was talking from personal experience, but the man had never mentioned a woman he had loved and lost in all the years they'd known one another.

"Julia is the answer to the future you fought hard to get away from your father to have. You really want to just throw that away? Always wonder what could have been?" Mouse asked.

"Mackenzie, Phoebe, and Piper already adopted her, and the guys and I like her too. She's hanging around, Domino. She's going to be part of your life. Do you want to sit back and watch as some other man comes in and sweeps her off her feet, or do you want to give both of you what you've been searching for; the other half of your hearts? You two belong together, she's perfect for you, and I think when you're not being a jerk you're perfect for her too. But it's up to you. Are you picking anger or are you picking love?" Surf asked.

Could it be as simple as that?

Could he set aside everything else? Julia's guilt over her parents' deaths, the way he had shut himself down to survive, her need to save the world by writing her stories, and his anger were all just hurdles along the way rather than the giant obstacles he had made them out to be?

* * * * *

October 11th
3:39 P.M.

"Hello, mi' lady, your carriage awaits," Surf announced as he came through Mackenzie and Bear's front door.

Julia laughed as she looked over at him, although a stab of disappointment hit when she realized nothing had changed, and Domino wasn't going to come and see her. The guys hadn't admitted it, but she'd thought they'd gone to try to talk some sense into that friend of theirs this afternoon, and she'd been kind of hoping it would work.

All afternoon she'd been trying to sneak glances at her phone, checking and rechecking that it wasn't on silent or do not disturb, hoping Domino might reach out to her. So many times she'd wanted to be the one to make the first move, but she wasn't sure how to do that while also not making it seem like it was okay for Domino to lash out and say cruel things.

Whatever the guys had talked about today obviously hadn't changed anything, or maybe she was just being incredibly selfish and self-involved to even think they had been talking about her at all.

"Hey, Surf," she said, shifting Mikey in her arms, preparing to hand him over to his mother.

"Still chilling with the baby, huh?" he teased.

"How could I not? This little guy is just perfect. He hasn't cried once, he gobbles up his bottles making the most adorable little snuffling sounds, and he smiles at me all the time when he's awake. Are you telling me this cutie-pie is not utterly addicting?"

"The baby sure, the diapers no way." Surf made a disgusted face that made them all laugh.

"The one and only time Surf changed Mikey's diapers he was gagging so much I thought he was going to be sick," Mackenzie said.

210

"That thing was gross." Surf started gagging at the memory.

"Did you call my son gross?" Bear growled as he came in from the kitchen. Despite his glower, his eyes were dancing with amusement.

"That end of him is and you know it, don't even try to argue about it. Besides," Surf said slowly with a sly glance Mackenzie's way, "I've heard you complain about how disgusting his diapers are."

"Hey!" Mackenzie slapped her husband's shoulder when he came to stand beside her chair. "Are you calling our son disgusting? Our *son*?"

Bear glowered at Surf then turned beseeching eyes to his wife. "You and Mikey are without a doubt the single most important things in my life. You two are my heart."

"Aww." Mackenzie grabbed Bear's collar and dragged him closer so she could kiss him.

"But those diapers of our son's are the most disgusting thing God ever created," Bear added.

They all laughed, and Julia stood carrying over the baby and passing him off to his mother. "Here, have your disgusting little bundle before he makes one of those gross diapers you guys are complaining about, and I stop thinking he's completely perfect. Actually, that would never happen, I am enamored." She leaned down to kiss Mikey's round little cheek. "Seriously, guys, best baby ever. For now anyway," she added with a glance at Phoebe. "I think perfect baby number two will be arriving soon."

As they said their goodbyes and she followed Surf out to the car, Julia couldn't stop thinking about babies. She'd always wanted kids, but it had always been in some distant, way into the future kind of way. Only she was thirty-two now, getting older and heading toward the end of her childbearing years. If she wanted kids, she was going to have to hurry up and start doing something about it, especially since she wanted a few.

Being an only child had its perks, but it also had its downsides.

Like the loneliness she'd felt after her parents' deaths, there had been no siblings to cling to as her life was turned upside down. The same loneliness of having no one to turn to now.

Domino.

The man had hovered in the back of her mind even while she was having fun with Mackenzie, Phoebe, and Piper.

Part of her wanted to ask Surf what had gone on today, if Domino was doing okay, but the other part didn't want to because that was admitting that she had now officially reached the stage of needing a go-between instead of asking Dom herself.

Blowing out a breath, she realized she was letting her pride get in the way.

"So, how is he?" she asked.

Surf glanced over at her as he turned a corner. "Struggling."

Well, at least she wasn't the only one. "And?"

"And he's trying, Jules. Really trying. He's battling against himself right now, and it's not easy for him, but I have faith that he's going to get there."

"Where is there exactly?" Was Domino's battle going to wind up with him deciding anger and emptiness were better than the possible pain that came with feeling? Or was he going to realize that life was all about feeling, and that risking loss couldn't be avoided no matter how hard you tried?

"Same place you are."

"What place am I in?"

"The place where you want it all. Marriage, a home, kids, growing old side by side. Domino wants that too. He just has to fight through the fear to admit it."

Her heart clenched for him because she knew fighting through your fears was one of the hardest things any person ever had to do. But the payoff was so worth it. She just prayed Domino didn't give up until he got there.

Reaching over, she grabbed Surf's closest hand and squeezed hard. "Thank you for whatever you guys did today. I just want him to be happy, you know? I want him to know what it's like to be loved. I hate that he's never experienced that before. I want to be the one to show him, I want to love him, all he needs to do is let me."

"I think that is starting to sink in."

Satisfied, she rested back in her seat, suddenly feeling the weight of exhaustion from the last week. Maybe things weren't quite as hopeless as she'd feared they were. "Good, I'm glad."

Letting her eyes close, they drove in silence for a few minutes. It wasn't until she felt Surf stiffen beside her that she opened her eyes and looked about. They weren't anywhere familiar. They hadn't come this way on the way to Bear and Mackenzie's house.

Something was wrong.

"What is it?" she asked.

"We picked up a tail about two minutes ago," Surf replied, his gaze darting between the busy street and his rearview mirror.

"Did you call the others?" While Domino had tried to veto the playing bait idea, she still thought it was a good one, and now with a tail following them maybe they could lead the Mikhailovs to a spot where Alpha team could ambush them.

"I'm about to," Surf replied.

Before he got a chance, their car was rammed from behind.

The force sent her jerking forward, only to be stopped and held in place by her seatbelt.

Next thing she knew a hail of bullets was raining down on the car.

Surf fought to keep control of the vehicle, but they veered off the road, narrowly avoiding a couple of preteens on their bikes, and slammed into a tree.

The impact jarred her but not enough that she was knocked unconscious or seriously injured.

"Stay in the vehicle," Surf yelled at her as he pulled out his weapon and opened his door, using it as protection as he began to fire at the men who had been following them.

Julia wanted to help, but she wasn't armed and didn't want to do anything that would put Surf's life in greater danger because of her. Last thing she wanted was for one of Domino's friends to die trying to protect her.

Although Surf kept firing, hitting some of the men attacking them if the cries of pain she could hear were any indication, there were too many of them.

Someone approached her side of the car.

Her door was yanked open, and large hands clamped down on her arms, trying to drag her out.

"Surf!" she cried out.

His attention darted her way, but men were still shooting at him, and he had no choice but to keep returning fire.

"Hold on, Julia," he yelled. Ducking down, he fired off a shot and hit the man trying to pull her from the car directly between the eyes.

Her reprieve was short.

That man dropped, but another appeared to take his place. Surf couldn't shoot at the men trying to grab her and the ones shooting at him all at the same time.

Julia wasn't going down without a fight.

If they wanted her, they would have to work for it.

Ramming her knee up, aiming for the man's groin, he pivoted at the last second, and her knee bounced painfully off his thigh.

"Don't be stupid, girl," he snarled as he grabbed a fistful of her hair and yanked hard enough that her scalp stung, and tears blurred her vision.

She clawed at the hand tangled in her hair as it pulled her out of the vehicle, then realized her energy could be better used. Changing tract, instead of struggling pointlessly, Julia curled her fingers into a fist, remembered her lesson with Domino at the safehouse, and threw a punch. With his hand in his hair, she couldn't get into the best position to punch through her whole body, but she connected solidly with his nose.

The man howled and released her, his hands moving instinctively to his bloody nose.

Julia dropped to her knees and tried to scramble around the car. If she could get in behind Surf, then his attention wouldn't be divided.

She was halfway around the car when more hands grabbed at her.

There were so many of them.

Kicking out at the nearest person, she got him in the knee, and he stumbled sideways. Another was there to grab her, shoving her down until she was on her back.

Fingers dug into her shoulders as he pulled her up and then slammed her into the unforgiving road.

The first blow stunned her enough that she stopped struggling.

The second made the world go hazy around the edges.

The third had pain screaming through her head and black spots dancing in her vision.

The fourth knocked her out.

CHAPTER TWENTY

October 11th
4:05 P.M.

All right, he could do this.

It was only a phone call.

Although from the way his heart was hammering in his chest, to Domino it felt like so much more.

It was stepping out over the edge of a building with no idea how tall the building was, whether there was anything to break his fall, or whether he was about to be dashed to pieces.

Either way, he had to do this.

Julia was too important to let slip through his fingers, particularly over something as stupid as his own fears. The woman didn't let anything stop her from going after what mattered to her, even if it put her very life in danger. While he might not blink at the thought of his life in danger, a danger to his heart was something else altogether. He'd spent a lifetime protecting it, but now it was time to lay it out there.

All or nothing.

Go big or go home.

Risking it was better than hiding it away. What was he protecting it from if he never used it anyway?

Domino reached out to pick up his cell phone to call Julia, to ask if he could come to Surf's and have dinner with her or bring her over here. He'd love to take her out on a proper date but with a hit out on her that probably wasn't the smartest idea. Before he picked up the phone it began to ring. Julia's name was on the screen, and he felt his fears recede. Even after he'd hurt her, she was reaching out to him.

Quickly picking it up he accepted the call. "Hey, little flame …" the rest of his sentence died on his lips when he saw an image pop up on the screen.

It was Julia.

Only she wasn't at Surf's house, and she wasn't smiling at him or even glaring at him ready to tell him off for the way he'd treated her the last time they'd been together.

Instead, she was in the back of a car, slumped against the window, her eyes were closed, and there was blood smeared in her hair and on her face, her bound hands rested in her lap.

"Hello, *bol'shoy brat.*"

Big brother.

Even before the camera shifted off Julia to the man sitting beside her, he knew who it was.

Kristoff.

Or Scar as he'd obviously started calling himself.

"What do you want?" he growled. How dare Kristoff think it was acceptable to abduct Julia. And not just kidnap her but hurt her in the process. His vision seemed to turn red, and it was hard to focus on anything but the anger thudding through his veins.

His brother would pay.

It was as simple as that.

"I think you know what I want," Kristoff continued in that perfectly calm manner of his that was even more infuriating. If the man was a monster, he could at least have the good grace to act like it. For once he'd love to see his brother cry or scream, lose his temper, something, anything, to prove he was human.

As children, Kristoff would never react when their father beat him or when he was made to watch an execution, not even when the gun was forced into his small hand, and he was made to kill his own mother. That was the moment when Domino had realized that his little brother was not normal.

"I want you to hand over your evidence on who killed Rosie. I want you to get the woman to talk and tell me who gave her the intel she has on the family, and I want you dead so there are no challengers left to the Mikhailov throne," Kristoff replied.

Is that really how his brother saw their family? As a kingdom with a throne. It certainly wasn't how Domino saw the Mikhailovs. To him, they were a blight on humanity, a stain on the earth, a plague of evil that needed to be eradicated.

Behind him Brick burst into the kitchen, no doubt to break the news that Surf and Julia had been ambushed and Julia had been taken. Waving a hand at his friend to silence him, he knew that as soon as Brick realized what was going on he'd call in the rest of the team. All they had to do was track Julia through the implant in her elbow. Looked like she was getting her wish after all. She would be playing bait, it just wasn't in the controlled manner they should have done it.

It would take them time to get to her, scope out the area where Kristoff took her, and time to figure out a way in that didn't sign her death warrant. All of that left plenty of time for Kristoff to inflict pain Julia couldn't even imagine.

So far, she'd been very lucky. Every time she found herself in danger something had happened to make sure she survived. Domino prayed with everything that he had that her luck would hold.

"I won't do that, Kristoff, you know that. I don't want to lead the family, that's why father had Rosie killed."

Kristoff laughed, a robotic, mechanical sound, nowhere close to true laughter. "You really are that stupid aren't you. Father would never have ordered that hit. He would have brought the girl home with you and used her to make you into the heir he wanted. I decided to remove her from the equation. I wanted you gone, out of the way. I was prepared to let you live, but now you are interfering with my plans."

"It's you, isn't it, Kristoff? You're the one who's masterminding this plot to overthrow the government. You used

Storm Gallagher and his survivalists, the family law firm to extort money for your cause, Pete Petrowski for access to weapons, and you've been setting explosions off across the country to create fear and instability. It's all you." To know his own brother was behind this, all the pain his teammates had lived through, not to mention all the innocent lives lost, was almost too much.

"You sound surprised, *bol'shoy brat*. You should have realized it. You know my only motivating factor in life is control. Everybody knows me only as Scar, the best mercenary in the business. The man you call when you want the job done, and you don't care how it gets done. Hiding in plain sight was the best way to stay anonymous. I'm not a threat, I'm just a yes man, although we both know I'm so much more than that. I'm the man who will one day soon rule the entire world."

"I won't let that happen, Kristoff."

"You can't stop me, *bol'shoy brat*. You were a problem I should have dealt with years ago, but I'm dealing with you now. I know you have a tracker on the woman. It's how you found us at the docks, but this time I want you to come, *bol'shoy brat*. It's why I took her, I know she means something to you. You won't risk losing her like you lost Rosie. I'll be waiting for you, and while I do, I'll be having a little fun with your woman. She is very beautiful." Kristoff reached out and ran his fingers through Julia's hair.

At the touch she stirred, her eyes opening slowly, filling with fear the second she saw Kristoff beside her.

Julia began to thrash, her movements clumsy and uncoordinated but filled with a determination that made pride bloom in his chest. His woman wouldn't give up, ever, no matter what, and he wasn't going to give up either.

"Hold on, little flame, I'm coming for you," he said.

She stilled, looking for him. "Dom?"

Kristoff must have moved the phone so she could see it, and her pain and terror-glazed eyes met his.

"I will come for you," he vowed, imploring her to believe him.

When she nodded, he let out a breath he hadn't known he was holding. He might have hurt her, but she still had faith in him, and that meant everything. "I love you, Dom."

"Oh, baby. I love you too." The words came so much easier than he ever could have imagined.

"Well, isn't that sweet? I'll be waiting for you, *bol'shoy brat*, enjoying the company of your beautiful woman. I wonder if her screams when I cut her open will remind me of Rosie's. Don't forget to tell your friend I look forward to reacquainting myself with the pretty blonde lawyer and the little girl." With a smile that lacked even an ounce of emotion, Kristoff ended the call.

Fear threatened to choke him now that his only tangible link to Julia had been terminated, but he clawed his way out from underneath it.

His girl was counting on him, and he couldn't fail her. He wouldn't. He hadn't been able to save Rosie and hadn't even realized the threat was so great until it was too late. But not this time. This time he was going to destroy his family so they could never hurt him, someone he cared about, or anyone else ever again.

Kristoff might think that he was going to win, but his arrogance would be his downfall because he had no idea who he was dealing with.

Prey security was the best of the best, and Alpha team was a family. When you messed with one of them, you messed with all of them, and Julia was part of that family now.

They would do whatever it took to get her back.

* * * * *

October 11th
5:12 P.M.

Julia felt like they had been driving around for hours, but she was floating in and out of consciousness, so it was hard to tell.

She was trying to be strong, keep faith, and believe in Domino. She knew he was coming, probably tracking her at this very moment while he and Alpha team worked out a plan where none of them died, and Kristoff Mikhailov's plot to destroy the government was stopped.

The problem was Kristoff knew about the tracking device and intended to use it to his advantage. Wherever he was taking her was someplace where he felt like he had the upper hand, where he was confident that he would be the one to come out on top.

He was underestimating Alpha team though. No matter where Kristoff was trying to set up his showdown, she would always put her money on Domino and his team. They were smarter, stronger, faster, better trained, and they could take on anyone and come out on top.

That thought kept her going until they pulled up outside a huge remote property. There were large wrought iron gates at the end of a long driveway. The driver climbed out and opened them before re-joining her, Kristoff, and another two men in the car.

They drove down the tree-lined driveway, but instead of going to the main house—an enormous gothic building—they continued around it, past a couple of other buildings, including a guest house, stables, and a large shed. Eventually, they stopped outside another shed, only this one was buried deep on the property, it was older, not dilapidated but also not in very good condition.

"Not quite what you anticipated for a final resting place I am sure, but nicer than the shipping container, yes?" Kristoff asked almost politely.

"Yeah, it's spectacular," she muttered with an eye roll. Kristoff was going to do whatever he had planned to do with her. He wasn't going to be provoked by her attitude, whether positively or negatively, nor was he going to be talked out of this. This was a person who did not function like regular people. He had worked through this plan no doubt in great detail, and his focus was on ensuring its success. She was but a tiny blip on his radar, he would torture her to try to get her to give up the name of her source and use her as a lure to bring in his brother, but he had no personal feelings toward her one way or another.

"The trees tower over the building. I'm told the display of fall colors they put on each year is quite beautiful," Kristoff said. There was an odd note to his voice which she took to be confusion. He couldn't personally experience the stunning fall colors in all their splendid glory, even though they were right in front of him because his brain didn't process information that way.

Knowing that almost made her feel sad for him.

What must it be like to live in the world but be constantly distant from everything? To never know joy, or even sadness, to never take pleasure in the simple things like the smell of the grass after rain, catching a snowflake on your tongue, or experiencing the beauty of a sunset. To never know the warmth and security that came with love or the bonds of friendship.

He was missing out on so much, and he didn't even know it. An empty life was all he had lived so far, and it was all he would live however many days he had left on this earth.

One of the men—not one she remembered fighting against when she was snatched—took her arm and pulled her out of the car. He looked bored with the whole thing, although the other man, who followed beside them, kept sending leering glances her way.

Inside the building was a large open space, for as old and run down as it looked, it was surprisingly clean and tidy inside. Even though there were no walls, the room seemed to be sectioned off into spaces, each corner had a bench with an array of tools set out on it, and a cold metal table with restraints attached.

Julia wasn't taken to any of them. Instead, she was led to a chair in the very center of the room. There were no tools of torture nearby, and for a moment, she allowed herself to breathe easy. Maybe Kristoff didn't plan to hurt her right away, or maybe he wasn't going to at all. If he had accepted that she wouldn't tell him who her source was then maybe she was only here to be used as bait to make sure Domino showed up.

That hope was quickly dashed.

"Strip her," Kristoff ordered.

The man holding her took a step back, and the other one stepped up. His eyes were small and beady, his breath smelled, and his hands were dirty as he took a knife and began to cut her clothes from her body.

He wasn't careful, and several times the blade nicked her skin. Not deep enough to cause any damage but enough to hurt. Still, she would take those cuts any day over the way he let his fingers brush against her inner thigh, or the way they lingered on her breasts as he cut away her sweater.

Once she was left in her bra and panties, she was shoved into the chair, the plastic zip tie at her wrists removed so her arms could be secured to the arms of the chair, her legs bound likewise. The cold metal cuffs around her elbows, wrists, ankles, and knees felt like manacles of death.

Claustrophobia hit her hard and fast.

Trapped.

Couldn't move.

Couldn't breathe.

Death coming for her.

Panic gripped her, and no longer able to think logically, Julia began to fight against the chair's hold.

All that achieved was sending it toppling over, crashing into the hard concrete floor. Her fingers had been curled around the ends of the chair's arms, and when she landed her pinkie was crushed between the metal chair and the concrete ground, the delicate bones snapping like twigs.

The pain was intense and instantaneous, and Julia choked on a rush of bile, only just managing to keep it down.

"Are you finished with your little performance?" Kristoff asked as he reached out and righted her chair. "That was childish and ridiculous," he admonished as though she were nothing more than a small child who'd had a tantrum over not being given another cookie rather than a woman staring a horrific death in the face.

"I won't tell you who my source was," she said, summoning her reserves of strength to bravely meet Kristoff's cold, empty gaze.

"They all say that, you know? They're all so brave at the beginning. Just like you were in the shipping container." Kristoff held her gaze as he crouched before her. "You did well. Better than I had anticipated. Holding up under that kind of pain takes guts, I'll give you that, but I thought we would try a different track this time."

Those dead eyes of his gave nothing away, and she gulped, wanting to ask what he was going to try next but at the same time dreading knowing the answer.

"I don't interrogate many women, but there is one thing I know for certain that is guaranteed to break even the strongest. Are you one of the strongest of women, Julia?"

No.

But she had to be.

Domino was coming, so long as Kristoff wasn't about to kill her, she could endure whatever she had to, so she was still alive when Alpha team arrived.

"I'm strong enough to survive anything you do to me."

Kristoff arched a brow. "Anything?"

"Anything," she repeated. Domino had said he loved her. Whether he'd been motivated by fear or not she chose to believe that he meant the words every bit as much as she had. No way was she giving up now when she had finally managed to crack through his hard shell and sneak her way inside his heart.

Jutting her chin out, she stared defiantly at Kristoff, silently daring him to do his worst.

Which he did.

"Do you know what will break any woman, Julia?"

She could guess.

"I think you do." He smiled, that same weird, empty smile that was all his emotionless shell of a person was capable of.

His hand moved slowly, deliberately, between her legs. Bound as they were to the legs of the chair, she was powerless to squeeze her thighs together to block out the coming intrusion.

He stopped just shy of touching her. "Do you want to tell me who gave you information on my family, Julia?"

Fear had her wanting to tell him what he wanted to know, anything to stop him from touching her there, but no way would she give up her source. Not to protect herself, not for anything at all.

Gathering every reserve of courage she had, she maintained eye contact. "I won't tell you, no matter what you do to me."

If her voice wavered a little on that last word, she made up for it by not blinking.

This monster in human skin wasn't going to destroy her.

"Maybe afterward then. Several of my men have expressed an interest in being allowed a little time with you. Perhaps I shall indulge them. A few of them have a reputation for being quite rough. I, on the other hand, can't promise anything either way. Nor can I promise you any pleasure, but then you already know I care nothing about other people's pleasure."

As his finger shoved its way inside her, Julia squeezed her eyes closed and did her best to block out what was happening.

She could do this.

She *had* to do this.

Domino had finally stopped fighting it, finally let her in, she wasn't going to make him relive his worst fear, losing another person he loved.

For Domino she had to endure.

Had to survive.

CHAPTER TWENTY-ONE

October 11th
5:43 P.M.

The woman was tough, Kristoff had to give her that.

Although her eyes were squeezed tightly shut, and a couple of lone tears trickled slowly down her cheeks, her body was lax, she wasn't fighting the intrusion of his finger inside her.

He added another and then a third, and she winced but kept control of herself.

Interesting.

She hadn't given in when he'd been whipping her at the shipping container the other day, and she wasn't now while he violated her. What would it take to make her sing like a canary?

Was she one of those people who could handle her own pain but not someone else's? Once he had Dominick, perhaps he could use him against her. It was obvious there was something between the two even before they'd uttered their pitifully, pathetic I love yous in the car. Or he could have his brother watch while Kristoff let his men have their fun with her. He was sure watching her violation would have his brother begging her to tell everything she knew.

Withdrawing his fingers, he watched as Julia sagged in relief. A stirring in his pants caught him by surprise.

Was he attracted to Julia?

The only woman Kristoff had ever been attracted to was his partner, his beautiful Dark Beauty. Her pitch-black eyes and midnight black hair that flowed down her back, contrasted violently with her porcelain white skin. Dark Beauty wasn't her name, but it was what he had always called her, she was the only woman to make him feel ... anything at all. Of course, he'd had sex with plenty of women over the years, some willing most not, but he was only ever attracted to Dark Beauty.

Until now.

Until Julia.

Perhaps it was because he knew she was Dominick's. Kristoff had always had a strange sort of compulsion to have what belonged to his big brother, *bol'shoy brat*. Perhaps it was because of his need for control or perhaps it was sibling rivalry. Their own Mikhailov brand of it anyway.

"Look at me, Julia," he commanded.

She gave a slight shake of her head.

Being disobeyed displeased him. Without thinking, Kristoff shoved the fingers that had just been inside her into her mouth.

At the intrusion she reared back in her chair, her eyes flying open. Kristoff clamped his free hand around the back of her head, holding her in place, forcing her to accept his fingers in her mouth.

Julia coughed and gagged as his fingers stroked the roof of her mouth, and he found the stirring in his pants growing, his body hardening.

"You might think you're tough," he said, leaning down so his lips were against her ear. "But I will break you. When you watch my men beat the man you love, you'll do anything to stop his pain, won't you, Julia?"

Her violent trembles confirmed his belief. Her own pain was something she could handle and control, but she felt a need to protect others. Especially someone she loved.

That was a weakness that could easily be exploited.

Between having Dominick beaten in front of her and having her raped in front of his brother, he'd have both of them falling all over themselves to talk. Julia would tell him about the snitch that had given her intel on the family, and Dominick would tell him what Prey and the government knew about his plot.

Easy.

"Scar."

Releasing Julia, he took a step back, noting the way her body seemed to fold in on itself even though she could hardly move, chained as she was to the metal chair.

"What?" he asked, turning to find his right-hand man standing in the doorway. He did not like to be interrupted so he knew the only reason Anton would be here was if it was something important.

"We need to finalize plans," Anton replied.

As much as he wanted to work the woman over until she gave him what he needed, he knew that she would continue to resist until it was Dominick receiving the punishment for her silence. His brother would soon be here, and then he could take his time and make sure he was thorough. A lot was riding on his plan, and he couldn't allow anyone to mess with it, especially his brother.

Dominick would come at him with everything he had, and with the weight and might of Prey Security behind him, that was a lot.

Still, Kristoff was confident in his ability, his men, his plan, and his resources.

Eagle Oswald and the rest of his family might be wealthy, they had handpicked dozens of men and women to work for them, cherry-picking the best of the best. With their vast fortune, they were able to arm their soldiers with top-of-the-line equipment, an armory that the military could only dream about. Prey developed new equipment regularly, and their teams were always armed to the teeth, often with things no one else had even heard of.

But Prey was missing something his men weren't.

Ruthlessness.

There was nothing his men wouldn't do to win. Simple as that. The same could not be said of Prey. For them, there was a moral code involved. They would do what they had to to live, to protect one another, and to save their target, but no more.

Unlike him and his men.

Kristoff believed that humans were merely another species of animal. He believed that right and wrong was a construct developed to try to subjugate the masses to create power for the elite. Survival of the fittest was a motto he lived by, he believed there was nothing you shouldn't do to advance yourself, and he surrounded himself with like-minded soldiers.

Wasn't that the purpose of life?

To work your way up the food chain until you reached the top spot.

That was his goal.

Top of the food chain.

In control of himself and everyone else on the planet. He would rule like a King. Better than a King because there would be no room for anyone to question him. Ruler of the entire earth.

Nothing was going to stop him from achieving that.

No one.

And certainly not his useless brother.

Dominick was weak. Always had been, even as a child. He made the mistake of taking their father's lessons personally. He'd allowed them to hurt him instead of using them to make himself strong, invincible.

Now that would be his downfall.

"You're right. There is a lot to finalize before Dominick arrives. We want everything to be perfect for *bol'shoy brat's* arrival." He said the words to Anton, but his gaze was fixed on Julia's. Fear was oozing off her, he could smell it, and it heightened his determination.

Brother against brother, only one of them could win.

Only one of them could survive.

There wasn't enough room in the Mikhailov family for both of them, and Kristoff was the only one who could take the family to the next level. Their father hadn't dreamed big enough or high

enough, he had been satisfied just to rule his own little kingdom, but Kristoff would have so much more.

He would have everything.

"Dominick won't save you," he told Julia. Placing his hands over hers, his hardened length jerked in his pants at her gasp of pain as his hand covered the pinkie she'd broken when she knocked her chair to the ground. Kristoff leaned in close. "No one will save you. I will gut you in front of Dominick after I torture you and let me men have their way with you. A punishment for him going against the family."

"Are you going to kill him?" she whispered.

"No. Dominick doesn't get to escape his pain that easily. I will break his neck just like I did to our father. Did you know that if you do it just right the person lives? Paralyzed but with their mind intact, hooked up to machines to breathe for them and provide them with nutrition, they can remain alive for a long time. Trapped. Locked inside their bodies with no way out. No hope, nothing."

Straightening, Kristoff ran a finger along the scar he received in his battle with his father. He had won then, and he would win now.

He was unstoppable.

Kristoff knew he did not possess a single fault, he was focused and dedicated. What others perceived as a weakness, his complete lack of empathy, was actually his greatest asset. It was through his ability to do whatever he wanted without guilt or remorse that he would achieve everything he had set out to.

No one stood a chance against him.

"It's time, Julia, time for the beginning of the end. Like dominos, everyone will fall. Dominick, Prey, the government, the world, everyone will fall, and my Dark Beauty and I will rise."

"Who is Dark Beauty?"

"She is my other half, the one who will rule the new world with me. A new world that begins tonight."

The final showdown was about to begin.

CHAPTER TWENTY-TWO

October 12th
12:00 A.M.

Go time.

Time to get his girl and bring her home where she belonged.

Time to end the Mikhailov family once and for all, his father and brother were done torturing whoever they wanted just to get their way.

Time to end this plot to destroy the government.

It all ended here.

Tonight.

At the place where it had all started for him.

For the first time in his life, Domino stood outside the Mikhailov estate and felt no fear, pain, or regret that he had been born into this life. He felt nothing.

His family's lingering hold over him had been vanquished the moment he opened the door and allowed Julia into his heart. She was the reason he could stand here, proud that he'd gotten out from under Konstantin's thumb. That he hadn't allowed the man to mold him into a monster, that even though he had struggled to understand and allow himself to feel emotions, he had still done good in the world.

Now it was time to step up and do what had to be done.

No more doing just what it took to keep himself safe and protect his identity. His identity was now out in the open. He was no longer hiding who he was or where he had come from. Instead, he was going to prove to the world that not all Mikhailovs were evil. It was time to undo his family reputation, remove its stain from the earth, and then build a new legacy.

One he hoped prominently featured the gorgeous redhead he was here to rescue.

"You good?" Surf asked quietly from behind him.

"I feel sick inside knowing my brother hurt Julia, but, yeah, actually I am. I'm not pushing her away again, I'm not running from what we have no matter how much it terrifies me. And I'm more than ready to bring down my family. This ends here tonight."

"Let's go get your girl."

"Surf," Domino fumbled for the words he needed, but in the end, he went with simple. "Thank you. For being there for Julia when I messed up."

"That's what friends are for." Surf clapped him on the back, harder than necessary. "Just don't do it again. You hurt her I'll hurt you."

Despite everything that was going on, the pit of fear over Julia in his stomach, and the anger toward his father and brother, Domino was actually smiling as Bear gave the order to breach the property.

Since he had grown up here and lived on the estate until the day of his eighteenth birthday he knew every single one of the property's weaknesses. Many times in the first eighteen years of his life, Domino had tried to find a way out. As a result, he knew not only the weaknesses but how and where his father and brother would post their men.

His father always had a thing for the elaborate, and while Kristoff's Scar persona was a well-known mercenary with an unbridled reputation for being the person to call if you wanted information extracted from someone, he knew nothing about fighting a war like this. His brother had zero battle knowledge and would no doubt fall back on their father's strategies, making Domino's simple plan the way to go.

Brick set off the explosion that would blow up the front gates, and a moment later, Alpha team, and Bravo team—who were here to provide backup—walked right through the main entrance and onto the estate.

Domino knew that Kristoff wouldn't be expecting that. Most of his brother's men would be stationed around the edges of the property, waiting for them to come in through the woods surrounding it rather than from the road.

Sure enough, no one was waiting for them as they moved quickly through the overcast night. The plan was for Alpha and Bravo teams to eliminate the Mikhailov army while he went in search of Kristoff and Julia.

There was no doubt in his mind where on the estate Julia was being held. The moment he saw that her tracker had stopped here on their family estate, he had known his brother would have her out in the remote shed hidden deep in the woodland that covered most of the property.

It was a place of pain and death.

Blood would forever stain the concrete floor, and the screams of those unlucky enough to find themselves prisoners of the Mikhailovs would forever haunt the walls.

That was the place he had witnessed his first murder.

Where he had been forced to participate in the torture of an enemy of the family when he was too young to even fully understand what torture was.

But he understood pain.

Just like he understood that his family had caused far too much. It was time for them to be stopped by whatever means necessary.

Domino had come here tonight fully prepared to end the lives of his father and brother. Those were two deaths he wouldn't be haunted by.

Sporadic gunfire burst out from around them as Domino, with Surf watching his six, moved toward the shed. That no one approached them or made any move to stop them even though he could sense presences nearby only confirmed that Kristoff was waiting for him.

His brother wanted a showdown, and he was going to get one, only it wasn't going to end the way Kristoff wanted it to.

When they reached the building, Surf remained outside while Domino entered. While he knew he was walking into an ambush of sorts, he also knew that his brother would be the only one in there besides Julia. Kristoff had no idea what he and his team were capable of, and his little brother had an innate need to prove he could beat Domino. He already knew his brother's plan was to taunt him and torture him and Julia while his army killed Domino's team. Kristoff believed that was easy, and once it was done, his men would come to join them in the shed. Surf was outside to make sure no one else entered the building.

This was between him and his little brother.

A showdown that had taken far too long to come about.

But he was done running and hiding.

It was time to face who he was and where he came from.

"Hello, *malen'kiy brat*," Domino greeted his little brother as he stepped into the dim light of the large room, his weapon trained directly on Kristoff's head.

Kristoff stood in the middle of the room, directly behind a metal chair. Julia was in the chair, her arms and legs strapped down, tape over her mouth, her eyes wide and frightened, but there was also trust in them.

She believed he would get her out of there, he wouldn't fail her.

His brother held a knife to Julia's neck, his insurance policy so Domino didn't drop him on sight. Despite Kristoff's arrogance and bravado, he knew his little brother was somewhat afraid of him. At least as afraid as a man with no emotions could possibly be.

"Hello, *bol'shoy brat*, it is about time you came home."

"This place was never a home, Kristoff, you know that. It was a place where we were both tortured and abused by the person in our life who was supposed to love and protect us."

Kristoff laughed.

It wasn't a human sound.

Hollow and empty, just like the man.

"Love, protect, do you realize how ridiculous you sound? That is your weakness, why I should have been the heir of the Mikhailov empire. You are too weak, I told father that many times, but he chose not to listen. Now he has no choice but to listen."

It was clear his brother was positively pink with glee about whatever he had done to their father, but Domino wasn't here to discuss Konstantin. He was here to get Julia free, take his brother into custody or kill Kristoff if that was what it came down to, then he would move on to eliminating their father.

"This is over, Kristoff, your plot to destroy the government will never work. We already took out Storm and the survivalists, shut down the money-raising scams you were using at the family law firm, and cut off your weapons supply when we took out Pete Petrowski. It's over, Kristoff. You may as well put the knife down and surrender. Your men won't win against mine. Prey is the best, already most of your army are likely dead. There's no need for you to die here tonight."

Once again, Kristoff threw his head back and laughed.

Julia's gaze bore into his, and he got the feeling she was trying to tell him something, but he had no idea what.

"*Bol'shoy brat*, once again you prove that you are not up to the task of ruling the Mikhailov empire, an empire that will soon span the entire globe. It is not father's plans you have been trying to thwart, it's mine. Father has not been in charge of the Bratva since the day you left. A man weak enough not to control his own offspring is not a man worthy of power. I have been running the Mikhailov Bratva for the last sixteen years, and the plan to take over the government was all mine. A plan I will not allow you to stop, *bol'shoy brat.*"

* * * * *

October 12th
12:29 A.M.

Julia could feel Dom's shock at his brother's words even from across the room.

Things might still be a little rough between them, they needed to talk through a lot of stuff and have clear expectations going forward, but she loved Dom.

The declaration in the car wasn't how she would have liked to have told him how she felt about him, it had definitely been spurred on by the fear that she might never get another chance, but it didn't change how she felt. She'd meant what she said, and even though she knew Dom's declaration of love was also born from fear, she also knew that he'd meant it.

He was here, not just to save her, but to kill his own brother and father if that was what it took to make sure his family never hurt anyone ever again. That his family couldn't hurt her or them.

"You've been running the Bratva all this time?" Domino asked his brother, clearly surprised at the revelation.

"Hiding in plain sight," Kristoff said, obviously pleased with himself. "Only a few of my most loyal men know the truth, to everyone else I'm just Scar the mercenary. But soon I'm going to be the ruler of the world. Everyone will bow done to me, I will control everything, anyone who doesn't comply will suffer the consequences."

To be honest, Kristoff sounded exactly like the kind of movie villain he'd named himself after. Scar from the Lion King had always amused her. He'd been over the top, silly in how he was willing to destroy his own land and pride just to be in charge. But now seeing a real-life version of the lion villain it was no longer funny. Kristoff didn't like that his brother was the heir and was prepared to burn down the world so long as he could have all the power and control.

There was no way they could allow him to walk free.

"You have to know my team is already wiping out your army as we speak," Domino said. He was slowly moving toward them, his weapon never wavered, holding it completely steady and pointed at Kristoff's head.

If it wasn't for the knife at her neck, she knew Domino would have already shot his brother.

She had to do something to get the knife away from her so that Domino could do what needed to be done. Bound as she was to the chair, she didn't have a lot of options. Earlier she'd knocked the chair down in panic, maybe she could try that again. It wouldn't be as easy this time because there was the chance the blade would slice through her carotid artery, and she'd bleed out in minutes.

No way she could do that to Domino.

Thrashing around to knock the chair over would take too long, and Kristoff would stop her before she could get it to the floor. If she summoned every ounce of strength she had left, she might be able to overbalance in one smooth movement.

Bottom line was the only way Domino could do what needed to be done was for her to no longer be Kristoff's human shield. She knew Kristoff's plans, how he wanted to use her against Dom and him against her, and what his ultimate plan was for Domino after she was dead, and she would rather die taking him down than do nothing and allow his plans to come to fruition.

Kristoff scoffed. "I have more men than you brought with you."

"More doesn't mean you're going to win," Domino said as he continued to close the distance between them.

"My men are ruthless, yours are weak. Emotional. They feel. It will be their downfall."

Fire sparked in Domino's eyes, and she could see he had his own breakthrough, finally understanding that emotion didn't make him weak it made him strong. It took strength to deal with pain, determination to wade your way through trauma, and the only way to heal was to feel. Julia knew from experience it was far from easy, the hardest thing you'd ever have to do, but the payoff would make it all worth it.

She just prayed she and Domino got a chance to experience that payoff.

"My men are honorable, they do what has to be done but take no pleasure in other people's pain. They don't torment for fun. They don't think wealth makes them better than others and therefore entitled to play with other's lives as though they were gods."

"But that's where you're wrong, *bol'shoy brat.* Money, power, and control, that's what makes a god."

And a god was exactly what Kristoff thought he was.

Unfortunately for him, he was as mortal as the rest of them.

Using every bit of strength and determination that she had, Julia wrenched the chair sideways.

It seemed to hover for a moment in the air.

The bite of the blade into her neck stung and she felt an immediate gush of blood.

This time she was careful to keep her fingers on top of the arm of the chair so they wouldn't get pinned when she hit the concrete.

Careful as she was, the landing was still painful.

Her shoulder hit first, sending a bolt of agony through her. Her cheek was next to strike the unforgiving floor, followed by her temple.

Julia was sure the bone beneath her eye cracked on impact, and her head hit with enough force to have her seeing stars, but somehow, she managed to cling to consciousness.

Kristoff uttered a curse as he realized he no longer had a

human shield, a bargaining chip, or a way to keep control of the situation.

As she knew he would, her fierce warrior didn't hesitate to spring into action.

Domino fired at Kristoff who spun at the last second and avoided being hit. The knife clattered to the ground beside her, narrowly missing burying itself in her side.

Still chained to the metal chair, Julia couldn't move out of the way and watched helplessly as a bullet slammed into Domino's chest.

If she could, she would have howled in agony at the pain of watching the man she loved die, but the tape on her mouth prevented the sound that echoed through her body from getting out.

The shot didn't so much as slow Domino down as he lunged at his brother.

Belatedly, she realized that Dom was wearing Kevlar.

Of course he was.

That was something she should have known, but thinking was getting increasingly difficult.

The brothers collided just a couple of feet from her.

Close enough that she could feel the whoosh of air with each traded blow.

Domino was bigger, stronger, and better trained, but Kristoff had a ruthlessness that made him a worthy opponent.

Never before had Julia felt so helpless. There was nothing she could do to help Domino, and she hated it. This was worse than the feelings of claustrophobia when she was trapped in the rubble after both explosions because this time it wasn't just her life hanging in the balance, it was the man she was hopelessly in love with.

Kristoff's fist connected with the side of Dom's head, momentarily stunning him, but before his brother could deliver another blow, he slammed his fist into Kristoff's abdomen.

As he doubled over, she saw Kristoff's hand reach for the knife he had dropped.

She screamed a warning to Domino through her gag.

Dom grabbed his brother's wrist as Kristoff flung the weapon out, bending his brother's arm back so the blade came toward Kristoff's neck.

Not going down without a fight, Kristoff kicked out, connecting with Dom's shin.

Both brothers went down to the ground.

Kristoff struggled, but Dom's superior strength won, and he pressed a knee into his brother's stomach to pin him down and buried the knife in Kristoff's neck.

"No!" A female voice shrieked behind her, and even though Julia couldn't turn to look she heard footsteps.

It had to be Kristoff's Dark Beauty.

"What have you done? You killed him. You killed my Black King." The scream was filled with grief-filled agony, and Julia realized that whoever this woman was, and however evil she might be, she had truly loved Kristoff Mikhailov.

"Stop, don't move," Domino ordered as he swept up his weapon and aimed it at the woman.

"Ty zaplatish' za yego smert' krov'yu," she screamed in what Julia presumed was Russian. "Tvoya smert' ne budet naprasnoy, lyubov' moya. YA prodolzhu nashu rabotu."

"Hands where I can see them, and ..."

Domino never got to finish his sentence because the world around them suddenly exploded.

"Julia!" Domino screamed her name as he flung himself toward her.

But it was too late.

The building was already falling down around them, and she had no way to protect herself.

She wished she could tell Dom one last time that she loved him.

Pieces of concrete and metal rained down upon her, battering her body, burying her alive, stealing her from this earth.

CHAPTER TWENTY-THREE

October 12th
12:42 A.M.

Pain.

For a moment, that was all Domino's world existed of.

But behind the pain was fear, not for himself but for Julia.

Trapped, bound to the chair as she'd been there was no way she could have protected herself from the falling debris. He'd tried to get to her in time but failed, watching in horror as debris rained down around them.

Now he had to get to her.

Frantically, Domino began to shove off the concrete and metal that covered his body and blocked him from the woman who meant everything to him.

Who owned him in every way it was possible to own another human being.

There wasn't anything he wouldn't do for her including learn to feel like a normal person. No longer would he shut out his emotions, no longer would he stoke the fires of his rage at the unfairness of his childhood. Now, for Julia, for the future he wanted with her, he would do whatever it took to learn to accept his emotions.

Shoving them away didn't make him stronger, it made him weaker.

Julia had taught him that.

As he bloodied his hands tearing through the wreckage of the building, he wondered who the woman was. Obviously, she was someone who had loved his brother, which in and of itself was

246

shocking enough. Who would love a man like Kristoff Konstantin?

Someone who was equally as dark and twisted.

You will pay for his death with blood.

Your death will not be in vain, my love.

I will continue our work.

The words the woman screamed at him when she saw him kill Kristoff.

He had no idea if she was dead or injured and buried in the debris along with himself and Julia, or if she had gotten out of the building as she set off the explosions. If she was alive, he prayed his team found her because if she got away, all of them were in danger.

Not only was someone still out there to carry on Kristoff's plan, but she also had a personal vendetta against him, Julia, and his team.

Which meant none of them were safe so long as she remained at large.

A foot appeared in the rubble, and Domino renewed his efforts to get to Julia. When he brushed a finger against her skin it was cold, and even with the layer of dirt and dust it was too pale.

"Julia?" he called as he grabbed a heavy piece of concrete and shoved it aside. Thankfully this building was old and only one room so the only thing that had collapsed on them was the roof.

It was still enough to do a lot of damage, but hopefully not enough to kill.

There was no response, and he doubled his attempts to get to her.

The knife that had been at her throat had cut her as she'd stupidly thrown herself out of the way, risking her life in the process.

Stupid.

Dangerous.

Reckless.

Why had she done that?

Didn't she know it would effectively kill him if he had to watch her bleed out before his eyes?

There had been no time for him to see how badly she was bleeding because he and Kristoff had shot at one another. Thanks to the Kevlar vest he was still alive, but more than enough time had passed for Julia to have died if the blade had nicked an artery.

"Julia," he called her name again as he uncovered more of her body. There were bruises on her beautiful, soft skin, small cuts, and marks that showed how she had fought for her freedom, for her life, for their future. "Come on, little flame, don't you dare go and leave me. Not now, baby."

Two minutes later, he shoved the last piece of debris out of the way and scrambled up to her head. The gash on her neck was about three inches long, it had bled a lot and was still sluggishly leaking blood, but there was nowhere near enough to indicate she had bled out.

He knew she was alive because her breathing was harsh and much too fast.

Fumbling in his pocket, he found a handcuff key and unlocked her ankles, knees, wrists, and elbows. It didn't go unnoticed that the pinkie finger on her right side was discolored and pointing out at an odd angle, indicating it was broken.

A growl rumbled through his chest.

Had Kristoff or one of his men done that to her?

Julia was limp and unresponsive as he held her in place, so she didn't fall once the restraints no longer held her in place. Domino eased her out of the chair and into his arms. Shuffling backward so he was sitting on his backside, leaning against some of the debris he'd pulled off Julia.

"Little flame, can you hear me?" Domino patted her cheek as he spoke, and finally, her lashes began to flutter on her pale, dusty cheeks.

"Dom?" The word was weak, barely more than a whisper of

sound but the knot in his chest loosened a little.

"Right here, baby," he assured her, leaning down to touch a kiss to her forehead.

"Kristoff?"

"Is dead, he won't hurt you again." Domino felt no guilt for ending his brother's life. Kristoff was a monster who wouldn't stop hurting people until he was dead. He wouldn't have put it past his brother to run the Mikhailov Bratva even from prison if he hadn't been able to buy his freedom.

"Dark Beauty?"

"Who?"

"The woman. What happened to her?"

"I don't know."

"Domino?"

He turned in the direction of the voice and could just make out Bear and Arrow. The explosion the mystery woman—Dark Beauty Julia had called her—set off wasn't a big one. There were still parts of the wall and roof standing, which meant his team should be able to get to him fairly quickly.

"We're over here," he yelled back.

"Julia with you?" Bear asked.

"Yes."

"Dom."

At the panic in her voice, he dropped his gaze to Julia. She was slumped against him, and she'd pressed her uninjured hand to her chest.

"What's wrong, honey?" he asked, struggling to keep fear from his voice. She was already panicking, she needed him to be calm for her.

"I can't breathe."

Was she having a panic attack?

Touching his fingertips to her wrist, he found her pulse racing. Just understandable shock over what had happened coupled with her fear of being buried alive, or something more?

There had been debris covering her. Had something hit her chest?

"You can breathe, little flame," he soothed, running a hand over her tangled red locks.

"M-my chest," she wheezed, her hand clawing at her skin as though something was sitting on her chest she was desperate to get off. Only there was nothing there.

"Arrow?" he called out, the panic that had loosened when Julia had regained consciousness now constricting his own chest.

"We're coming," Arrow called back.

"She says she can't breathe."

"So tight," Julia mumbled, her hand still trying to claw at herself.

Catching her hand, he cradled it in his, smoothing his thumb across her knuckles in an attempt to calm her. "Just hold on, baby," he ordered. No way was he letting her die now with help so close.

"Dom, I love you." The words were said quickly as though she feared she might not get a chance to say them again. Her green eyes met his, stark with fear, and his heart cracked into a million pieces.

"It's going to be okay, baby."

"If it's not, I want you to know I meant what I said in the car."

She was slaying him with her every word. "I know you did, little flame. I meant it too. I'm sorry for what I said, for hurting you, so damn sorry. I love you too. You taught me what love meant, and I won't let you go, baby. I won't let you leave me, not like this."

Her gaze shifted, begging his forgiveness, and Domino knew she believed she was dying.

"Arrow," he screamed, needing the medic here now.

"Almost there."

Almost wasn't good enough.

He wasn't letting her die here.

"Okay, let me look at her," Arrow said a moment later as he appeared beside them and reached for Julia.

Domino didn't want to let her go. Only did because he knew the medic was her only chance.

"What's wrong with her?" he demanded as Arrow checked her vitals and examined a bruise forming on her chest.

"Broken ribs, punctured her lung," Arrow answered sharply as he rifled through his med kit.

"But you can save her, right?" he asked desperately.

"I'm going to do everything I can," Arrow promised. The medic pulled out a needle and tubing.

Julia's breathing was quickly deteriorating, and he could see she was fighting to remain conscious. Her gaze bounced between him and Arrow, and he could read her terror as easily as his own.

"Hey, sweetheart," Arrow said, voice soft, calm, and soothing, "I'm going to put in a chest tube. It should make it easier for you to breathe, then we're going to get you to the hospital. You just hold on, okay? We need to keep you around to wrangle the tough guy here."

Her lip curved slightly, but then she winced and cried out. "N-no air."

"Hold on, little flame. Just look at me and hold on." When Julia fixed her gaze on his, he held it, took her hand, and threaded their fingers together. "You got this, baby. I won't give up on you so you can't give up on me. Deal?"

"D-deal," she gasped out, her breathing labored.

"Do it," he said to Arrow.

Julia cried out as Arrow inserted a chest tube between her ribs, into her collapsed lung, then her eyes fluttered closed as she passed out.

"We need to get her to the hospital," Arrow said as he moved to start an IV. The controlled concern in the medic's tone did little to ease Domino's own concerns.

The guys helped him carefully gather Julia into his arms to

carry her out of the rubble, and as he held her close against his chest—against his heart—a lifetime of repressed emotions came pouring out, and tears trickled silently down his cheeks.

There was no way he could deal with losing this woman.

* * * * *

October 13th
5:16 A.M.

This time when she surfaced closer to consciousness, Julia actually felt awake.

She wasn't sure how long she'd been here in the hospital, but they'd kept her sedated for a while, and even after that, her battered and weakened body had been able to do little more than sleep or drift in a sleeplike haze, content to just lie in her bed and stare at Domino.

He hadn't left her side. Even when she was sedated, she had been able to feel his presence, the echoes of his shouts to anyone who tried to make him leave seemed to penetrate even through unconsciousness.

Now she blinked open eyes that still felt much too heavy and found him asleep in the chair beside her bed, his hand covering hers, his grip tight even in sleep. Her body was completely wiped out from the crazy ride of the last ten days. She'd been blown up twice, shot at twice, tortured, kidnapped twice—three times if you counted Domino holding a gun to her head and making her drive to be interrogated by his team—and now she needed time to recoup and recover.

When she shifted slightly to try to find a more comfortable position, wincing at the pain in her broken ribs, Dom immediately snapped awake.

"What are you doing? You shouldn't be moving," he said, always the protector.

"Sore," she croaked.

"Want me to call the nurse to give you more pain medication?" he asked, already reaching for the call button.

Julia lifted her hand, ignoring the tug of the IV inserted in the back, and touched his. "Don't need painkillers, just uncomfortable."

His gaze softened, a little of the worry fading. "Then you should have woken me so I could help."

"You need rest too." Her tough guy was a hero, but even heroes eventually hit a brick wall if they didn't take care of their bodies.

Ignoring her comment, his large arms slipped behind her, carefully supporting her weight and shifting her position slightly. "Better?"

"Mmm." She gave a content moan as she snuggled as best she could with broken ribs, a concussion, broken finger, cracked cheekbone, and bruises covering a good proportion of her body into the mattress. "Yeah."

"Good. Go back to sleep."

When he moved to reclaim his seat in the chair, she curled her fingers around his. "Lie with me, please." Julia knew it was the only way he was going to get any rest and he badly needed it.

"Don't want to hurt you." He reached up and gently brushed a stray lock of hair off her forehead, tucking it behind her ear.

"Please."

"Julia," he started.

"Don't call me that."

"What do you mean? It's your name." A furrow appeared on his brow, and she could tell from the worry in his deep, dark eyes that he was concerned the head injury was messing with her.

"For everyone else. Not you. You called me little flame, baby, honey at the estate, but now you only call me Julia." While she didn't remember having bad dreams, she remembered jolting awake, her chest tight, cold sweat dotting her brow, her heart racing, the machines around her bed shrieking their protestations. Each time she'd woken, Domino had been there, whispering her name, calming her, soothing her back into sleep.

But every time he had called her Julia.

It made her feel like there was this great chasm between them. One she didn't know how to cross.

Still touching her temple, she felt his hand jerk against her, then his fingers curled into a fist. "I messed up. Hurt you. I don't know how to fix it. I want to. I want you to know that I will try to never hurt you again. I want to make it up to you, but I don't know how, and I'm worried that I don't have it in me to learn. All I know is that I want to take all your pain and make it mine so you never have to hurt again."

"That's the first step to fixing things. Now get your cute backside on the bed and lie down with me."

"Little flame," he warned, and everything inside her went soft. She'd known she needed that connection but hadn't realized just how badly until the words fell from his lips.

"Now, Dom," she ordered.

With an indulgent smile, he slipped his arms around her again and moved her to one side of the hospital bed. It hurt her battered body, especially her chest, but she didn't care. The best medicine for her right now wasn't the chest tube, and it wasn't the IV giving her fluids and painkillers, it was being in the arms of the man she loved.

"Am I hurting you?" he asked as he stretched out beside her, careful to avoid all the tubes and wires, and then settled her against him.

"This is perfect."

Domino was on his side, his arm pillowed beneath her cheek, her face turned so her nose touched his chest. She was still on her back because that was the best position for her broken ribs and punctured lung, but she was close enough to her man that his heat infused her with a pleasant warmth, and his strength was a comforting presence.

"Kids at school used to call me a witch because of my red hair and green eyes. They used to say that I did black magic and cast a spell to kill my parents."

Against her, Dom went completely still, and she could feel fury coiled tightly inside him. "I made you feel like it was your fault when I said you had a death wish. That's why you ran away."

Sugarcoating things wasn't going to help either of them or their relationship in the long run, so Julia nodded. As she spoke, her fingers rested against his stomach and began to stroke the lines of his six-pack. "I don't have a death wish. I don't want to die. At first, after I lost them both and had to adjust to a whole new way of living, I admit there were times I wanted to. Thought it would be easier. But I remembered the kind of people they were, the things they had taught me, and I realized that living my life to the fullest was the best way to honor them. I want to live, Dom. I can't promise I won't continue to go into dangerous situations because writing about things the world needs to know is who I am, but I want you to know that I'm committed to a life with you."

"Baby, I want a life with you, and I promise I will become the man you deserve."

"Oh, Dom, don't you know? I fell in love with the man you are. You're not your father, and you're not your brother. You are a man who is capable of feeling and loving. I know because you already love me, and whether you acknowledge it or not, you love your team, their wives, and kids. You are a good man, the best, protective, fierce, loyal, and when you hold me like this I feel safe."

"I will always keep you safe, little flame. I won't ever let anyone hurt you again."

Everything that had happened and almost happened crashed down upon her all at once, hitting her with the force of a million tornados. Her breath hitched, and tears welled in her eyes.

"Dom?"

"What is it, baby?"

"I don't think I'm okay."

He was silent for a moment. "I don't think I'm okay either."

Those words reassured her more than anything else he could have said. "Kristoff he … he put his fingers inside me. I tried to be brave, but I was terrified. He was going to have me raped and tortured in front of you to make you talk. I could have handled that, but … he was going to hurt you, and I think I would have given up my source to protect you," she admitted her greatest fear. Enduring pain herself to protect someone who had given her intel was one thing, but to watch the man she loved hurt … Julia didn't think she was strong enough for that.

"I was trained to withstand torture, and I would have taken whatever abuse my brother dished out, but I think I would have broken if he made me watch his men violate you," Dom admitted.

"I would have taken anything to protect you."

"I would have taken anything to protect *you*, little flame."

"I don't know how to be okay with everything that happened."

"It will take time, baby. Time to heal physically and psychologically from what my family put us through, but you know what?"

Julia sniffed. "What?"

"I know how we'll both be okay."

"How?"

"By holding on to one another and never letting go."

She smiled despite the tears trickling down her cheeks. "And you thought you wouldn't know what to do if you were in a relationship. What you said just now was perfect and exactly what I needed to hear."

"I love you, little flame." His lips touched her forehead, lingering for a moment as though he didn't want to break the contact.

"I love you too, my toughest tough guy."

Against her forehead his lips curved into a smile. "Sleep now, baby."

Julia yawned and shifted closer. "You too."

"All right, little flame."

"My job to wrangle you, remember?" she teased as sleep pulled at the corners of her mind. She gave into it, content in the knowledge that her body and heart were safe in the hands of the man she would love for all eternity.

CHAPTER TWENTY-FOUR

October 13th
3:33 P.M.

"Can I expect you will now be watching me like a hawk at all times no matter what I'm doing?"

"Yes," Domino answered Julia's question without hesitation.

Always, but especially with a direct threat hanging over the heads of everyone on Alpha team. With Kristoff's Dark Beauty still out there, determined not only to carry on their plan but also to get revenge on him and his team for the death of her King, all of Alpha team were on high alert.

Eagle had grounded them until Dark Beauty was found and eliminated as a threat. So, unless there was an emergency, for the foreseeable future, he and his team would be working solely on uncovering the identity of Dark Beauty from right here at home. Julia, Mackenzie, Phoebe, and Piper would all have around-the-clock security.

Mouse and Phoebe had even made the decision for her to leave her job and homeschool their daughter Lolly until this situation was resolved. Mackenzie ran her own business so could work from home, and Piper worked at Prey where she would be surrounded by top-of-the-line security and escorted to and from the building by Arrow.

Julia could also work from home—his home—and besides her priority would be this case anyway. She had wanted to expose the link between his family and the explosions, something she could now do, but he knew it wouldn't be enough. She was like a bloodhound, and now that she had a whiff of blood she wouldn't stop until they exposed every single person—many were already in custody including his father—involved in Kristoff's plot.

For now, they all had to lie low and be careful, and if things got worse, they would all move to Prey's building, which housed several apartments, and their families would be secure around the clock.

Family.

For the first time in his life, Domino actually felt like he had one. His team had always been there for him, but what he had with Julia was different.

Special.

Precious.

Something he wouldn't allow to be broken or damaged.

"Earth to Dom." Julia clicked her fingers—somewhat awkwardly given the IV was still attached to the back of her hand—in front of his face.

"Sorry, what did you say?"

"I said," she started with exaggerated patience, "that you watching me like that every second of the day could get old. Fast."

"Too bad."

"Too bad?" she spluttered. From the look of love and mild amusement in her eyes, along with a little spark of lust, he didn't think she minded all too much that he would be glued to her side for the foreseeable future.

Or forever.

"Yes. Too bad. Now eat your soup." She'd been stable for the last twenty-four hours, and although the chest tube would remain in for a couple more days, and she would be in the hospital for a few more days after that, she was doing well. Well enough that she was being allowed her first meal. Liquid diet only, which she'd complained about, claiming she felt like pancakes. Noted. That was the first meal she'd get when he got her home.

"It is good," Julia admitted somewhat begrudgingly as she took a small mouthful.

"It won't be long, and you'll be back up and around, home again." They'd already talked about it, and Julia was going to move in with him as soon as she was discharged, neither of them liked the idea of being apart.

Julia waggled her eyebrows at him. "I have plans for you when we get home."

"Little flame," he said, exasperated. "You know it's going to take weeks for your ribs to heal, that means no sex."

"Whoa, cut the sex talk," Mouse said on a laugh as he opened the door to Julia's hospital room.

"You up for some visitors?" Arrow asked, making a beeline for the bed where he picked up Julia's wrist, checking her pulse and earning himself a bemused glower from the patient.

"Guess we have to be since you're all here," Domino grumbled as his entire team, their partners, and kids all piled into the room.

"How are you doing?" Piper asked Julia, following her boyfriend to the bed.

"I'm hanging in there," Julia replied honestly.

"If you want to talk, I'm here." Piper shifted her focus to him. "For both of you."

The psychiatrist was a good friend, one that had reminded him of Rosie which is why it had been so easy to step up and help a few months back when she was being stalked. Although he wasn't sure he would take her up on her offer—Julia was the only one he felt comfortable opening up to—he appreciated her offer more than he could put into words.

"Thanks, doc," Dom said.

"Of course, that's what family does, and we're all a family," Piper said, leaning into Arrow when he slipped an arm around her shoulders.

"Speaking of our family, where's Surf?" Julia asked.

Everyone else was here. Mackenzie had snagged the chair he'd been sitting in, and Bear was scooping Mikey out of his stroller and settling the baby in her arms. Lolly was buzzing around the room while Mouse and Phoebe attempted to remind her they were in a hospital and she needed to keep things quiet. Arrow and Piper were on the other side of Julia's bed, and Brick was standing guard by the door, but Surf was noticeably absent.

"Is everything okay?" he asked. Other than gathering information on what had gone down at the Mikhailov estate the day before, including learning what Kristoff had done to their father—who was now in police custody—he hadn't had time to check in with his team. His priority had been, and still was, Julia. Still, if something was wrong, or Surf was in trouble, he wanted to know about it.

"Said he had something to take care of," Bear told him.

"What exactly?" Domino asked. Of all the guys on his team, Surf had been the one to bond the most with Julia, and he was surprised the man hadn't come along with everyone else to check on her.

"Breaking up with Lila," Surf answered for himself as the door swung open and he stepped into the room. The man looked terrible. There were dark circles under his eyes, which were missing their usual spark.

"Who's Lila?" Mouse asked.

All of them looked confused, except for Julia, who just looked sad. "You ended things with her? I thought you really liked her. What happened?" she asked.

"Wait, you know who he's talking about?" Domino asked.

"Yeah, he told me about her while I was staying with him. I don't understand why you broke up with her though," Julia said.

Surf crossed the room and kissed her cheek. "You doing okay, darlin'?"

"Hanging in there but tired, so don't make me ask again," Julia replied.

"Nice guilt trip," Phoebe said with a snicker.

"What's a guilt trip?" Lolly asked.

"It's like when you wanted a sleepover, and you kept telling Phoebe and me in that sad, whiny voice that all your friends have had sleepovers at their house, and you were the only person in the entire second grade who had never ever not even once had your friends come and spend the night," Mouse told his seven-year-old.

"Oh." Lolly nodded like that explained it.

"So, out with it," Mackenzie prompted.

"Well," Surf hesitated, then sighed and dragged his fingers through his blond locks. "So, you guys know about my, ah, issue," he said with a glance at Lolly, "since what went down a few months back."

"Yeah, we're aware," Arrow said, "kind of why we're surprised there's a Lila."

"Not as surprised as I was, trust me. It totally came out of left field. We just clicked right away. It was like all of a sudden no other woman could compare to her."

"Is she pretty, Uncle Surf?" Lolly asked.

"Yes, squirt, she's gorgeous. Long blonde hair and the biggest, bluest eyes I've ever seen. But she's also sweet, kind, and she makes me laugh, and most of all she makes me happy."

"So, you ended it because …?" Julia asked.

"Because we're all in danger. Kristoff's Dark Beauty is out there, and she's made her intentions clear. Because of that, we all need to be careful and adjust how we go about living our lives. How can I ask her to step into this mess when we've only known each other for such a short time? That wouldn't be fair of me to put her in danger like that, it would be selfish. So, I did the only thing I could and broke up with her."

"That sucks, man, but probably for the best," Mouse said, clapping him on the back.

"I'm so sorry, Surf. I know you really care about her. And I'm sorry about the tears," Julia said as they streamed down her cheeks. "I can't help it, I'm just a mess right now."

"Understandably," Domino reminded her as he perched on the bed beside her and carefully folded her into his embrace. This woman was his heart and soul, she'd taught him what it meant to love and let people love him in return, and for that alone she would own him forever. "But you have all of us. Alpha team is a family, it took me a while to fully grasp what that meant, but I get it now. No one messes with us and gets away with it. Kristoff's Dark Beauty won't know what hit her because Prey always gets the bad guy."

Jane Blythe is a *USA Today* bestselling author of romantic suspense and military romance full of sexy heroes and strong heroines! When she's not weaving hard to unravel mysteries she loves to read, bake, go to the beach, build snowmen, and watch Disney movies. She has two adorable Dalmatians, is obsessed with Christmas, owns 200+ teddy bears, and loves to travel!

To connect and keep up to date please visit any of the following

Amazon – http://www.amazon.com/author/janeblythe
BookBub – https://www.bookbub.com/authors/jane-blythe
Email – mailto:janeblytheauthor@gmail.com
Facebook – http://www.facebook.com/janeblytheauthor
Goodreads – http://www.goodreads.com/author/show/6574160.Jane_Blythe
Instagram – http://www.instagram.com/jane_blythe_author
Reader Group – http://www.facebook.com/groups/janeskillersweethearts
Twitter – http://www.twitter.com/jblytheauthor
Website – http://www.janeblythe.com.au

Faith is being sure of what we hope for and certain of what we do not see.

Hebrews 11:1

Made in the USA
Monee, IL
20 August 2023

41323074R00159